BREAKFAST IN BENIDORM

BY KEN BIRCH – AUTHOR & VICTIM

Certificate of Copyright

This certificate is issued under the attestation of The Copyright Index in accordance with international copyright laws. It verifies that registration has been made for the work identified below, and confirms the date on which the proof of copyright was witnessed by The Copyright Index.

James Anderson
Registrar of Copyrights

Registration Number
CI-2739968556

https://copyrightindex.com/verify/

Copyright Holder

Name of Copyright Holder   Kenneth Birch

Year of Birth   1944

Address   42 Cervantes Drive, Erskine, Erskine, Wa, 6210, Australia

---

Copyright Details

Registration Number   CI-2739968556

Date of Registration   12 March 2025, 03:09 GMT

Title of Work   breakfast in benidirm

Nature of Work   comidy book

Year in which work was created   2024

Country in which work was created   united kingdom

Description   word documet

Contents

Dedications i

Chapter 1 – In The Beginning... 1

Chapter 2 – The Start of Something Big.......................... 22

Chapter 3 – Decorating Is Fun 34

Chapter 4 – The Plague.. 47

Chapter 5 – The Wonders Of Flight (Day 1) 57

Chapter 6 – Benidorm – The Grand Arrival (Day 1)........ 72

Chapter 7 – Restaurant Of Culinary Surprise (Day 1)...... 93

Chapter 8 – Come Dancing (Day 2) 109

Chapter 9 – Sun – Sand- Sea & The Trot's (Day 3)....... 134

Chapter 10 – Awaiting Christmas Eve (Day 4) 155

Chapter 11 – Father Christmas Ho Ho Hic! (Day 5) 165

Chapter 12 – Christmas Fare – The Bird Has Flown..... 187

Chapter 13 – The Battle Of Flemington 199

Chapter 14 – Life Balloons On Boxing Day (Day 6) 215

Chapter 15 – Men In Black – Back On Track (Day 7) .. 232

Chapter 16 – Our Bavarian Saviour (Day 8) 253

Chapter 17 – The December Fest..................................... 262

Chapter 18 – Going Home (Day 8).................................. 276

Chapter 19 – Return To Reality 291

In Conclusion – A Better Way... 307

Dedications

In loving memory of my dearly missed Mum and Dad, Tiggy and Len, and my beloved wife, Judy, whose kindness, love, and sparkling humour brought light to even the darkest days.

To my wonderful children, Karen and Graeme, who weathered it all with strength and grace, and to the dear friends who shared in the sunshine, laughter, sangria, and those unforgettable breakfasts in Benidorm.

Chapter 1 – In The Beginning

I was born of Tiggy and Len and came into this world on the 29th August 1944 in the middle of the night at the Islington General Hospital in London.

The war with Germany was in full swing, and as misfortune would have it, an air raid on London was going on at the time. The German Luftwaffe were doing their very best to drop down as many bombs as they could on poor old London, seemingly busy trying to prevent my birth.

Mum told me in later years that while I was being born, all she could see were huge flashes of light, like a firework display, through the large blackout-curtained windows at the end of the bed.

I guess on the positive side, it must have taken her mind a bit off the proceedings going on lower down where the Doctor and Nurses were rather busy trying to drag me into the world with an overlarge set of forceps. I've still got the marks in my head!

Eventually, the good doctor prevailed, and out I came, much to the apparent relief of everyone involved. Mum swore the bombing stopped almost immediately, as if the Germans just threw in the towel once they realised I'd made it. Honestly, I can't blame them—anyone would be exhausted trying to keep me out of the world.

As fate would have it, years later, I found myself working at Dornier in Germany, right in the factory where some of those very bombers that terrorised London were made. Yes, the same planes that once rained bombs down on my head and all of London. Nothing says "irony" quite like clocking into work at the birthplace of the machines that once tried to ruin your first day on Earth.

Time marched on, and I was duly christened Kenneth Francis. Why Kenneth? Well, Mum had a soft spot for Glenn Miller, but since every other baby was being named Glenn, she figured "Ken" was close enough without following the herd. She threw in Francis as a nod to her other favourite, Frank Sinatra, because, naturally, naming me after her musical heroes seemed perfectly reasonable.

The whole celebrity naming thing always struck me as odd. It's as if everyone was trying to give their newborns some jazz or swing credibility from the get-go. Frankly, I've never understood it—just one of life's many little mysteries, I suppose.

So, having been born, had my head squashed and bent in the process, and survived an air raid all in the space of my first few hours of life, things could only get better.

Fortunately, they did, and after the due days of the post-birth rest period, my Mum and I were dispatched home to Pinner Park, where I spent the next six years of my childhood.

Pinner Park was a nice part of the world; it was one of the 1930,s developments built in the new outer London suburbs.

The area was quite posh, where people spoke proper English, and most appeared to work as Civil Servants or in other offices or in their own businesses.

Life was good for us after the war and I continued to live happily in Mum and Dad's nice house and played in the very large garden.

My Dad, known as Len to everyone, had decided to move the family out of the home in Wembley as the bombing was getting worse in London and was gradually extending to the outer regions. Dad thought it would be safer in Pinner being just that bit further out and was a bit less risky.

As luck—or sod's law—would have it, just months after we moved in, a chunk of shrapnel, about the size of a dinner plate, decided to pay our roof a visit. It sliced straight through, broke into bits, and ended up decorating the bedroom floor upstairs. Not satisfied with just one mess, it took out a nice chunk of plaster from the kitchen ceiling on the way down, which then showered the kitchen floor. Quite the gift from above.

I remember the story Gran told me in full detail about the hell of a bang she heard from her bedroom. This was quickly followed by a great commotion she heard coming from downstairs when Dad discovered the mess on our floor. He was not given to bad temper, but on this occasion Gran heard him stomping about downstairs shouting at what he was going to do to Germans if he got hold of one of them.

Eventually, Mum had to step in and bring him back down to his usual, mild-mannered self before he headed off to work. In Dad's calm state, he was a fairly quiet man, not liking to make a fuss of things. He was quite tallish and thin with swept-back shiny black hair. His slim face sported a thin moustache, which was always kept in perfect trim.

He was rarely seen out of a suit and sporting a full collar and tie. His head always sported a Trilby Hat. He was considered by Mum, with a special pride, as one of the smartest men in town.

Dad's job in life was to organise demolition in London and would have to travel all around London organising lorries to take away what was left over from bombed-out buildings. He was not expecting to clear demolition from our house as part of the bargain.

Dad had been with the same Builders Merchants since he left school at the grand old age of 13. There wasn't a more loyal supporter of "the Firm," as he called it like it was some secret society instead of a demolition outfit. He was an honest, dependable bloke with a knack for organisation and a natural talent for managing people. His crew—whom he fondly referred to as "His Men"—respected him immensely, and for good reason. Dad could get things done, whether it was clearing debris from war-torn London or, unfortunately, from our own home.

Mum and Dad first met in their schooldays; Mum was just eleven and Dad twelve, it was love at first sight, proper romantic stuff. Mum always told me she saw Dad, then fell in love and did everything possible to make him notice her.

Her patience worked, and they married just before the war, spending their honeymoon in Germany of all places. Even visiting the Zeppelin factory as their holiday pictures revealed.

They, like the hapless British Government, thought everything was going to be all right!

Dad had been called up to the Army just after the outbreak of war and was soon doing his basic training for coastal defence, manning giant anti-aircraft guns.

He used to have us in stitches in later years as he recalled a lot of stories from his training period. The favourite one was when he and his fellow soldiers were required to march about with broom handles, instead of guns, over their shoulders. This was usually accompanied by a pea-brained Sergeant shouting furiously, with eyes bulging as he marched them around the square.

They didn't have many guns in England, Dad explained, so in those days, broom handles had to do instead of the real thing.

You can imagine the scene of thousands of German Soldiers storming the beaches of good old England with Dad with his merry band of troupes repelling the invaders, yelling and swinging their broom handles about over their heads.

Just as well, the Germans didn't know just how badly prepared England was for war!

Years later, the TV series Dad's Army became the success we all know now; Dad always said one of the writers must have done training at his camp.

Dad's other favourite story was about the meal arrangement during training. One hundred or more blokes would have to sit down together in a big wooden shed to eat.

They would queue up with their plates, which had two divisions, one for dinner and the other for pudding. The first division would be filled with some horrible slop, which would be something in gravy. This would be accompanied next by lumpy rice pudding or something equally revolting in the other division.

Dad said you had to walk slowly back to your table to avoid the stuff swilling around, breaching the weir separating dinner and pudding.

After eating came the washing up. Dad described the horrific scene of a number of buckets at the end of the room full of cold water where you had to wash your plate. Apparently, after the first ten or so blokes had dunked their plates in the washing-up bucket, the water became like thick, smelly soup, with all the bits of dinner floating about on the top.

Dad was always a bit particular about his food, so by the end of his six-week army training, he'd come back a good deal thinner—a little unintended "military diet," I suppose. His brief army career mostly consisted of driving the Colonel around various gun sites, usually in the dead of night, with gunfire lighting up the sky. Quite the scenic route.

One night, as they were dodging bullets, the Colonel—a man Dad always described as the definition of a "thorough gentleman"—asked him what he did back in "Civi Street." When Dad casually mentioned he organised demolition in

London, the Colonel nearly choked. "What the bloody hell are you doing driving me about?" he exclaimed. And just like that, Dad's army days were numbered.

In three weeks, he was out of the army and back with Sabey's Mum and the endless piles of London rubble. Mum was thrilled to have him home—albeit a leaner version of the man she'd sent off. I suspect she wasted no time fattening him back up.

My Mum, in contrast to Dad's thin frame, was a large woman by any standards. Her Doctor said to her, when consulting about a slimming diet, there was nothing wrong with her figure only that she had a lot of it.

She had dark brown hair and hazel eyes, which always had a sparkle. Her face was quite pretty and was rounded and jolly looking.

Mum was also a very kind person and had the great ability to make people laugh. She had such a very happy disposition and could always face the world with a big, genuine smile. Consequently, she had many friends both outside and within our large family.

Mum's name was Kathleen, but everyone called her Tiggy—a nickname that stuck from childhood. She worked as a tracer, first for Hawker Aircraft and later for Handley Page Aircraft, producing the most beautiful drawings of all kinds of aeroplanes and their intricate parts. She had such a gift for it that, by the end of the war, she'd been promoted to Chief Tracer. In later years, she worked from home, tracing gauges for Smiths motor and aircraft equipment. I suspect that watching her work so skillfully, with me often peeking over her shoulder, sparked my own love for engineering drawing.

By 1943, Mum and Dad sensed that Germany's defeat was only a matter of time, and they figured it was as good a moment as any to start a family. Soon enough, Mum was expecting, and they patiently counted down the months to my grand entrance—the one involving bombs, forceps, and a bit of commotion, as you've already read.

The war finally ended in 1946, and thankfully, we all came through unscathed and healthy. For Mum, the real joy came when her brother Matt returned home safe and sound after his time in Coastal Command. He'd flown countless dangerous missions and earned the Distinguished Flying Cross and Bar (DFC) for his bravery. But if we were hoping for thrilling tales, we'd be disappointed; Matt spoke little of his adventures as if facing death in the skies had just been another day at the office.

It was not till far later years that I learned that he, as Navigator and his Pilot, had led the longest-distance raid into Norwegian Fiords where Hitler's flotilla of ships was in hiding prior to entering the English Channel. They luckily returned home safe from the action, but sadly, others of his Squadron did not. Heroes one and all!

Matt and his wife Marjory lived with us in Pinner Park with my Nan, Alice. The house was very big, and we all had a lot of fun together. Matt was often away for long periods as he was post-war employed as a Navigator at the British Overseas Aircraft Corporation (BOAC), travelling back and forth across the Atlantic.

Time marched on, and in 1950, Mum and Dad decided it was time for a change. For reasons known only to them, they picked Preston Road as our new home. It was a relatively new area, full of houses built around the 1930s. Not quite as posh as Pinner Park, mind you, but apparently good enough for Mum and Dad.

At the age of six, I left with a heavy heart. Saying goodbye to my little friend, Elisabeth Peatfield, my constant companion, was hard enough. But the thought of leaving my cosy school to go to some strange new place miles away, full of unknowns, filled me with dread. It all felt a bit dramatic, but in my six-year-old mind, I was certain life as I knew it was over!

Preston Road was a strange sort of place. It was another part of the sprawling London suburbs some 3 miles from Wembley with its famous stadium.

The place was a mass of small roads and cul-de-sacs mostly named after places in the Lake District.

We lived in Inside Gardens, which was a small cul-de-sac filled with semi-detached houses. The vast majority sported various types of hedges, like little fortress walls around their properties and defining their boundaries.

We found the folk in the area were generally very strange, although, by good fortune, the neighbours on either side of us were pretty decent. They kept themselves to themselves a bit, but that was the pattern of things in highly Conservative Preston Road.

The residents offered little communication between themselves but could often be seen peering out from behind their net curtains to spy on each other.

As a kid, I remember my best mate, Ricky Basciano, and me constantly playing out in the street. All sorts of miserable old men and women would be moaning and groaning at us for various crimes like standing on the pavement outside their houses or playing in the road with balls.

These miserable 'Snobby types' abounded in our area, filled with levels of self-importance as regularly displayed. Sadly those 'Castle Custodians' who had bought their own houses truly considered they had also bought the whole road with it.

We even had a Residents Association with a monthly book, which was full of dos and don'ts for living in the community. Things like lowering the tone of the area were mentioned frequently.

A cardinal sin was putting out washing on a Sunday; this was a prime magnitude of worry to the Resident Association and involved endless paragraphs on the subject within its unforgiving pages.

Yes, Preston Road had far more than its fair share of self-appointed Guardians of Public Morals and Behavior, and I could go on forever about this foreboding place.

Mum and Dad found endless amusement in the *Residents Monthly*, eagerly flipping through each new issue to read the latest rules and regulations, which inevitably led to bursts of laughter. These articles typically started with lines like, "It has been observed..." I often wondered just who these mysterious "observers" were, though I suspected a few of them lived right on our road.

TV was only just hitting the market, and hardly anyone had one, so I figured these observers filled their time with reading, radio, and—well, maybe not much else. The radio back then was mostly the stuffy BBC, with presenters so prim and proper you'd think they were born with marbles in their mouths. And judging by the neighbours on our street, any hint of romance was strictly off-limits. The mere thought of a little Sunday morning hanky-panky in Arnside Gardens would have probably sent them into shock—no roaring passions here, that's for sure! I can't imagine what the sound of any Sunday morning hanky panky in Arnside Gardens would have done. No roaring orgasms here!

Certainly, the Resident's Association monthly would, without question, have tried to discourage that sort of going on!

To add to the quirks' of living in the area, our street had its own little rituals, the most hilarious being the weekly visit of the rag and bone man. He would come around on a Thursday on his horse and cart, bellowing out 'Rag bone, Rag bone' at the top of his voice. This would be the alarm to all the local gardeners.

As the rag and bone man came down the street, you would see nothing else moving; however, you knew that behind many of the net-curtained bay windows, they, 'The Observers,' were watching.

They were just waiting for the horse to stop and discharge a pile of lush garden fertiliser onto the road. Within a few seconds of this event, and just when the horse and cart had moved a respectable distance away from the pile, from behind the hedges and out like cats, The Observers would spring! Fully equipped with shovels and sticks in hand, they would make a beeline for the precious golden gems.

The spoils would then be divided up between the lucky people whose houses were near enough to get to the plunder first. They would quickly make their way back home with a steaming cargo for their rhubarb or beans.

Thank God they never invited us for dinner. As a young lad I loved rhubarb and custard but shuddered at the thought of ever eating any of it grown in our street.

I remember the classic *Steptoe and Son* series and the unforgettable Rag and Bone Men. One scene that stuck with me was when Harold listened to his dad's take on life, where he mused, "I used to think horses were amazing creatures. You put grass in one end, the horse works all day, and then shits out fertiliser at the other end to make new grass."

I guessed the same applied to cows but pondered why horses dropped round balls, and cows did pancakes like giant pizzas.

I was into pizzas at an early age. My best mate, Ricky, who lived at the end of our Road, had Italian parents. His Mum, Paulina, used to make them for Ricky and me till our stomachs were fit to burst. No McDonalds in those days.

But back to Cows pancakes. My Dad used to say they were made round and flat so dogs could roll in them easily. Now, there's a thought for another time!

When I'd take my wire-haired terrier, Buster, out for a walk over the golf links, he'd make a beeline for the cow patties every time. I tried everything to keep him from finding one, and most days, I could outsmart the little devil, but every now and then, he'd stumble upon a big, juicy one. And boy, did they stink once the crust was broken!

I absolutely hated it when he did this, but thankfully, there was a pond nearby. All I had to do was toss a stick in, and Buster would dive right in, happy as could be. After half a dozen dips, most of the "pancake" would be washed away, though he'd still reek of pond water—sometimes just as bad, so it was a bit of a Hobson's choice.

Being a small dog, Buster was easy enough to bathe in the tin tub out back, though scrubbing him down was always a labour of love (and a bit of frustration). Still, by the end of it, he'd be back to his former glory—at least until the next trip to the links.

My Dear little mate

BUSTER

Giving Buster a bath was always a battle of wits—and I usually lost, ending up nearly as soaked as he was. Why is it that dogs, typically limited to four legs, seem to sprout another half dozen the moment you try to put them in a tub? You'd get his front legs in, then reach for the back ones, only for the front to pop right back out. All I ever seemed to do was chase an endless number of legs, never managing to keep all four in the tub at the same time.

Why don't dogs like baths? Toss a stick into a filthy pond, and they're in there like a shot, but try to bathe them, and suddenly it's World War III. Logic, it seems, doesn't factor much in a dog's mind. Buster ran purely on fun and food. His "fun" often included attacking the TV whenever another four-legged creature showed up, leading to absolute chaos in the house. But his real speciality was the "Pal Meat for Dogs" ad—just the sound of it would send him flying downstairs to pounce at the TV screen. Mum and Dad didn't find it as amusing, and more than once, Buster got a little smack for his enthusiasm.

When visiting some other households, I have found, witnessed, and wondered the strange antics of our canine friends. Why do they embarrass their owners by licking their balls when any newfound friends come around for tea, wrapping themselves around the Insurance man's leg as he comes to visit, or even worse, shoving their noses where they shouldn't when someone sits down in a chair?

I grew up with many imponderables in my head, and to this one, I have never reached a sound conclusion, or it's 'Just Dogs!'

=========================

I lived on Preston Road until I finally made my escape—
to get married! On 29th March, I tied the knot with Judy and
moved to Dunstable, following the advice of my mate Ricky,
who had moved out earlier after his escape into marriage two
years before.

I met Judy at work. She worked in the Print Room and
used to make copies of our drawings while also being the
part-time telephonist during lunch break.

I was a young draughtsman and designer at the time, sort
of following in Mum's footsteps, and had landed this job
after being made redundant at 21. This was Harold Wilson's
doing, our then Prime Minister, who decided that Britain's
premier world-beating aircraft project, TSR2, was to be
cancelled.

We were going to buy American F111s instead (the
bastard).

I thought the sun shone out of Harold's arse until then.
On the upside, this twist of fate led me to Elliott Brothers
and, more importantly, to Judy Cowell. Within days of

starting the new job, I found myself in the Print Room. There she was, running the print machine, slim and pretty, with these big eyes that looked straight at me—and that was it. I was done for.

I was shy at a tender age and used to go red at just about every conflicting event. It was a few weeks later that I met her again in the pub at lunchtime during our Christmas office break. We ended up having a drink together, and we got talking. I was too shy to ask her out, and when I got home after work was really cross with myself for not doing so.

My Dad asked what was up, as he noticed I must have been really pissed off.

'I met this girl at work,' I explained. 'I like her.'

'Ask her out,' Dad advised.

I sort of shuffled in an embarrassed way. Dad said I was stupid and if I liked her, I should go around to her house and ask her out. He then followed on, giving me various reasons why I should.

Finally, I thought, Sod it! I'll go! So I got in the car, and off I went, speeding into my new tomorrow!

The next instant, I was standing outside her front door, feeling I wanted the ground to open and for me to drop into the hole.

After ringing the doorbell a few times, I heard the turning of locks, first one, and then another until the thud of a final one.

I was to learn later that my future mother-in-law had a thing about locks.

I was in sweat by this time, and by the time the door opened, my stomach was full of that sinking feeling. Pull yourself together, I thought to myself. The door opened slowly, just a few inches, until it was restrained by a chain. Next, I could just make out half a lady's face, about 4 feet, nothing inches off the floor, with one eye peering at me through the crack.

'Hello,' she said, 'who is it?'

I paused for what seemed like an hour before stammering,

'It's Ken from Judy's work, is she in?'

The door closed a bit, and I heard the chain being removed. The door opened slowly to reveal a small, thin-faced be-speckled woman.

She had long grey hair spilling down over her shoulders and peered up at me in a strange sort of way. I introduced myself, cautiously blurting.

'I'm Ken from Judy's work.'

She looked me up and down a bit and then turned her head around.

'Jude,' she bellowed down the hall, 'It's Ken from your work!'

She then turned her head back in my direction, looked at me again, and grinned.

'I'll see what she's up to.' She said, then turned and walked off, with a waddle in her step, down her hallway.

After what seemed like an eternity, Judy came to the door.

I stammered out the sentence.

'Fancy coming out tonight, Jude?' which was about all I could manage.

To my surprise, she said yes and started my new world ablaze!

I picked Judy up at 7:30 on the dot in my pride and joy—a Ford Anglia 100E. This car was the bee's knees: a sleek two-tone red and white body, chrome go-faster stripes down the side, and hand-painted whitewall tires. I really did cut a dash back then!

The weather outside was dreadful—cold, raining, the kind of night that only winter could pull off. But off we went into the darkness, undeterred. That night, we ended up meeting Judy's friends at a pub called the Thatched Barn in Boreham Wood. It was a great evening, full of laughs, and around 11:15 pm, we headed back to the car so I could take Judy home.

Playing the gentleman, I opened the door for her, got her settled, started up the engine, and went to pull away… except we didn't. The car stayed exactly where it was, wheels spinning uselessly in place.

"Oh, God," I groaned, "we're stuck in the mud!"

As it happened, the pub's car park was packed, so I'd parked on a little patch of ground just in front of the tarmac. Seemed like a good idea at the time—doesn't it always?

I got out of the car to look for assistance, and I could see the friends we were with standing in the car park waiting for their pickup. I ran over to beg for assistance, and after the expected jokes, they came over to give me a push. Judy got out of the car to join the others, and I started the car again.

Soon there were five bodies all pushing at the rear of the car whilst I let up the clutch. Thank God we moved forward. I drove ten or so feet onto the side roadway.

I got out to say my goodbyes and walked around to collect Judy, only to find her and my newfound friends standing in a solemn line like some honour guard. As I got closer, my heart sank—the streetlamp light revealed the full extent of the disaster. There was Judy, along with everyone else, completely streaked in mud. It was all over the girls' party dresses, smeared up the blokes' trousers—it looked like a mud bath gone wrong.

Panicked, I lurched forward, hankie in hand, making some futile attempt to dab off the mud, but it was hopeless. I managed a stammered apology, then another, then a dozen more, and finally grabbed Judy's hand as we made a quick exit.

I got her into the car, her lovely dress now wet and muddy, and all I could think was, *That's it. She's going to hate me. She'll never speak to me again.*

I whispered, 'Why can't I die?'

Instead, as I drove off, she started laughing quietly at first.

I looked round at her and bleated out in a sort of stammer.

'I'm so sorry,' I said, then quietly waited for her response. She just carried on laughing, almost until we arrived back at her house.

I still hardly had the gumption to speak, but as I drew the car up to her driveway, I just managed to utter another apology and said,

'I'm so sorry about tonight. I have really messed up!'

'Don't worry so much; it was only a bit of mud on the clothes, I guess it will all wash off, so no real damage done!' She continued once again, with laughter still ringing in her voice, I've had such a good time tonight. I don't care a fig; you can take me out again if you ask me nicely.

I quickly jumped in on hearing this surprise request,

'How about tomorrow evening for a nice meal out? It's the least thing I can do.

That will be really nice; how about picking me up at 6 pm, if that's ok with you?'

'Oh yes!' I quickly replied, and with all done and dusted, I opened her car door, and she disappeared onwards to her porch way.

As I drove off to my home, I exclaimed to my inner self, 'Thank God for the Gin & Tonic!' which had clearly kept Judy in high spirits, so to speak, and my thanks for the company of a lady with a great sense of humour!

Judy and I continued many happy outings, and an engagement to marry followed quickly. Three years later, after endless saving up, we were married and living in our new semi-detached house in Dunstable. Within a few months of our honeymoon, Karen, our daughter, was on the way.

Karen was born as a beautiful baby in Luton and Dunstable Hospital.

I still remember the strange feelings of joy and bewilderment at becoming a father, especially having a daughter, which was so small and so precious to hold!

A few days later, Judy and baby Karen were finally released from the hospital, and I drove them home at a snail's pace, determined that nothing would disturb our precious cargo. The proud grandparents were waiting at the house, eagerly watching as I pulled up the driveway.

After the initial "oohs" and "aahs" over Karen, Judy launched into her thoughts about the hospital, declaring in no uncertain terms that she would *never* have another baby in "that bloody place!" And true to her word, she never did!

In two more years, our son Graeme was conceived. After some struggle and nine months of anguish, Graeme came forth, ejected from his mother onto the middle of our bed into the hands of the waiting midwife.

I'll never forget the joy on Judy's face when she heard the word "boy!" Tears filled her eyes, and her arms lifted instinctively as if she could already feel him close. The midwife wrapped up little Graeme and handed him to Judy, who held him so tightly as if she'd never let go.

Seemingly hearing the sounds of joy, the little face of Karen appeared at the slightly open bedroom door.

'Come and see your new Brother!' I said quickly and beckoned with my arm outstretched.

And just like that, the Birch family—Dunstable Branch—was complete.

This brings us to where this story truly begins, just three and a bit years after Graeme's birth on 7th March 1973.

Chapter 2 – The Start of Something Big

It was a sunny September Sunday morning in 1976 when Judy and I were preparing for a weekend trip down to Mum & Dad's in Preston Road.

Being a very close sort of family, Judy and I never left it too long for visits down home, as we called it, to see my Mum & Dad and Judy's mum. It was great to see everyone but equally nice to leave Preston Road, which had changed little in the six years since we left. I always thanked God that Judy and I had escaped to Dunstable those years earlier.

Judy had swiftly bundled the kids into our little Singer Chamois Sports—a rather posh Hillman Imp, mind you. This zippy little motor was about the size of an Austin Mini but with a bit more flair. Made by the long-gone Rootes Group, it was their cheeky response to the Mini craze of the day.

Now, let's be honest—a half-hour trapped in that compact box with noisy kids was usually enough to drive you spare. But today, all was blissfully calm as we whizzed off at 10:30 am, breezing down the M1 en route to Mum and Dad's.

We aimed to visit them every other week. They adored having the little ones around and were always happy to babysit, giving Judy and me a rare chance for a night out or a catch-up with friends. Plus, we'd swing by Judy's mum's for a chinwag and a good cup of tea—always a lovely finish to the day's outings.

We arrived at about 11.15 am. I thought wickedly; good timing, just right to drop off Judy and the kids, grab Dad, and then off down the Windermere Hotel for a pint or two.

I turned the car into the drive, and within seconds, as usual, Mum was first out of the door as we pulled up.

Typically, she would leap out of the door, which was no mean feat as she was a large woman, always waiting to give us all a hug and then chatter on about our journey. She would always ask a flurry of questions like how we were all, what the journey was like, and numerous other things our lovely Mums go on about when not meeting for a while.

Dad would always trail a few paces behind Mum, making a beeline for Judy and the kids to offer his quiet, understated greetings. With the usual formalities wrapped up, I'd give Dad a knowing wink—our well-rehearsed signal to slip off to the Windermere Hotel for a few pints.

"Well, that's enough chatter," Dad would say, his tone decidedly cheerful. "Let's let the ladies handle the dinner, and we'll see to more pressing matters at the Windermere."

"Well, go on then," Mum would reply, grinning from ear to ear. "Go and have your beer, but make sure you're back in time for dinner!"

With that all-clear, Dad and I were out the door in a flash, into the Singer, and speeding down to the pub quicker than you could say "cheers."

Mum & Dad

The Windermere was a 1930s pub built next to the railway station. It was a Courage Pub, and I was weaned on drinking in this fine establishment.

Courage Alton Bitter was our drink, two shillings a pint, good real ale; a few of them on a Sunday lunch would really get you glowing and ravenous for your Sunday roast.

The landlord was a large, jolly Irishman, John who boasted his brother was Joseph Locke, the famous Irish Tenor who they made a film of a few years back. 'Hear my song,' I believe.

Certainly, singing was in the family, and John could sing well and held many a Friday night concert with the locals, 'Doing their turns,' as my Mum used to call it.

We arrived at the Windermere, and Dad and I hurried in, having built up quite a thirst, and waited in eager anticipation for our pints to be pulled. We sat down at our favourite table like one does. A few of the old lads were in there, and the conversation turned as usual to what the Government was doing wrong, a few jokes, and the inevitable football.

Dad, Len to his friends, seemed in very good form; he was a quiet man usually, tending to require drawing into a discussion (unless it involved Queens Park Rangers) when he could go on for ages, yawn, yawn! But today, he was chatting away about all sorts of things, Mum, kids, work, you name it. I began to wonder what he was on, apart from the pints, which were going down rather well.

Dad, described in modern terms, was a good old boy, a real 'Diamond Geezer.'

He was always smart and generally wore a suit, even at weekends. In the height of summer, Dad would still have on his jacket, shirt and tie, the full rig out.

A Trilby hat was always present, cocked proudly on his napper, 'What a Dapper,' my dear Dad was.

This clobber still remained during the weekly ritual of mowing the lawn. Dad would parade up and down the back garden, suited up, Trilby on head and puffing away at a small cigar jutting out from the side of his mouth.

His passion was Queens Park Rangers, having been introduced to the club at the tender age of nine by Uncle Horace, his brother-in-law.

Dad would religiously go to Loftus Road, the QPR ground, every Saturday when they were playing at home. QPR was Third Division at this time and would often lose. Poor Dad would defend them to the hilt and, on Sunday, would buy the News of the World and the Sunday Mirror and scan the sports pages for any comments on his beloved team. If they were mentioned adversely, he would always comment with phrases like.

'Where was he sitting? He must be blind,' and 'What do they know about bloody football?'

QPR never had more loyal supporters. Dad's crowning moment was to come in a few years when QPR made the League Cup Final at Wembley Stadium and beat West Ham, a First Division team. Dad went to the match that day with Ricky and me for support.

Although I was not a real football fan, I felt I had to go with Dad. It was such a big day for him, and he was always a little disappointed that I did not share his love of football.

The game got off to a bad start for QPR, who were down by a goal quickly in the first half, which soon came to a conclusion.

Despair could be felt all around the great stadium. Dad was muttering about his team having to get their fingers out and other less printable phrases about the other team.

The second half, by contrast, had hardly re-started when, as though possessed, QPR came fighting back.

After what seemed like an eternity, their valour was rewarded, and they came through like champions to an even score.

The sheer electricity of the fans, all at fever pitch, was staggering, I certainly had never experienced anything like this in my life, and in the crescendo of the last few minutes of the game, their star player took the ball and scored the final winning goal.

That day, QPR proudly carried off the League Cup; I remember my dear Dad, almost speechless, walking out of the Stadium with Ricky and me at his side. I swear to this day, three feet off the ground.

As usual, time passed quickly in the Windermere, and 2.30 pm was soon upon us.

'It's chucking out time,' Dad said as the final bell went; let's get off to that Roast Beef and Yorkshire pudding. No guesses for anyone that we were a traditional English family,

'None of that rotten foreign muck!' as Dad called it, on our table.

Mum took a different view and loved all the pasta and sauces, but poor Dad was English, plain and simple. Mum always wanted to please him, so Roast Beef, Suet Pudding, Bacon, and Eggs, plus gross-smelling Kippers, were the norm in our house.

Mum was a good cook, and as we left the Pub I was starting to get that feeling of anticipation of good grub to come.

We arrived back at the house quickly, Dad still in his jovial mood as we opened the front door and walked into the hall.

'We're home,' cried Dad, and with that, Mum replied.

'Dinners ready, it's very special today.'

I began to wonder what was so special. Mum always did a grand table for us, and as I walked into the dining room, the table looked great with all places neatly set, the silver and well-polished candelabra proudly standing in the centre of the table, but this was normal for Mum's Sunday lunch. I drew Judy to one side, and I whispered in Judy's ear.

Has Mum said anything, 'What's so special about today?" Dad is like a dog that's found his lost bone!'

Judy replied, 'Mum's been strange too. It's like she is waiting to announce a pool win or something, but I know no more than you.'

Mum came bustling into the dining room.

'Well dinners ready, all get up to the table places quickly!'

'Len!' she called out, noting he was absent and had disappeared to the loo.

'Hurry up, it's going on to the table.'

We all assembled, Judy managed to get Graeme and Karen to sit down and we then waited in anticipation for Mum's special delights.

Within just a few minutes, Mum, with Judy's assistance, had duly delivered the steaming plates. The fine aroma of cooked beef was all around, and my mouth began to salivate as I looked at my piled-up plate of delights.

Mum, at last, sat down, sat with us, and looked over at Dad, who had hurriedly returned to the room.

We had barely started eating when Mum spoke up sharply.

'Len, are you going to tell them now?'

'Tell them what,' I immediately thought, having sensed before that something was afoot, then all flashed to the conclusion, 'It must be the pools!'

I turned my head quickly in Dad's direction to note him paused, sat up straight, ready spring to deliver his message.

He started in his usual official manner for this sort of thing, hesitantly at first, then in confident stream.

'Your Mother and I have something to tell you,' He announced,

'We have just had an Insurance policy come out from Prudential, and guess what, it's done so well we have got so much more than we expected, so we decided to give us all a treat.'

A treat, I thought, presents, some cash perhaps. In our low and impoverished state of early marriage, Judy and I were grateful for anything.

Dad carried on, "Your mum and I thought we'd do something special this year. So, for Christmas, we've booked us all into a hotel for eight days in Benidorm, Spain!"

Judy and I just looked at each other, completely taken aback.

Little Karen piped up in her squeaky voice, "What's Benidorm, Mummy? Is it far away?"

Judy smiled, her face lighting up. "It's in Spain, love, another country where the weather is always warm. Your dad and I went to Spain on our honeymoon, but we haven't been back since you and Graeme came along!"

I said in a sort of shocked delight, 'It's just wonderful!'

Judy felt a tear coming and gave Mum and big hug and then got up and went round to Dad and gave him the same treatment.

'When do we go, Dad?' I asked quickly, barely being able to talk because of the excitement in my voice.

'We leave home and fly off just three days before Christmas,' Dad replied excitedly,

'I've booked it with the blokes from work; they go every year.'

With his audience of us four eagerly waiting, Dad continued to further explain the situation and went on quickly.

'Dennis, my old workmate, suggested that now I had some money, why not join their little group for the Christmas trip?'

'Dennis said that he, his wife Florrie Jim, and Doris were all booked, so why not join us and make up a great party.'

'Well, Mum and Dad,' I exclaimed, 'I knew you were going to tell us something, but we had no idea it was going to be as wonderful as this. I just can't take it in!'

I continued, without hardly a space in my voice, and looking towards Judy and Mum cried out with such joy.

'What a great holiday we are going to have, and only six weeks away, oh! Dad, Mum, what a fantastic surprise, we are so happy!'

Dad slowly got up from the table, looked at me with a grin all over his face, and said in almost a whisper,

'I've got the brochure with our Hotel in it; I'll just pop out to the kitchen and get it to show you where we are going.'

With that he scurried off quickly to return with the brochure we were now dying to see.

He sat down and slowly opened the pages until he came to the one which had the corner folded over.

'Here it is!' Dad exclaimed, 'Our super Hotel is called the Flemington, and we have ten glorious days!'

Strange name for a Hotel, I thought, a bit sort of Yuk sounding!

Dad then put the open pages in front of us and quickly put his finger on the Hotel picture.

It was Dad's practice not to let you read certain things for yourself; he seemed to get great pleasure explaining everything personally to you, particularly on matters that he was excited about. This one certainly came high on his 'I'll show you category.'

As the presentation unfolded, Dad explained, like an expert salesman, all the outstanding features of this jewel in the crown of Benidorm.

From the spacious restaurant where the Chef proudly boasted of his pride in the range and standard of the cuisine to the spacious bedrooms, with a balcony overlooking the famous Levante Beach. The rooftop, swimming pool and the ballroom, where there would be nightly dancing and entertainment. If this was not enough for a fabulous holiday, Dad continued on to the grand finale.

'There's a special Christmas dinner,' he explained, 'The Hotel is putting on the full works, just like we have in England, and afterwards, a special party night in the ballroom!'

Judy and I looked at one another, hardly being able to contain our excitement. Mum turned to us and, with a grin, said,

'What do you think of that?' and turned to proudly look at Dad, the instigator and planner of this wonderful event.

Karen and Graeme, taking all this in, had been strangely quiet then Karen piped up.

'Will Father Christmas come, does he go to Spain?'

'Of course he does,' Judy quickly replied and looked at Dad anxiously for confirmation.

Dad sat up quickly, having been put on the spot, and without hesitation confirmed.

'Father Christmas will definitely be coming; I've written him a letter!'

Thoughts quickly flashed through my mind.

'What would a Spanish Father Christmas be like?'

Spanish men are usually thin. It would take a hell of a lot of padding to look the part!

I wondered, would he say 'Ho Ho Ho' in Spanish and would he breathe garlic all over the children?' I further realised that Hotels in Spain don't have chimneys.

I realised the whole scenario of Father Christmas would have to be re-examined, and knowing more questions would undoubtedly come from Karen, I made a mental note to talk to Judy, Mum, and Dad about this one when the kids were asleep.

We continued with our Roast Beef dinner, which seemed that day to taste like no better Roast Beef in the world.

The rest of the day went so quickly, and before we knew it, Judy and I, plus the kids, were waving Mum and Dad goodbye, and we were off in the little Singer Chamois, which had now almost taken onto the feel and space of a Rolls Royce!

We were so elated the journey seemed to take only minutes, and quickly, we were turning into our road in Dunstable and pulling up the drive to the garage. We soon got in and put the kids to bed, hoping Father Christmas would not be mentioned.

Luckily the subject did not arise further as tiredness had taken over and little eyes were starting to close.

We crept out slowly from each room and eagerly moved off and into our bedroom. Thankfully, Judy and I were soon tucked up and comfortable in bed.

The room felt silent as a changing scene from our hotel night experience of noisy corridors and people talking loudly.

As Judy settled down, she said to me in a happy voice,

'What a wonderful day! I just can't wait for the next six

weeks to pass, it's going to be Heaven, all that beautiful sunshine, sandy beaches, and wonderful evenings!'

We were so happy that night and cuddled together and quickly drifted off to a beautiful, deep sleep, completely oblivious to what fate had in store.

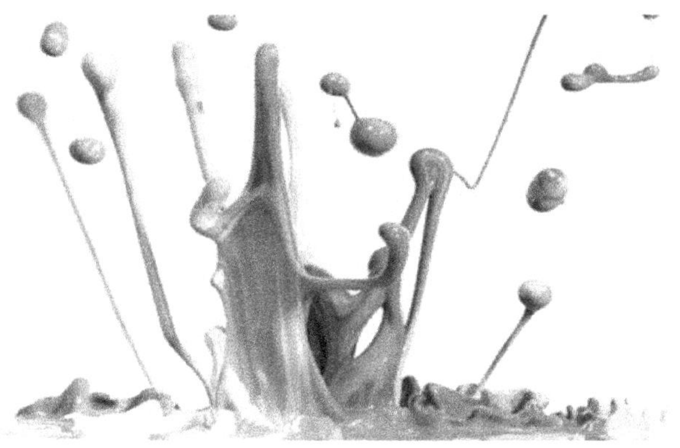

Chapter 3 – Decorating Is Fun

After a long day Judy and I had just got the kids up to bed. After the usual return trips for drinks of water, I'm hot in bed, can't sleep, can we watch the telly a bit longer etc, we started to relax.

Just as Judy had made a cup of tea and I sat down with a glass of my infamous homemade beer, Tom Caxton's Best Bitter, I recall, the bloody phone went.

'Who's that,' Judy called out.

'As if I know,' I replied with my usual curt kind of response to questions like that, 'Go and answer it and find out!'

I've never understood why people say 'Whose that!' when a phone rings.

Same applies to, 'Who's at the door?' not to mention, 'Who's this letter from?' while staring at it unopened. More and more, it just goes on.

Judy got up, sighed, looked at me, stuck out her tongue, and walked over to the phone.

'Hello Mum, 'It's Mum,' she said, looking at me, and then went into a long conversation as the ladies can do.

I concentrated as best I could on the telly, sipped my beer, and hoped the kids would not have heard and come downstairs.

But this night, we were lucky, not the sound or sight of them, 'Thank God,' I thought to myself.

After what seemed like an eternity, the telephone conversation petered out,

'See you Saturday night, take care, love to Dad, yes I'll give your love to Ken, Karen & Graeme.'

'Yes, they are in bed now. Goodnight, see you Saturday, sweet dreams, looking forward to seeing you, etc., etc. etc.

It's always been another great source of mystery to me; why do some people take so long to finish a telephone call. I imagined Dad sitting in his chair at home, thinking the same as me.

I made a mental note to discuss this with him and my Uncle Charles when we got down to the Windermere Pub at the weekend or on Friday night if we got to Mum and Dad's early enough.

'Bye Bye,' I heard Judy say in conclusion.

She put down the phone, plonked herself down in the chair, and looked at me.

'Guess what,' she exclaimed, 'Dads started decorating the hall, and it's only three little weeks to go on our holiday in Spain.'

She continued. "Mum wants it finished so that it's all nice when she comes home.'

'Trust Mum!' I replied, raising my eyebrows and nodding my head in agreement.

Dad had previously told us Mum was planning the pre-Christmas decorating of the hall, stairs, and landing. Quite why he was pressed into doing this now was a mystery to me as we were to be away so soon.

'I would have thought they would have waited until after Christmas to do the decorating!' I questioned Judy, 'What a strange thing to do now!'

'You know Mum!' she replied, 'Always thinking of the next job for poor old Dad.'

'If I know Mum, she will have Christmas again after we get back from our holiday.'

'I guess you're right,' I said in agreement. 'Mum will invite all her friends round for a great big party to tell them all about our adventures, and I guess she will want to show off the new painting!'

'Well,' said Judy. 'As they already have that bumpy wallpaper Dad had decided to paint it over with emulsion paint.'

She continued, strangely and pausing sentence as if she might be thinking the plan was rather odd and explained.

'They have chosen two colours, one for the wall up the stairs and the other colour for the rest of it!'

'That's novel! I hope it looks ok when it's finished; you know what an old fusspot my mother is with decorating!'

The thought of two different colours slapped onto thick, bumpy paper filled me with a kind of wonderment. As a kid, I'd grown up with years of home decorating, and my parents often took a rather peculiar approach to this part of household life.

Dad, bless him, was a top-notch decorator. He'd spend hours painstakingly stripping walls, hanging wallpaper, washing down with Sugar Soap, rubbing down paint, and doing all the other little bits and pieces that made the difference between a shoddy job and a decent one.

Sugar Soap was used a lot on Dad's day, and he used to swear by it. I remember mentioning the name many years later, and some daft bloke thought it was a sweet of some kind, silly sod.

Mum, in her usual supervisory role, would pop up at regular intervals to inspect and offer the full benefit of her advice and opinions on the progress and quality of the job.

"Len, you've missed a bit over there!" was one of Mum's favourite lines.

"Do you think it'll dry patchy like this?"

"I hope that wallpaper settles back to the wall, it's got a lot of bumps in it!" And so it went on.

Over the course of a decorating project, my Dad—who, by nature, was as placid as they come—would start to get a bit "miffed off." I was fully expecting our visit over the weekend to be a good laugh. Dad would be telling me stories like,

"Old Hawkies have been at it again; she could spot a fly on the wall at 100 yards! She should try decorating!" More would follow, I was sure.

My mind quickly pictured Mum in the hall, carrying out her routine inspection of the works, Dad rolling his eyes and saying to himself,

'Yes dear, no dear, three bags full dear,' and hoping she would return to the kitchen quickly.

Thinking of poor old Dad slaving over the paint pot, I turned to Judy and asked,

"How about we head down to Mum and Dad's tomorrow for the weekend? I'm guessing Dad's going to need a break from the 'helpful' critique."

"Sounds good to me," Judy replied without missing a beat. "I'll call Mum now and check if it's alright."

So, the usual long-winded chat ensued, but it more or less confirmed that our visit was a go. And, of course, I knew Dad would be counting the hours until we arrived—he'd need a pint or two just to survive Mum's next round of 'decorating advice.'

The evening drew on, and with phone time concluded, our bedtime had quickly arrived. Wearily, we departed the living room for our quiet (don't wake them up), crept up the stairs, and quickly into bed. As I drifted off to sleep, I had happy thoughts of chats with Dad over a pint or two and the expectation of Mum's fine dinners with roast potatoes and Yorkshire pudding. My mouth watered.

My sleep was both welcome, and sustaining, realising quickly as I awoke and feeling in such Great Spirit, and happy now it was Saturday, and no work today.

I had also awoken to a beautiful September morning, the sun shining beams of sunlight through the gaps in the curtains. I thought of the day ahead and felt so pleased we were off down to Mum & Dad's for the start of a great weekend.

I looked towards Judy to see her eyes slowly open. She smiled at me in a happy way and then got up quickly from the bed.

Judy was soon up and away, bustling in and out of drawers and wardrobe, preparing for our weekend trip.

I followed, at a rather slower pace, to assist with the Kids.

Our teamwork paid off, and they were duly bathed, dressed, and breakfasted in quick order and ready for the off at 10.30am.

Judy's haste to get ready was especially noticeable, just that bit more paced than usual. I had realised that it was surely due to the desire to see just what Mum and Dad had got up to with the decorating.

It all just happened like a greyhound out of the trap as Judy quickly loaded the kids into our little Singer Chamois Sports, and we sped off down the M1 and on to Mum and Dad's.

We tried to visit at least once every two weeks. They loved seeing the kids and would also babysit so Judy and I could go out on the town or visit friends. We could also pop into Judy's Mum and see her and chin wag over a cup of tea.

It was a pleasant, uneventful journey; no one was sick, and the kids didn't argue. The traffic for a Saturday morning on the M1 was surprisingly not heavy, and I thought happily to myself, I'm looking forward to this weekend!

If we got to Mum's early, as it looked like we would, I could give Dad a rest from the decorating, and we could go down the pub for a few jars.

I said to Judy as she stared strangely through the car window as if fixated on something that was quite puzzling.

'I bet poor Dad's well fed up with his decorating by now!'

Thinking that this would further smooth the path for Dad and me to go early to the pub.

'Yes, I bet he must be tired, what with going to work all week and decorating when he gets home!' she replied and continued.

'I bet Mum's been doing her usual inspections. I suppose you should take him out for a pint before dinner,' She suggested.

I quickly seized the opportunity, nodding my approving head.

'Perhaps that will be a good idea,' I answered in anticipation,

'You really don't mind if we pop out for a little while?'

'No, I can have a good old chat with Mum all about holiday preparations,' she replied, 'I know you men don't want to think about things like that!'

So this had all the makings of a good weekend, and I felt a happy sense of well-being.

In no time, we were turning the corner into Mum and Dad's road and quickly pulled into the drive. The front door swung open before we even had a chance to park, and there she was—Mum, bounding out like she'd been waiting by the door for hours.

True to form, she leapt out as if launching from a starting block, ready to give us all a bear hug before bombarding us with a flurry of questions. "How was the journey? Did you get caught in traffic? Did you stop for a break? Why didn't you call me when you left?!"

You know, the usual inquisition, all wrapped up in the kind of enthusiasm only a mother could muster about when they have not seen you for a week or two.

'How are you all,' she greeted us warmly as we opened the car doors to get out; Dad was surprisingly absent.

'Fine,' I said, 'I suppose Dad is up the ladder with a paintbrush in his hand?'

Mum laughed and pointed her finger in the direction of the open doorway where Dad was obviously otherwise engaged with a brush.

'You got it; Dad's well into the painting now!'

With that, Judy and I got Karen and Graeme out of the car only to be rained on with hugs and kisses from Mum.

'Where's Granddad?' Karen asked, 'He usually comes out with you, Nanny' she anxiously continued.

'You heard your Dad,' she replied, 'Granddads' up a ladder.

We stepped up the small drive and into the hall only to see Dad at the top of his stepladder, paintbrush in one hand and bucket in the other. I could see he had been busy and had so far painted the wall down the side of the stairs blue. He turned around, waving his brush in greeting.

'Hello,' he smiled at us and looked grinning at Karen.

'How are you Karen and you Graeme? I'll just get down off these steps!'

Dad looked in a rather precarious position with a brush in his right hand and a bucket in the left.

He hastily shoved the paint bucket onto the top of the steps and scrambled down the few rungs to the hall floor. In his rush, Dad had completely forgotten about the bucket lurking by the last step of the ladder. We quickly discovered that the paint—peach, of course—had other plans. It shot up in a glorious eruption, like some sort of volcanic disaster, as Dad's right foot plunged straight into the bucket. The paint, now airborne, found a new home—down his trouser leg and splattered some of the walls.

A loud cry of "Bugger it!" echoed through the hallway.

Poor old Dad, now flailing in fury, raised his arms in a kind of helpless rage. But with his foot stuck in the bucket, he wobbled like a toddler learning to walk, reaching out for the stepladder for support. And then—everything happened in an instant.

The bucket which Dad had placed down on the top of the steps, a bit too quickly for comfort, wobbled and then toppled off the step, fell forward, and hit poor Dad on his left leg.

Within an instant paint was everywhere, down his trouser legs, up the wall, over the floor. Dad just stood there, covered in peach down one leg and blue down the other, his face a sort of ashen colour and stretched taught.

I looked at Mum and Judy. Karen and Graeme stood with mouths open. I felt an overwhelming reaction to laugh. I could see Judy's mouth starting to curl up. Mum was similarly ready to break.

Dad just stood there, with paint brush still in his hand, looking like a small boy who had trod in dog poo or wet his pants.

It was too much, I felt my body start to shake and I could stifle the laughter no more.

Judy looked at me and put her hand to her face. Her shoulders were starting to move in an uncontrollable fashion, and within seconds, Mum, Judy, the kids, and I were reduced to convulsions of laughter.

Dad was very clearly not amused by this and said hotly,

'I'm glad you lot can laugh, I'm going to clean up!'

He removed the bucket from his right leg and turned to march in the direction of the kitchen.

The following event, while not quite as dramatic as the bucket falling from the ladder or the Dad's foot in the bucket, brought its own special finale.

In his haste and anger, poor Dad had unwittingly planted his best foot straight into a roll of wallpaper, which lay coiled up like a snake ready to strike. This small, seemingly innocent move triggered a chain reaction. The wallpaper unrolled at breakneck speed across the hall while the spilt paint splashed everywhere like a Jackson Pollock gone rogue.

None of us had the slightest clue what to do next. Judy and I lost it completely. She grabbed onto me, arms flailing, convulsing like a demented disco dancer caught in a time loop. I was shaking so hard I thought I might soil myself.

But honestly, the sight of Dad's face was enough to fuel the flames of laughter. I swear we must've stood there, laughing like maniacs, for what felt like an eternity. Meanwhile, Dad, caught in a moment of pure confusion, just stood there frozen, probably the wisest thing to do under the circumstances.

Mum, sensing Dad might explode at any second, was first to compose herself. She advanced towards him and said in encouraging words.

'Len, just stand still, and I'll get some cloth to wipe the paint off your legs!'

She quickly scurried off to the kitchen while making a great footwork effort to avoid the mess over the floor. She returned in seconds with some old cloth and immediately set to onto Dad to wipe off the paint. I managed to blurt out a few words of encouragement,

'Dad, it's only emulsion. It will wash off in no time!'

This did little to remove the stern look on Dad's face.

Judy quickly turned to Dad and announced.

'It's ok, Dad, we'll soon clear this mess up!' She continued.

'When Mum finished wiping you down, we can get those painted trousers off so you can go up to the bathroom and clean up properly; it will all wash off!'

Ken and I will clear up the paint and paper mess, so don't worry. Get up to the bathroom with Mum, and you will soon feel better.

With a look of grudging agreement, Dad sighed heavily; he then turned round slowly and said to everyone in a grunted voice.

'This accident is not funny, all me paints gone and half me paper!'

He little realised he was in considerable danger of starting us off again, but Mum, realising this, quickly pulled off his trousers and led him, all pants and skinny white legs, up the stairs and to the bathroom.

This, under the circumstances was the wisest thing to do.

'I don't think I've seen anything so funny for years,' I said to Judy. 'Poor old Dad, he looked so helpless, I feel so sorry for him.'

She nodded, still laughing,

'You'd better get Dad down to the pub when he's cleaned up, buy him a few pints to calm down and cheer him up!'

'Yes, that sounds the best idea,' I quickly replied.

'Under the circumstances, I'd better get him a few, and if I know Dad, he will soon be laughing about this!'

I looked around at Karen and Graeme, who had been holding one another throughout this happening; both were giggling as Kids do at the sign of something funny.

'Don't laugh anymore, you two!' I said firmly, 'It will upset Granddad; he will be down here in a moment.'

'Sorry Daddy said Karen, but poor Granddad did get rather a lot of paint over him, but we will not say anything!'

True enough, just a few minutes later, as we were clearing up the last of the paint dregs, Dad came marching down the stairs.

Dad was sporting a big grin on his face and shining in a new smart trousers and jacket. Following behind was an equally smiling Mum. All seemed back to normal.

'Come on, son!' Dad said, 'I think I deserve a good few beers after all that!'

With a nod from Mum, who had now observed the clean-up with apparent approval, we made our goodbyes to leave.

Dad pointed me in the direction of his car and we moved outside and towards his Ford Escort we called 'The Yellow Peril.'

This car travelled all around building sites and would generally show heavy mud streaks on the tyres and body. The inside was similarly mud-coated on the carpets. With Mum's heavy decorating programme, it was clear Dad had no time for the car.

Within minutes, we were quickly seated in Dad's car and, in no time, into the Windermere for the start of our weekend's bevvy and the pleasure of Mum's big but delayed roast dinner.

The Yellow Peril

Chapter 4 – The Plague

The next weeks leading up to Christmas went like lightning; Judy and I were saving like mad. I worked as much. I squeezed in as much overtime at overtime at Rolls Royce as I could. Steadily, we put together a little pool of cash to see us through the holiday. Everything was wonderful.

It was one week before our departure. I was sitting at work by my desk, when the phone went.

My workmate Dave picked it up, looked at me and said.

'It's for you Ken, it's your misses.'

'I wonder what she wants.' I replied, 'Usually, a phone call at work heralds some disaster like the washing machines leaking, the kid's locked in the toilet, the car won't start, or some other drama too horrible to contemplate.'

I thought, 'Best get up and get to the phone.'

'Hello Judy,' I said in anticipation, What's up?"

"Ken," Judy replied; her voice was tense, and I immediately knew something was wrong.

"It's Karen," she said, "This morning Karen felt a little poorly, then by the afternoon she was starting to get a temperature and to get a rash over her face and back."

"Oh my God," I said, "what's the matter.'

'I think it's chicken pox,' Judy exclaimed. 'I saw Maureen next door and her two have just had it, and they had the same symptoms!'

'What are we going to do?' I said quickly. 'We go on holiday next week!'

'I'm going to get the doctor round tonight,' Judy replied, 'He will soon know what it is.'

It felt like a hit on the head from a thunderbolt and out through the feet. Poor Karen, sick just one week before our holidays start,

'What could we do? We were really stuck!'

My thoughts went to the strange hope of some Godly salvation with an anticipation of a God-like answer to our misfortune.

'Maybe Karen will recover quickly; kids do.' Perhaps that's it?

I tried to convince myself that all would be well, and then we could still go, but what about the spots? Everyone would notice and think Karen had got the plague or something!

The next few awful, wracked hours at work took so long to pass, grinding at me till I was able to get on my way home.

What were we to do? A thousand thoughts went through my mind, holiday in ruins, Graeme getting sick the next week, why was God doing this to us? What sin had we committed? All my hours of overtime for nothing!

Oh, woe is me, I thought, falling into the trap of self-pity.

The slow, ticking clock finally reached my goal, and soon, I was out of the building and running to my car, furtively driving home to see what fate awaited us.

I went straight to see Karen when I arrived home. The poor kid was very hot and sweaty, and her face was covered in spots. I took great pains not to look hard and let her think she was too bad.

It seemed like hours until the Doctor came. Fortunately, it was Doctor Pike who called; he was Judy's favourite and had looked after her during both pregnancies. He was a God in her eyes.

He entered with his customary haste, stethoscope dangling around his neck as was his normal way.

'Well, where's the patient,' he asked as he briskly walked into the hallway.

'She's upstairs,' replied Judy, and up the three of us went into poor Karen's bedroom.

Dr. Pike quickly examined Karen and confirmed the worst.

'It's chicken pox; by the look of it, she will have to rest for a few days, but it doesn't look like a bad attack. See what she is like later in the week.'

'What about Graeme? We are supposed to be off on holiday to Spain next week,' Judy anxiously asked.

Dr. Pike paused and then put his hand to his chin. He turned to look at Judy and said, to our everlasting relief.

'Well, Karen should be ok; she is not contagious now the spots are out, but as for Graeme we will just have to wait and see, he may not get it.'

With that to ponder, the good Doctor headed down our stairs, out of the door, and off into the night to another waiting patient. And so, for us, the nightmare began. Would Graeme get the Pox?

Judy immediately called Mum and Dad with the news. Mum, in her wonderfully optimistic way, dismissed it as a mere hiccup,

'Chicken Pox is not much; I remember when Ken had it, he was up and running about after 2 or 3 days, spots went after a week or so.'

'But what about Graeme? What happens if he gets it,' Judy questioned quickly.

'We don't know that,' said Mum, but it doesn't always follow he will get it; some kids are resistant, Ken's cousin Susan was always with Ken when they were little kids, and when he got it, she never followed, so you just don't know!'

It was good listening to Mum; she had great wisdom in these matters, so after this little chat, Judy and I felt so much better.

'Let's check what happens in the next few days?' said Judy after collecting her thoughts for a few moments.

'Karen may be alright like Mum said,' I can always cover her spots with lotion so she doesn't look too bad!'

I agreed; there was little we could do. We were in the hands of fate, and fate could be a hard master, I thought to myself.

With just three days left before departure, Karen was back

to her cheerful, bouncy self, though still rocking a slightly polka-dotted look. The spots were fading, but not fast enough to calm our nerves. Judy and I exchanged knowing glances—decision time. Do we stay or roll the dice and go? The next few days seemed like a year. Karen was still with a temperature; Judy kept dosing her up with 'Beechams Powders', the great cure for all sweaty ailments.

Sure enough, by the third day, Karen was out of bed, running around like nothing had happened! 'What about the spots,' I wondered.' Poor kid looked very pasty too. The more we looked at her face, the more spots we could see.

The anxious Judy also examined Graeme hourly, but so far, he showed no symptoms of anything and was running around and into mischief like usual.

It finally reached a point of three days to departure. Karen, by this time, was well again, back to her normal happy little self, just spotty, but even these were fading fast. Judy and I both realised it was decision time, to stay or to go.

'What are we going to do,' I asked Judy in the sort of way that let her know we had really come to the crunch.

'Well, Karen seems alright to me now; the Doctor said she is on the mend; just keep her quiet a few more days.'

'But what about the spots,' I asked nervously. People will think she has some horrible disease or other; what will we say? They may not let us into Spain.'

'But Karen is okay now; she's not infectious according to the Doctor,' Judy said in a reassuring sort of way.

'If you are worried, let me see if I can cover the spots over. They are getting better each day, and by the time we go in three days, they will probably be nearly gone.'

With that Judy went upstairs and returned a few moments later with a bottle and some cotton wool.

'What's that,' I enquired hesitantly.

'It's calamine lotion,' Judy replied, 'I'll try some on Karen now and see if it works.'

Karen was duly summoned and, after some mild resistance, let her mother daub a little on her face. The transformation had to be seen to be believed. She looked almost normal.

'Thank God for Mums,' I thought.

'Well, what do you think of this,' Judy asked proudly.

'You've done the business,' I replied happily, 'what a star; let's phone Mum and Dad and tell them to book our taxi.'

'Benidorm, here we come!'

The great day arrived so quickly and with the usual panic of last-minute things to do.

Karen came down from the bedroom, all dressed up in her holiday gear, having just been sorted out by Judy.

'Spots, I see no spots,' said I, 'Karen, you look lovely, but don't scratch your face!'

I walked out to the car; it was cold enough to freeze off a brass monkey's nuts. I scraped the ice off the windscreen and then put the cases in our little car.

With Judy duly seated and Graeme and Karen safely strapped in their seats we were ready for the off, down to Mum and Dad's.

I had just started the engine when Graeme cried out

'Mum, I want to go pooh-pooh!'

Judy was not very happy at this prospect and said crossly,

'Can't you wait till Nannies?'

'No, Mummy, I want to pooh-pooh now!' was the lad's urgent reply.

With so many things packed into the car it was no mean feat to remove enough of it to eject Graeme from his seat.

'You know!' The full compliment that every Mum and Dad needs for kids on holiday. The driveway is now littered again.

Judy took him inside and back into the house.

I contemplated being rich enough to buy a Cortina Estate, big enough for all of us.

'Still dream away, son,' I thought, on my low wages another two years at least.

At least we are going on holiday, and we have overcome the major setback; we just can't let a little pooh-pooh spoil the start of a wonderful day.

Judy returned with a smiling Graeme who I duly bolted in position and re-loaded the car. With the engine started and smiles on our faces, we sped off to Mum and Dad's, thinking life was so good and contemplating the wonderful Christmas in paradise.

We were a mere five minutes from Mum and Dad's when Karen screamed out the dreaded words no parent wants to hear on a car journey.

'I feel sick!'

I quickly looked into my rearview mirror just to witness a stream of puke, flowing like a fountain, bursting from her face.

This cascaded all down her brother, whose face now had the look of sudden and extreme shock. Instantly, he shrieked out loudly,

'Karen sicked on me!'

He sat imprisoned by his safety seat, arms outstretched and waving like a pirouette.

Judy turned round to view this latest disaster.

'Couldn't you wait?' She rasped out angrily, 'Why didn't you ask Daddy to stop.'

'I'm sorry, Mummy, it just came!' she replied with a tearful sob.

Fortunately, we arrived at Mum's quickly. Graeme was still screaming and trying to move his arms out of his harness.

'I'm all sticky,' He squalled out. 'I want to see my Nanny!'

Karen was crying, with periodic intervals of heavy sobbing.

We quickly poured ourselves out of the car. Fortunately, Mum was outside and, from the commotion, quickly realised what had happened and grabbed Karen to take her inside first.

Like the good Mum she was, Judy pulled the reserve clothes for Graeme from the bag and, once inside the house, quickly calmed him down while my shitty job was cleaning up sick from the car and getting out the rest of the luggage.

The taxi arrived thirty minutes later, and as though nothing had happened, we were quickly loaded and off to the Airport, thinking nothing else could go wrong.

The rest of the journey was uneventful, but excitement thickened the air, accompanied by something from the Taxi driver.

It became apparent as the journey progressed that the Driver had a dreadful personal problem. This caused me to subsequently lower the window a little to let some fresh air get in.

Mum was busy chattering away about everything when suddenly Karen advised,

'It's smelly in here, Daddy. Is that why you've opened the window?'

'What is the smell, Daddy?' she continued.

'I don't know, darling,' I quickly replied, hoping we could dump the subject quickly, but to no avail.

'It's horrible smelly Daddy,' Graeme piped up,

'Yes, we must be near a dustbin place,' I said, trying to divert the problem out of the car.

'But it's been smelly since home, Daddy,' Karen retorted, seemingly determined to get to the bottom, or should I say the armpit of the subject.

'That's enough now,' Said Mum, coming to the rescue.

'We will soon be at the Airport, and we can all have a nice drink with our friends.'

Karen and Graeme carried on the rest of the journey giggling most of the time; I think they thought Granddad had farted.

I looked at Judy often, who had become rather quiet.

'What's up Judy,' I questioned in a concerned sort of way. Judy touched her face; I immediately looked at Karen, who had obviously been wiping her face a lot, revealing the last vestiges of the spots we had tried so hard to cover.

Judy quickly delved into her bag and reached in for the lotion and cotton wool. In seconds, the bottle top was off, and to Karen's cries of, 'Oh Mum, not again!' the lotion was quickly daubed on.

'Karen, be very careful not to go wiping it off again,' Judy requested strongly, but I knew this was like telling the wind to stop blowing. Karen was a far too busy little person to keep still for very long.

Mercifully, the taxi reached the airport in a short while, and I, for one, breathed a sigh of relief, waiting anxiously to get quickly into a BO-free zone!

Chapter 5 – The Wonders Of Flight

(Day 1)

The taxi glided—or maybe crawled—into the Departures area of the ever-chaotic Luton Airport. Finally, we had arrived, and not a moment too soon. The driver eased to a stop, and we all spilt out like popcorn from a too-full bag. Judging by his less-than-thrilled expression, he wasn't exactly sad to see us go, but to his credit, he did help hoist our overstuffed cases onto a trolley Dad had triumphantly discovered nearby.

With the luggage loaded and Dad handing over the cash, we made our grand entrance through the airport doors, ready to tackle the madness of the departure area—armed with a trolley, a little bit of hope, and probably no idea what was coming next.

Luton Airport wasn't exactly the crown jewel of the Luton and Dunstable area—its reputation for delayed flights and questionable service preceded it. Walking in, it was hard to miss the drab, uninspired décor. The vibe? Let's just say it wasn't screaming "welcome!"—more like "brace yourself."

Scanning the area for some clue of where to go, my eyes landed on a large board hanging from the ceiling, still a good distance away. It looked promising—flight information, perhaps? As we got closer, I noticed the letters on the board flipping and rolling at breakneck speed, as if they had somewhere more important to be. Squinting didn't help much, but hey, it added to the adventure, didn't it?

I turned to Dad, who I could see had the flight tickets in hand, with fingers outstretched, looking for our flight number.

'It's Monarch, 161to Alicante', Dad informed us.

Just as Dad had called out the flight number and I tried to follow the line to the check-in number, the board rotated, and all the letters scrambled; when it stopped the line I was looking at had changed. Suddenly, flight B161 to Alicante was BA007 to Nice. The board spun again, and I quickly scanned it, but to no avail. Happily, after a few minutes of this pantomime, the board rolled onto our flight number, and I discovered we were to go to check in at gate No. 5.

'It's gate No 5!' I informed the family, who were all looking a bit agitated, as travellers do in strange places, and to admit, I was also feeling a bit in that vein. I put it down to our earlier events.

Dad responded quickly by giving directions,

'It's best we go to the check-in; I said we would all meet up there, and Dennis said we could then wait together in the bar.

'That sounds like the best plan,' I quickly replied, 'Let's get settled by the bar!'

Just as we were about to march off in the direction of the check, a loud 'Hello, Len' bellowed from behind.

We all turned round to see Dennis making a beeline towards us, with Florrie trailing close behind, pushing a trolley for all she was worth.

Dad waved, and quickly, Dennis was upon us, hand outstretched to greet us.

Dennis and Dad had worked together for close to 30 years, tied like surfs to The Firm, where they had both been almost since birth or so it seemed. Dad had been with The Firm since the age of thirteen, and Dennis at sixteen.

Dad was, at this point, working alongside the company representative and Dennis, running the sand and ballast plant. They had been solid workmates from the very beginning, united in their mutual grumbles about "The Firm" and the general goings-on—an expression Dad used often. Their camaraderie seemed to thrive on shared frustrations and a good dose of sympathy for each other.

Dennis was a great bloke, East End of London and proud of it. He was of average height with a stocky build. His head was slightly balding and beneath this, he had a rounded sort of face which looked well lived in. Dennis had a certain presence about him and you sensed that nobody messed with Dennis.

Dad always liked him and would often describe him as forthright and that you knew where you stood with him.

To say he could call a spade a spade was no exaggeration, as many an unsuspecting person would learn as our holiday unfolded.

Florrie was, in contrast, a fairly quiet lady, larger than Dennis, more on the way to Mum's generous size but not quite.

She had red hair and a round, friendly face, which I learned could turn quickly into laughter.

She had a bit of an old-fashioned way about her, according to Dad.

Mum and she always got on well at the times they had met on the annual firm's do's, and although this was the first time they had spent a holiday together, I guessed they both thought they had enough in common to have a good time.

Anyway, Mum could talk enough for two or, on a good day, three or four. Dad used to say Tiggy could jaw the hind leg off a donkey.

Florrie, however, was not far behind in the talking stakes and within minutes Mum and she were talking away about all and everything.

With greetings over, Dennis informed us in his normal rough voice,

'Jim and Dorris are at the check-in already!' He continued,

'They travelled together with us in a hired mini bus but have gone on a bit ahead to find out everything we must do at the check-in. We held back waiting for you all to arrive!'

'Let's get checked in now', said Dennis excitedly, and turned round to look at Dad, then continued.

'When we get checked in, Jim, Ken and I can have a quick one in the bar.'

I realised the wisdom of this man quickly. I had only met him before a few times when I collected Mum and Dad from the Firms Do's. Most times, they were in the latter stages of 'Having a good time', so there had never been the opportunity for a 'Get to know you session.' However, Dad's reports were highly favourable, and Dennis's suggestion of the bar was a good starting point. I began to feel well into the party mood already.

Mum, hearing this opportunity for a pre-flight drink, piped up with some gusto,

'What about us? I could do with a drink, and I bet Judy would like a Gin and Tonic!"

Well let's get checked in and be quick about it', said Dennis.

'If I know Jim, he will be waiting at the bar by now.'

This combination boded well for me at the very start of the holiday, and within a wink of an eye, we were through the check-in and into the bar area.

Greetings were duly administered, and without further ado, Jim was up at the bar with Dennis getting the drinks in.

They were back quickly with a loaded tray on which I could see a few pints.

Drinks were passed to the ladies who were busy listening to Judy's stories of Chicken Pox and car sickness. Our turn was next, and soon, we were all pints in hand and into the holiday spirit.

Dennis sure could down a pint, as I was quick to learn; no keeping up with this, I thought to myself. Still, I had eleven days to try!

I did not know Jim and Doris but had heard a lot about them from Dad who had met them a few times before when visiting Dennis and Florrie's house.

Dorris was a tall, thin woman about 5ft 8 inches tall. She was very smartly dressed in a green two-piece with a nice brooch in her lapel. She was quite thin-faced and had light grey hair. I noticed she spoke very quietly but with a London accent, more refined than Dennis or her husband, Jim.

She told Mum she had a job at the RSPCA and jokingly said she liked looking after soppy animals that's why she had married Jim.

Jim, by contrast, was a little chap, slight in build, with a thin face and a good head of dark brown hair. He was a smart man who complimented his wife. He sported a blue blazer, grey trousers and polished shoes. Dad had told me it was a good laugh and everybody liked him. He was also a war hero and had escaped from a German prisoner-of-war camp in 1943.

He had escaped twice from camps; the first time, he was caught and was seriously beaten by the German guards. They had hit him so hard that his jaw was fractured, and two of his fingers were broken. Apparently, this did not deter him, and he didn't give up. The second time, he escaped through a tunnel he had dug with his mates.

In spite of searches all night by the German guards with dogs, two of them got away and made it to a safe house in

France, where they were helped to get back to England by boat.

Dad once told me that Jim hated the Germans, and I reckoned that was understandable. He also mentioned that Jim didn't like to talk about his ordeal, so I decided there, and then it was a topic I'd never raise unless Jim brought it up himself.

A few minutes passed, and then Dennis chimed in. "I suppose we should check when we're boarding the plane; the thing might take off and leave us behind on its way to Spain!" he quipped, adding quickly, "I'll go and check the departure board!"

With that, Dennis got up and scurried off, leaving the rest of us.

"Well then, bottoms up!" said Dad with a grin, glancing pointedly at Mum, suggesting she might want to finish her drink. Mum took the hint and quickly drained her glass just as Dennis reappeared, announcing that it was nearly time to board.

Before he could finish, the crackly airport speaker system spluttered into life, grabbing everyone's attention.

'Would all passengers booked onto Monarch Airways flight 161 to Alicante move to boarding gate 3'.

I looked at Judy, who was busy controlling our two very excited kids, who were getting very fidgety in their seats and said.

'Well, love were off, how is Karen's face?' Judy sat upright as though I had shocked her a little with the unexpected question; she looked quickly down to where Karen was sitting,

'She looks okay.' Judy observed thankfully, 'I think the lotion has done the trick, so I guess it's time to face the journey to the clouds.

Jim said with an upbeat note of urgency in his voice, 'Come on, you lot, or we will miss the plane!'

With that advice from Jim we made our way to the departure gate, showed our boarding cards and quickly we were onto the outside. I could now see the whole aeroplane. 'Wow!' I thought, 'It's a Boeing 737, what a beauty!'

The aircraft were newly in service in the UK, and Monarch had decided to add some to their fleet, just behind British Airways, which was the UK launch customer. I felt a good deal of excitement building up as I realised I was soon to be flying in this fantastic aircraft.

A man in a bright yellow jacket appeared seemingly out of nowhere, gesturing for passengers to head towards the set of stairs leading to the open aircraft door. We were lagging a bit behind the main group, but he soon strode over to us and swiftly ushered us across the tarmac and into the plane.

"What plane is this?" Judy asked me, her voice tinged with worry.

Without thinking, I quipped, "Just some old crate, past its best, I'm sure!"

The look on her face made me instantly regret the joke. Knowing Judy's fear of flying, it was a poor choice of words. I quickly backtracked, trying to sound reassuring.

"I'm only joking, Luv. It's a Boeing 737—not very old, and one of the safest planes ever made."

Her response came without missing a beat: "I think I'll have a large gin and tonic and try to relax!"

Clearly, my attempt at reassurance hadn't landed quite as I'd hoped. At least the gin and tonic might help!

We soon boarded the plane and stowed our bags in the overhead lockers, sorting ourselves into our seats—two rows of three, as I noted. I settled Karen next to Mum and Dad, then strapped Graeme in by the window next to Judy, with myself in the aisle seat.

Dennis and the others had seats further up in the plane. From where I sat, I could just make out the top of Dennis's slightly balding head peeking over his seat, which reassured me that everyone was in place and ready for takeoff.

The air hostesses did their bit, showing you how to put on the life jacket and to put that strange red tube in the mouth to blow it up.

This, I noticed produced a guffaw of laughter from a group of young bloke's sitting in front of us. It also produced some slight redness on the face of the nearby air hostess, and she quickly withdrew the tube from her mouth.

After a few minutes, the engines whined to life, the sound steadily growing as they started up. Soon, we were trundling down the runway, ready for takeoff. The aircraft made a quick turn, and then the engines roared with power as the pilot prepared to lift us into the sky.

In an instant, we were racing down the runway, and I felt Judy's hand clamp tightly onto my arm.

As the plane climbed higher and broke through the clouds, the flight smoothed out, and we levelled off into a clear, steady cruise. I glanced at Judy, who seemed more at ease now, though her hand was still resting on my arm—just not with the same vice-like grip. I placed my hand gently over hers, and she turned to me with a sheepish grin, her nerves giving way to quiet relief.

After a short while the speakers crackled with the words I wanted to hear.

'The cabin staff will now be serving drinks from the trolley.'

It seemed to take ages for the trolley to arrive at our seats. As it finally approached, I could see two absolutely gorgeous girls known as trolley dollies. I later learned from a friend who worked on aircraft maintenance at the airport.

The first one leaned towards me and asked so nicely,

'Would you like something, Sir? Would you like to drink, Sir?'

I have to admit that unworthy thoughts instantly flashed through my mind.

'A Scotch and Lemonade for me, please, Gin and Tonic for my wife and a coke for Graeme,' I replied, trying to compose myself and put further naughty thoughts out of my mind.

Judy must have sensed in some way what I was thinking, and as I passed Graeme's coke and the Gin and Tonic to her, she scowled as only a woman can.

'That's a fair Gin and Tonic,' I said quickly, trying to divert her attention.

'Yes,' Judy replied, scowled again then turned to Graeme with his coke.

I quickly picked up my copy of the Daily Mirror, sipped my drink and decided to keep quiet for half an hour.

I was concentrating on my paper when a voice piped up from above my head.

'This is your Captain speaking, Captain Halton. We are soon to pass over the Pyrenees, and ground control has advised me there may be some slight turbulence, so please fasten your seat belts and remain seated!'

A few people were standing, and the duty-free trolley was in mid-path at this point; nobody seemed in any rush to get seated. The pilot was just being cautious, I guessed.

Within a moment the aircraft shuddered slightly, causing Judy to return to gripping my arm. Then again, the huge beast quivered; my drink was slurping about the glass and over my shaking hand.

I noticed people more urgently seeking their seats, as most now seemed intent on getting strapped in.

I looked at Judy and Graeme to reassure myself and privately.

'Only a little bit of turbulence, love, it will soon stop when we are over the mountains!'

No sooner had I finished my attempt at comforting words than the aircraft gave a sudden, violent shudder. It trembled and, without any warning, plunged downwards with such ferocity that my glass flew out of my hand. Nearby, the flight attendants—"trolley dollies," as some call them—gripped the nearest seats, their expressions betraying the same alarm I was trying to suppress.

The plunge seemed to go on forever, an endless descent into chaos. Just as I braced myself for the worst, it stopped abruptly, like we'd slammed into an invisible wall. A deafening crack—sharp as a whip—rang through the cabin as though something critical in the wings had given way. The aircraft lurched wildly to the left, then to the right, throwing us all into a disorienting, stomach-churning sway.

My mind raced with images of the captain in the cockpit, wrestling with the controls in a desperate bid to keep us airborne, like a scene from one of those nail-biting thriller films. For a terrifying moment, I couldn't shake the thought that we were seconds away from the crash we all dreaded.s

The aircraft shuddered again, then within an instant, we were level and all shaking had ceased like nothing had happened.

The trolley dollies started composing themselves, picking up things from the floor which had been strewn in the disturbance.

I looked at Judy, who had gone as white as a sheet, then to Graeme. Nothing heard from Karen, Mum and Dad. Nobody spoke.

I could just see Dad's balding top, his head so still. I tapped him with my hand-stretched over the top of his seat and said.

'Are you all ok? That was a bit of a fall; I hope all is well.'

I heard Mum's voice in quick reply but not in her usual tone,

'All ok over here just dropped my flipping G & T, but the Kids are just laughing about it.

After a few seconds, Captain Halton announced, in a matter-of-fact voice, as you might read out a menu.

'Sorry about the turbulence; we are away from this now, but please remain in your seats with your belts secured.'

As if anyone is going to get up after that, I thought!

The captain continued in exactly the same reassuring tone,

'We expect to be landing at Alicante in approximately 30 minutes; I will advise you all again just before we land.'

The rest of the journey was completed in comparative silence. I noticed Judy's knuckles were quite white as she continued to grip my arm. Even Mum was speechless for once. More drinks were received with a considerable level of welcome.

It seemed like hours before we heard from the Captain again, who, in his perfect, reassuring manner, advised us we would soon be landing in just a few minutes and hoped we had enjoyed the flight, apart from the earlier problem.

I had visions of the wings falling off on landing, or worse, the undercarriage collapsing or even a fire. But then I consoled myself with thoughts like these aircraft are built pretty strong, and the Boeing 737 has a superb safety record.

I felt the bump of the landing, followed by the noise of the engine in reverse thrust as we sped along the runway and then started to slow down.

The greatest sound to be heard was the clapping from the passengers, it was like thunder, and I guessed every one of our grateful travelers must have been thinking that our Captain Halton was a hero. 'It's a miracle,' Judy said as the colour started to return to her face, no doubt with the help of the additional G & T's from our beautifully recovered 'Trolly Dollies.'

You could feel the atmosphere of relief at the light and so very safe landing. People were talking, getting their belongings from the bins, and an air of relief filled the cabin.

I stood up and looked at Karen to see how she was and noticed her face. The lotion was gone, and spots like craters on the moon seemed to be everywhere. I sat down quickly and gently touched Judy's arm.

'Judy,' I called and quietly whispered in her ear, 'Karen's face, the spots are everywhere.'

Judy quickly stood up and leant over the seat and I could see something in her hand. I quickly worked out that Judy, with great dexterity, had reached quietly into her bag for the cotton wool and camouflage lotion.

Within seconds, much to protest from Karen, Judy was sat down again and advised me the face was repainted to its original mask.

Luckily, Calamine lotion dries quickly, and by the time many of the other passengers had walked down the aircraft aisle to the exit, Karen's face was looking fine.

It was soon our turn to leave the plane, and with a mixture of happiness and relief, the six of us trooped forward and down the steps onto Spanish soil and into the welcoming sunshine of Spain.

Our journey was over, all seemingly in the wink of an eye.

It seemed hard to imagine that from leaving the cold of England just a few hours ago, we could have been involved in a real 'Air Catastrophe!' splattered all over the ground below.

I gratefully considered the good Lord had been merciful and spared us from such a dreadful fate.

Looking towards Judy and the kids, I could see they were all ok and gestured. We put steps forward to follow the other passengers being ushered onto a large coach; waiting to take us to the terminal building.

Dennis and the others were already inside, and we walked forward to join them on the few remaining seats.

'What about that flight,' Jim said rather loudly to us.

'God help us!' I replied, 'I thought we were going to crash!'

Dennis looked sternly, replying, 'So did everyone else!'

There were no further comments from anyone, and the coach moved off with a jerk and swiftly took us to the terminal.

As we approached the building, I could see it looked quite nice, clean and new-looking. The coach drew up at a large entrance, and we all got off to enter and move on to collect our baggage.

Our earlier fears of being stopped by Spanish Plague Control Officers were unfounded and we trotted through passport control and on to retrieve our luggage and then Customs without a hitch.

So here we were in Spain, together and safe with kids, Mum, Dad and friends, ready for our coach journey to our Hotel and the paradise yet to be unveiled.

Chapter 6 – Benidorm – The Grand Arrival

(Day 1)

We came out of Customs into the arrivals hall, a big open space buzzing with people. We stood with some other passengers, waiting for our Holiday Rep to spot us.

"Sunrise Holidays!" a voice called out.

I turned to see a young, blonde, cheerful-looking woman heading towards us, dressed in a red jacket and white skirt. She had the kind of energy that made it seem like nothing could go wrong on her watch.

Dennis piped up in his usual loud voice, "It's our Courier!"

Then, turning to Dad, Mum, Florrie, and the rest of us, he added, "I'll go over and let her know it's us."

With that, he marched off briskly, full of purpose and enthusiasm. Unfortunately, Dennis being Dennis, he'd only taken two or three steps before disaster struck.

In his haste, he completely missed the bag lying right in his path.

"Oh God!" I cried, seeing it unfold in slow motion—but far too late to stop it.

His foot caught the bag, and down he went, arms flailing as he sprawled forward in a spectacular heap, hand outstretched like a tragic hero reaching for poor Miss Sunrise as he fell.

Why Dennis's hand had to land where it did, on the poor girl's boobs, only fate can tell. In clutching for support, his fingers gripped the cotton material of her blouse and ripped the front as he fell downwards. They both ended up sprawled onto the floor.

'Christ Almighty!' I heard Dad call out.

Dennis and the poor girl were in a bundle, both trying to get up at once and both impeding the other.

When they eventually scrambled to their feet, Miss Sunrise was frantically holding her jacket closed to conceal her bra, not to mention her embarrassment.

I looked at Judy, trying to suppress my giggles at the scene in front of us. She was no help as I could see she was very near bursting with her hand clasped over her mouth; all the people in the hall seemed to be transfixed on the poor fallen girl.

Dennis, who was now standing limply in front of her, seemed to be trying to apologise, but as he gestured towards her, she flinched back as if to expect a repeat performance.

Miss Sunrise looked so very shocked and continued to hold her jacket tightly across her chest.

Suddenly, a woman of grandmother's age stepped forward and declared,

'Don't worry, Luv! I've got a couple of safety pins in my bag; let's go to the ladies and sort you out!'

Miss Sunrise looked so relieved, she blurted out.

'Can everyone wait here a minute? I'll be back with you as soon as I can.'

With that, she sped off, trailing the older helper behind, off into the direction of the ladies toilets.

I looked around; everyone previously trying to conceal laughter was all in the midst of giggles, close conversation, and wild gestures.

Dennis stepped towards us and was immediately taken to task by Florrie, who red in the face rasped.

'How could you do that?' she looked fiercely at Dennis,

'Can't you look where you are going, poor girl, you made her so embarrassed?'

'I didn't see the bag; it was just an accident,' was Dennis' sheepish response, trying to minimize the whole affair, but without success.

Florrie continued, 'It's those drinks on the plane, I hope you're not going to be like this the whole of the holiday!'

At this point, Mum stepped in, feeling rather sorry at Dennis's predicament and pronounced.

'Florrie, it was just an accident, as we could all see; the poor girl was not hurt, it could have been worse.'

Jim piped up and, still with stifled laughter, blurted out.

'Yes, Dennis could have pulled off her bra as well!'

We all started to laugh again, realising Jim had got a point.

I turned in the direction of Miss Sunrise's departure to see she was walking towards us, seemingly as though nothing had happened. Granny must have done a good job, I thought.

She was soon upon us and quickly introduced herself as Sharon from Torquay and would be our Rep and helper during our holiday.

After taking our names and accepting yet another apology from Dennis, Miss Sunrise briskly marched us toward the car park to locate our coach.

"All of you heading to the Hotel Flemington; you're on coach 21," she announced, gesturing for us to follow her and climb aboard.

As we approached, the coach driver hopped down from his seat, all smiles and efficiency. Sharon introduced him as Carlos, and he wasted no time hauling our cases into the cavernous hold under the vehicle, his movements so swift and practised it was like watching luggage ballet.

After some shuffling and mild chaos, those bound for the Flemington were finally seated. Sharon did a quick headcount, her eyes darting across the rows as though she were taking stock of a particularly unruly class. Satisfied no one had wandered off, she gave Carlos the nod. With that, the coach rumbled to life, and we were off.

Within seconds, we were speeding, and I mean speeding, off in the direction of Benidorm and the Hotel Flemington.

The journey passed quickly as we accelerated out of Alicante and along the coast road. We had not been to this part of Spain before, never mind in winter, and I marvelled at the trees and flowers, all looking so bright and fresh in direct contrast to England, where we had just left, so cold and barren.

I sighed and contemplated our next day's full of fun, sea, sand and sangria.

We soon approached Benidorm, and it was much bigger than I had imagined. The coach veered off the wide carriageway and wove its way into a maze of narrow streets, eventually reaching a particularly steep incline.

I glanced ahead and felt a twinge of dread, already guessing that this hill would be a real test of stamina at the end of a long day. The coach powered upward, turning left and right so many times I lost track before finally entering a long, narrow street flanked by tall buildings.

Some of them were clearly flats, their balconies festooned with laundry flapping lazily in the breeze. I leaned towards Judy.

"Is this it?" she asked, her voice laced with concern.

"I don't know," I replied, frowning. "I thought we'd be near the sea!"

Before either of us could speculate further, the coach pulled over to the left and came to a stop. Sharon stood up, tapped the microphone she held in her hand, and raised it to her lips. She paused for a moment, letting the silence build, then finally made her announcement.

'Well, folks we are here at your Hotel,' indicating to a building on the corner of the road.

All heads turned quickly towards that direction. From the coach, it was very difficult to see anything as the road was narrow, and the building loomed very close to the windows.

'We can get off the coach now,' Sharon requested.

With that, most of our holidaymakers rose to their feet as if sensing they needed to see the Hotel without delay.

One by one, we shuffled off the coach. Dad looked decidedly sheepish, his eyes darting nervously toward Mum but not daring to say a word. Before long, we were standing with the rest of the passengers, forming a loose group in the street. Everyone seemed to be doing the same thing—glancing up and down the road and then over at the Hotel with various degrees of scepticism.

"Bugger me," Dennis muttered loudly enough for half the group to hear. "I wasn't expecting the bloody Ritz, but this neighbourhood looks a bit grim."

Mum, ever the optimist, piped up with, "I'm sure the Hotel is nice inside," though her tone carried just a hint of doubt.

Judy, meanwhile, clung tightly to my hand, her grip firmer than usual. "Let's get the cases in and have a look," she said, her voice low and clearly worried.

With that, we trudged towards the entrance, the street behind us offering no reassurance and the Hotel ahead holding all the promise—or peril—of a Pandora's box.

I nudged Dad, who was staring at the peeling paint on the side of our Hotel and the pitiful wonky sign, Hotel Flemington, hanging precariously from two bits of angle fixed to the wall.

We picked up our cases and made our way across the road and into the crowd that some of our fellow travellers had now formed at the bottom of the steps leading inwards. The doors at the top of the steps opened, and a rather small but portly man emerged.

He had a round face and a large black moustache that took up an over large portion of his face.

'He must be the Manager,' Dad observed, who turned out to be quite correct in his initial assessment as the next sentence confirmed.

'Welcome to the Hotel Flemington, I am Julio, the Manager,' he declared in a mild and flowing sort of accent.

He gestured towards us with an over-large wave of his hand and a similarly large smile.

'Please come into the Reception for registration,' he requested.

Our party moved onwards and into the Hotel lobby. It was bigger than the outside would lead us to believe and, while looking a bit past its best, was at least clean and tidy. The Christmas spirit was clearly visible and captured in the decorations, festooning walls and ceilings!

White marble tiles covered the floor, which led to a small curved reception desk on the right-hand side and a lift on the left.

I noticed the lift had a sign pinned to the door, which I could barely see, but it appeared to be written in Spanish, which I would be at a loss to understand. But signs on lifts invariably mean it's broken.

Julio soon cleared up that little matter by announcing in a loud voice.

'We are sorry, but today the lift has broken, but we hope it will be okay tomorrow.'

People started to mutter, contemplating lugging suitcases up flights of hotel stairs.

'Stuff this!' said Dennis loudly, 'I hope we are not on the bloody top floor.'

'We must be if there is a sea view,' I commented, realising quickly that only the very top floors could be able to see over the surrounding buildings.

We gritted our teeth and waited to sign in to get our keys from the young Spanish girl in reception. I noticed she was very attractive and smiled in greeting to everyone as they checked in.

There was quite a queue waiting to register, and after what seemed like hours, we were finally clutching keys and able to contemplate the stairs.

'We are all on the sixth floor at the top of the Hotel,' Dad announced with a heavy voice.

I noticed that no staff seemed available to help anyone so off we went to commence the long accent to the summit. Jim was only a little bloke, and to see the size of his misses' suitcase defied belief.

'How the hell are you going to get that thing up!' said Dennis jokingly.

'You can help!' was Jim's reply.

'Let's send the girls and kids up in front to open the doors and we can do this in relays,' said Dad, ever the organizer.

This would have been a good idea if most of the other guests had not thought along similar lines.

The staircase was not very wide and had a rather large number of sharp bends. I considered the sight of so many people humping their belongings along like a trail of ants would have seemed amusing if it was not happening to us.

'What a crappy start to a holiday!' I heard Dennis comment to Dad, 'Let's get this lot upstairs and go and find the bar; we are going to need a bloody drink by the time we have finished!'

About half an hour later, the last of the cases were upstairs, and I had not yet even looked at the room.

I noticed Judy was standing by the open door of room number 603; she was looking a bit blank. I picked up the first case and walked a few steps to join her.

'Well, here we are,' I said as she moved over to let me go through the door.

As I pushed further, the door moved about three-quarters of the way open and stopped abruptly. I pushed and, feeling resistance, put down the case and stuck my head around as I negotiated the narrow opening.

My eyes hesitantly took it all in, seeing four beds side by side. Graeme and Karen were standing up on two of them. The only gap was between the half-opened door and the first bed. At the end of the row of beds was a space of about 2 ft 6 inches, which contained a balcony door at the end, and I guessed the bathroom door at the side wall.

'What the Hell!' I exclaimed with my hands outstretched.

'You can't swing a cat round in here!'

We both entered through the gap and into the room.

Judy said, 'I didn't want to say anything until you came in and saw for yourself, but the bathroom's okay!'

'Shall we sleep in the bath then?' I replied, 'It's probably going to be more comfortable than the beds.'

With my initial shock, I hadn't noticed Karen and Graeme now bouncing up and down like fury on the beds.

'Look, Daddy,' said Karen, 'I like this room, it's nice. We can all be together,'

'Well, I'm glad you're happy,' I replied in a sniffed-off sort of voice, thinking that this holiday was not going to be exactly a second honeymoon for Judy and me.

At that moment, Mum poked her head round the door, raised her eyebrows and slid through the gap and into the room.

'Good God!' she blurted out, 'How did they get four beds in here?'

'With a shoe horn,' I replied to Mum's amusement.

'I wondered why the Kids' special holiday offer price was so low but now understood. A one bedroom suite for two had now become a Christmas special sleeping a family of four.

Dad had also planned to come to join us, but seeing there was no more standing room just stood with his head around the door, looking in.

'It's a bit tight, isn't' it,' Dad observed with understatement.

Not wishing to seem ungrateful, Judy spoke up quickly,

'Well, Dad,' I suppose it's full at Christmas time in the Hotel, and we got a big discount for a family room.

'But it's the same size as ours,' Dad went on,

'It's just got two more beds in it!'

'Don't worry, Dad, we will be okay,' I said reassuringly; we only sleep in it, and we can get dressed in the bathroom.'

'Yes,' Judy added, with a sort of reassuring tone.

'I'm only little, we can manage; let's wash, brush up and find the bar, I'm thirsty.'

With that, Dad shrugged, Mum sighed, and both departed to their room.

There wasn't much else to say about our room. It was clean and bright, at least, and after enduring a camping holiday in North Wales with the rain pissing down and locals who wouldn't so much as nod in your direction, this felt like sheer luxury by comparison.

I quickly decided to stop dwelling on it—this was our home for the duration of the holiday, and there was no point wasting energy wishing it otherwise. Instead, my thoughts turned to something far more promising: the Bar.

"Let's get changed!" I said to Judy, and we wasted no time making ourselves presentable. Karen and Graeme got a quick cat's lick and a promise before we headed downstairs in search of liquid salvation.

After what felt like a trek across half of Benidorm, we reached the reception area. Scanning the room, my spirits soared as I spotted a sign that read *BAR* in gloriously bold letters.

Walking in, we were greeted by the sight of the rest of our group, drinks in hand and roaring with laughter. Judging by the grins and the sheer volume of their merriment, I could only assume they were enjoying an animated recounting of Mum and Dad's opinion on our less-than-Ritz accommodations. It was good to see someone was making the most of it already.

'Bit cramped up then!' Dennis said with a broad grin on his face, 'Let's get you and Judy a drink, I think you need one.'

'A bottle of Gin for me!' was Judy's answer and continued,

'Still, we only sleep there, so it won't be too bad.'

The bar was surprisingly spacious, a large square room clad in dark wood panels, each decorated with ornate Spanish motifs neatly centred like they'd been measured to perfection. The walls were adorned with oversized pictures of idyllic Spanish countryside scenes—rolling hills, whitewashed villages, and vineyards basking in the sun, no doubt meant to remind us why we'd come here in the first place.

The floor was white marble, cool and gleaming, dotted with chairs and tables that looked comfortably inviting. To the right stood the bar itself, an impressively long counter staffed by a short, stocky Spaniard with a round face and the inevitable moustache.

We'd later come to know him as Jose. He had a cheerful air about him, laughing and grinning as he served drinks, clearly enjoying his role as the purveyor of much-needed spirits. "A happy barman," I thought to myself. *This could bode well.*

It seemed most of our fellow travellers had the same idea as us—the bar was already buzzing with familiar faces. I figured the initial shock of arriving at *this* Hotel had driven everyone to the same conclusion: a stiff drink was in order to soothe the nerves and make the situation look a little brighter.

While everyone was chatting about the climb up the stairs, the dreadful flight and Sharon's accident, I scanned the room to notice our fellow holidaymakers and to get a better idea from my first apprehensive assessment of the airport and coach journey.

Some I recognized from our coach journey but most other people in the room were strangers to me. I realized they must be from another Tour Company or were staying here for more weeks than us.

The more I surveyed the people around the room, it slowly dawned on me that most were in their very advance years. Ladies with blue rinsed hair abounded and many of the men were balding or were having a love affair with the Brylcream bottle.

Not many of the inmates looked very happy, and some had very sullen looks on their faces.

'Oh God,' I quietly whispered, 'I hope we haven't arrived at the Benidorm Geriatric rest home!'

Still, I thought, all things have compensation, and the beer was going down well. Certainly, a few old folks would not worry us.

I had nearly finished my well-earned drink when I heard Dennis shout out in his normal loudish voice,

'Let's get them in; at least the beer is ok here!'

'I'll help you!' I quickly replied and got up from my seat to follow Dennis, who had started briskly on his way to the bar.

As we approached to wait our turn the barman was just finishing serving a large bald-headed man. The barman was quickly over to us and said, smiling broadly, in a very welcoming way.

'Good evening, I am Jose; can I get you a drink?'

'Not half,' said Dennis very quickly, as though his life depended on it. He then leaned forward against the bar as if to re-enforce the words.

'You can start with four large beers, please!'

As the foaming jugs were put in front of us, I seized the opportunity and asked Jose.

'How long have you worked here?'

He looked at me and grinned as though expecting some odd consequence from his answer.

'Four years now,' he replied and continued.

'I came here from Barcelona, where I was born, but its more fun in Benidorm and many more bar jobs!'

I continued with my probing to get more info and questions.

'There are many English people here, but most seem rather old!'

Jose looked at me and, with a wry smile, leant towards me and, in a low voice, replied,

'Yes, there are many old people here; the hotel caters for them, especially the Old Time Dancers.'

Jose continued, seemingly happy to provide more details.

'Some of the people stay for the winter; we also get many guests from Germany.'

'Oh my God!' Dennis instantly uttered, 'I hope there are none this week, what with Jim being with us, you know what he thinks of Germans!'

I turned to Dennis, after I could see some other Guests at the bar looking at us, and said rather abruptly.

'Dennis, be quiet, Guests can hear!'But Dennis just continued.

'Can you just imagine our holiday filled with Old Time Dancers prancing around and Jim's problem with the Germans?'

Dennis then sighed and, in a lower tone, thoughtfully said,

'Let's get the drinks over to the table and have a sit-down; it can't get much worse!'

We returned to the others, who were all in conversation and passed the drinks around. Dennis and I sat down, not quite knowing what to say about our new information.

My thoughts were interrupted by a nudge from Judy,

'Have you seen this lot?' She whispered, 'They all look like a bundle of fun!'

I nodded in agreement, and Judy continued,

'What are those people looking at over by the wall?'

She pointed discretely to a small group of men and women, looking at what seemed a notice pinned to the wall. It appeared to be just freshly posted.

'Perhaps it's the restaurant arrangements,' I said and gestured to Judy to go and look with me.

We walked over to the other side of the room, which we could see was now attracting not only attention from us as others were coming in our direction.

I stood behind a particularly large lady who was peering at what we could see as a poster. I leaned over to the left to get a view and to read - Entertainment in the downstairs ballroom.

My eyes immediately followed further down and, to my horror, onto the first line, confirming my worst fears. Nightly Bingo, followed by, Old Time Dancing, three times a week.

My heart sank; I searched frantically for something Judy or the kids might enjoy and, to my relief, read, "Father Christmas on Christmas morning and Children's entertainment on Boxing Day." Final relief was provided when my eager eyes saw, "Christmas Party Night from 7pm in the hall. Live music and dancing."

'Thank the Lord!' I said out loud and turned to Judy, who was still trying to see the notice but, being quite small, could not view the man standing in front of her. I conveyed the news first, informing her about the Bingo and the Old Time stuff.

She looked at me aghast, 'What about a Disco?'

'No Disco was mentioned anywhere,' I said, although, 'We have a dance Christmas night, but I can't see any Disco.'

At Judy's and my age, a Disco was our idea of an evening's fun. We both liked dancing, but not Prehistoric Old Time stuff, especially with a load of old geriatrics prancing about.

I took Judy's hand and led her back to our lot at their table.

We were out of earshot of the other residents, and I said quietly to Dad, Dennis and Jim, who were grouped in serious drinking mode,

'Guess what? They've got sodding Old Time Dancing three times a week in the ballroom.'

'I hate that bloody lark,' said Dennis, scorning quite quickly,

'Florrie and Tiggy don't mind a quick step or a waltz now and then, but not all that old fart stuff!'

'Same for us,' Jim said in strong confirmation.

'I don't like dancing much anyway,' Dad added.

This was always a bone of contention with Mum as she likes to trip the light fantastic now and then, especially at the Firm's "Do's."

Dennis turned to Florrie, Mum and Doris, who were engaged in heavy gossip.

'Girls!' Dennis interrupted in a slightly overloud voice, as was sometimes, unfortunately, his way, fully demonstrated at the Bar.

'Ken and Judy have just looked at the entertainment board, and guess what; they have Old Time Dancing three times a week!'

'What about the nightly entertainment?' Florrie questioned,

'It said in the holiday brochure that we have some nightly entertainment!'

'Perhaps that's it,' Jim quickly piped up, 'Maybe their idea of entertainment is watching a load of old geriatrics doing the Can Can or something?'

The thought of this lot of old ladies doing a Can-Can was too bizarre to contemplate.

'Most of this lot look like they will have a coronary if they move about too fast,' I quickly commented. 'Still, you're St. John Ambulance trained, aren't you, Judy?' I joked, 'Imagine giving the kiss of life to any of this lot.'

Judy looked at me in a sort of repulsed way and did not comment.

I paused for a moment, then related the good news about the Christmas night dance and the children's entertainment.'

'Also, there is nightly Bingo,' I related to Mum with a slight grin on my face and continued.

'You like that, don't you? Perhaps one of the old boys will trip you round the floor on his Zimmer frame.'

'I have heard they have them with big wheels on now,' I continued, which brought a round of laughter from everyone.

'I don't need some old boy, thank you,' Mum quickly retorted.

'Your Dad dances with me sometimes and questioned, don't you, Len?'

Dad replied with a grin, 'I try to, dear, if my poor old feet aren't playing me up.'

This seemed on top of everything else to get us all laughing and contemplating another visit to the bar.

Judy looked over at Karen and Graeme, who were sitting at the next table playing quietly for once with some small toy cars we had bought with us from England.

'They've got children's entertainment in the hall during the week, she told them, and 'I think they have a magic man. Also, Father Christmas is coming.'

'That will be okay for you two,' said Mum, in her ever-enthusiastic way.

Karen looked round at Mum and said with a beaming smile,

'I like magic; this is a nice Hotel Mummy.' Graeme looked up from his car on the table, and his eyes fell on Judy.

'Mummy, when is Father Christmas coming here?' he enquired excitedly.

'On Christmas morning,' Judy replied. 'He is making a special trip to Spain for all the Children who won't be home for Christmas; he is coming on his sleigh with six reindeer pulling it all the way.'

Karen and Graeme looked wide eyed, as only young children can at the expectations of this magical red cloaked figure with a sleigh filled with children's presents.

I looked at Karen and Graeme and felt a warm glow inside. After all our troubles getting here to Spain and all the worry, there, in the beaming faces of our two children, the Christmas spirit was seen to have finally arrived.

I was soon woken from my dream by Florrie who quickly reminded us all saying rather loudly.

'We have all been looking at the Bar, Drinks Menu and the entertainment, but what about the restaurant and eating? It's 6pm and I am rather hungry.'

Dorris added very quickly and in an equally firm voice,

'I looked at the restaurant times on the board by the restaurant door; it said diner was at 6pm, so perhaps we should move on in.'

As I looked round towards the restaurant, I noticed people moving through the two large restaurant doors at the end of the room, which I realised must have just been opened.

I turned to Mum and Dad and said with some enthusiasm,

'I think the restaurants are opening, don't know about you, but I'm getting famished, shall we go in?'

It seemed like, in our rush to get the thoughts of the journey over and our shock on arrival to Flemington, we had lost sight of basics like eating.

I stood up slowly and readied myself to make a start to the door, which was now being opened by a very pretty girl dressed in a fetching black and white costume.

Judy likewise arose and held out her hand towards the kids, who had been surprisingly quiet for the half an hour we had been in the Bar. I looked to see Karen's face still good under its thin camouflage of Calamine lotion. All seemed okay; that was until Karen's voice cried out!

'I'm hungry, mummy, we haven't eaten for ages!'

'So am I,' Graeme responded in firm agreement.

I quickly realized that we had briefly neglected our two charges while we had been a bit over-engrossed with our friends. I felt a little ashamed and tasked myself to be better and more watchful.

I got a grip on the situation and softly called out,

'Come on, you two Kids, let's go to eat!'

'Good idea; I think we all must be pretty hungry,' I heard Jim call from behind, followed by similar words from Florrie.

As we all started to move forward, I was suddenly filled with a strange feeling of mixed expectation towards what lay ahead.

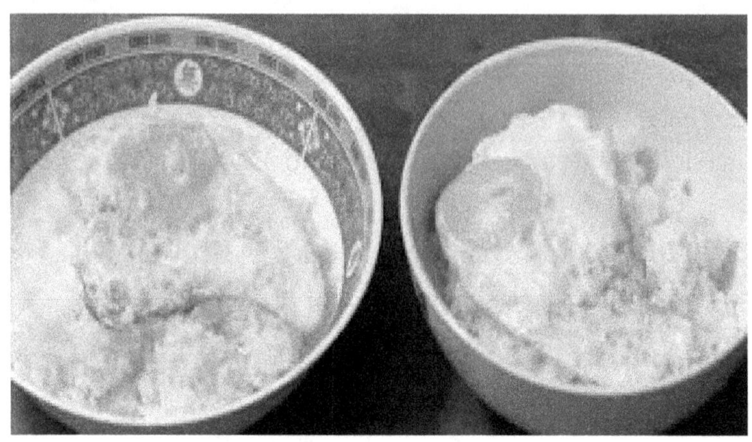

Chapter 7 – Restaurant Of
Culinary Surprise (Day 1)

We made our way to the restaurant door, joining a small line of guests waiting to get in. As we waited, Judy looked at me, curious.

"I wonder what the food will be like?" she asked.

"I bet it'll be great," I replied, trying to stay upbeat. "The brochure said the chef has a good reputation."

"Oh, just like the Entertainment Manager's reputation?" Denis chuckled behind us reminding us all of the less-than-thrilling weekly lineup of Old-Time Dancing nights!

We shuffled closer to the front of the queue, where what I could only assume was the Head Waiter stood, clipboard in hand, pointing like a maestro conducting an orchestra—albeit one made up of tables and chairs. He was expertly directing diners to their designated spots with the gravitas of someone who clearly took their table allocation duties very seriously.

The restaurant, however, was a bit of a surprise. For a hotel of this size, I'd expected something a touch grander. Instead, it felt like they'd crammed about fifty tables into a room clearly designed for thirty—cosy if you're being generous or downright claustrophobic if you're not. As I scanned the room, it was obvious the place was almost full, diners wedged in like sardines but seemingly too polite to complain.

And then it was our turn. The Head Waiter turned his attention to us, clipboard at the ready. I sized him up and couldn't help but think *Another short arse!* Honestly, where were they recruiting these vertically challenged maître d's from? It was starting to feel like a theme.

'Is every bloke so small and skinny in Spain, and why do they all have a moustache!'

These points I had remembered fondly from our earlier Spanish holiday; as previous memories were starting to emerge.

This waiter, however, had a certain presence about him, a bit of a "Master of all he surveyed!" Like the Captain of a grand ship.

I noticed he gestured frequently to any waiting people with a rolling hand movement, and while he did so, not appearing to smile much. He walked over to us and introduced himself to Dad as Manuel.

'What is your room number?' he asked,

'It's 604,' Dad replied Mr and Mrs Birch, and 607, Ken and Judy and the children.

Manuel looked hurriedly down the list, then up the list and then down the list again and then paused for a moment. He then announced,

'Room 604 should be at the 6pm sitting and Room 607 on this sitting for 7.30p.m.'

He looked at us as though we had done something to really upset the smooth flow of his restaurant.

'It's on the list, the rooms are on the list,' Manuel went on.

'What list?' inquired Dad in a surprised and rather narked-off tone.

Manuel continued, 'The list is made in Reception; we have two sittings, one at 6pm and one at 7.30.'

Dad replied quickly, 'No one asked us or told us about the sittings.'

Manuel continued, appearing to be a little irritated by this,

'Well, room 604 is at this time, so you will be at 7.30.'

'But we are together as a family,' Dad replied firmly! Clearly now getting a bit vexed with this.

However, this just did not seem to register with Manuel who seemed to be becoming exasperated with this questioning of the Hotel arrangements.

'No, No!' he carried on in an even more impudent voice, which was starting to really grate.' 604 is at 6pm, and 607 is at 7.30p.m. It's on the list.'

At this point, Judy, who had remained surprisingly quiet so far, stepped forward to face Manuel.

'Oh Dear God!' I thought, knowing sometimes to my cost what my misses could be like when vexed. She squared up to him, looked straight into his face and directed her index finger at his chest. He reeled back at this like it was some kind of sword.

'Now look here!' Judy spurted out and stared straight into his eyes with all the ferocity of a Cobra about to spit its venom. She then thrust her finger further forward at Manuel, who flexed back even more.

'We have come here as a family for Christmas!' She continued.

'If you think you are going to put us on different sitting for our meals, you've got another thing coming!'

The onslaught continued, and Manuel went bright crimson!

'Now stop messing about and get us a table together, Cos, I don't give a damn about your silly meal arrangements!'

I thought Manuel was going to burst. His whole body was tensed like a spring. I sensed his whole Spanish manhood was on the line at the thought of this little English woman pointing at him and telling him what to do.

'It's my Restaurant!' He blurted out, 'I am Head Waiter!'

'Well, it's my family!' Judy rasped back at him,

'You should sort out your Restaurant to suit what's best for us!'

Various guests by this time were staring at the scene. Waiters and Waitresses previously flitting as they do from table to table were transfixed on the scene. Even Mum was quiet for once.

I could see this was now a severe problem of authority and decided we had reached an impasse.

Was this time to unwrap my "Mr. Mediator" soothing skills, taught to me by my mentor Foreman at work, Jack Cannon!

He had helped so much in honing my approach to Forman, Trades and others who found my rather young and admittedly brash manner far too aggressive. Jack's training paid off, and I used the soothing skills often on the shop floor at Rolls Royce, generally with loud, hairy-arsed Foremen. These guys would always get angry about something or other when mere mortals like me dared to enter their 'patch!' as they referred to their dutied areas.

So onwards, with soothing, I stepped forward and gently got between Manual and Judy.

'Manuel,' I said quietly, trying to be as low-key as I could, and turned to face our poor cross man.

'This is now the way for us to behave at Christmas, our family time; I am sure you have family, Manuel and would not be happy to be separated from them for your special holiday?'I continued,

'Do you have family,' I asked.

'Yes, my Maria and three sons,' Manuel replied crossly.

I replied quietly, 'I'm sorry we got cross, but we have been travelling with our children for a long time now and are a bit tired, so could you please try and do something for us?'

This seemed to calm him down a bit, and I noticed the crimson colour going fast from his face. I carried on,

'I'm sure it's difficult to fit everyone into your restaurant.'

Manuel paused momentarily and looked again at the list now quivering in his hand.

'I think I can fit you all in on table 10 tonight,' and continued, 'I will see if we can keep this table for the rest of your holiday.'

I nudged Judy as I said, 'Thank you, Manuel.'

I looked at Judy, then heard a grudging and quiet 'Thank you' drifting from her lips.

Manuel paused momentarily to compose himself.

'Follow me,' he said and, with a wave, ushered the six of us to table ten.

As we strolled across the restaurant floor, I couldn't help but notice a po-faced old hag glaring at us with a look of pure disapproval, as though we'd just strutted in wearing pyjamas and muddy wellies. Well, I wasn't in the mood for her nonsense. So, I met her judgmental stare with a look that could curdle milk—one part snarl, two parts "try me."

It worked a treat. Her head shot down like a guilty schoolchild right as her soup spoon was en route to her mouth. The timing was impeccable. Startled by her own poor coordination, she jerked upwards, sending the spoon's contents cascading down her chin and straight onto the front of her dress.

I couldn't help but grin. *Serves her right, nosy old bag!* I thought. It was a small yet deeply satisfying victory. Dinner and a show, all in one.

I looked around for Dennis and the others, who were now fronting a long queue, which I guess had built up while our table problem was being resolved. Dennis was in discussion with Manuel, which I could only assume was about being on the same food sitting as us.

Thankfully, in a few moments Manuel was soon ushering them over to one of the only tables which were still empty for our sitting.

'Thank God for that', Mum said wearily as she sat down at our hard-won table, 'let's all get tucked into a great meal; I'm starving.'

Likewise, we all followed Mum's lead and got seated with Karen and Graeme suitably placed between me and Judy; where table manners could be controlled and monitored.

The waiter arrived quickly and, in typical fashion, was short and sporting a small moustache. He bowed slightly and introduced himself as Silvio, followed by giving us a broad, welcoming smile.

We later found out he was Manuel's brother.

He shrugged his shoulders a little, turned over the palms of his hands uttering, 'I'm sorry, we are very busy with many guests for Christmas, I will get your soup.'

I looked over to our friend's table and could see they were being served by a very beautiful, young, dark-haired girl.

'What a lovely figure!' I observed. I just couldn't resist staring until Karen's little voice piped up.

'Daddy, why are you looking at that lady?'

'I'm not darling,' I quickly replied, 'I'm checking if the others are all okay.'

Judy gave me a strange look, not really believing the white lie I had just tried to get away with. Her look quickly turned to one of disapproval.

Fortunately, Silvio arrived with a large tureen, which he gently placed onto the table centre while announcing,

'Enjoy your soup dish,' then went away as fast as he had arrived.

Mum placed her fingers onto the rather large-looking spoon in the tureen and lifted it up to view the contents it held.

'Looks a funny colour, like a sort of yellow,' Dad was quick to comment! 'Not sure I'm going to like this stuff!'

'Oh, I'm sure you will like it when you try it, you old fuss pot,' Mum said rather abruptly and started to serve it out to us hungry bodies round the table.

I quickly tried it while blowing a little to cool the contents, which surprisingly tasted quite nice.

'Nice soup, Judy,' I said and bent my head quickly downwards in its direction to try more as my hunger had now increased after my first taste and enticing smell from the soup. I looked round to see Dad and the kids tucking in with Dad actually appearing to be enjoying his.

'This soup is very nice; can I have some more, Mummy?' Karen's voice urgently inquired.

'Ok,' Judy replied, 'It's quite nice soup,' and duly took the spoon and re-filled Karen's bowl.

I thought it seemed all were satisfied so far; what a good start!

Our next course was seen arriving in small tin dishes and my curiosity grew as to their contents. I did not have to wait long as Silvio came up quickly and placed before me a dish containing nothing but peas.

I looked quickly at Dad, who we know didn't like 'foreign muck,' as he called it, at the best of times.

Dad's face straightened as he stared down as Silvio placed his and the rest of the dishes down on the table.

'This is a special Spanish dish,' Silvio informed while quickly moving off.

'It's special, alright!' Dad responded with a firm frown,

'Is it Smedley's or Bachelor's? Special dish, my arse!'

'Len,' Mum quickly responded, 'the children!'

I can hardly say we tucked into the peas with gusto, but being in our state of hunger, almost anything would do. So, with reluctance, we completed our peas; Dad just pushed his to one side in disgust.

I wondered whatever we would get next from our Gourmet Chef. Pig's trotters on toast perhaps, something smelling horrible of garlic, or maybe a sheep's eye floating on a sea of spaghetti!

I saw Silvio coming towards our table carrying an even bigger tureen than our soup arrived in. He put this down in the centre of the table and, with a flourish, as was his waiter's way, we were to learn, removed the lid. Inside was a sort of casserole looking strange mixture?

'Don't like the look of that,' Dad commented very predictably.

Mum picked up the large spoon provided and plunged the murky depths of the bowl to bring out a piece of dark-coloured meat with a few lumps of egg attached to it.

'I'm sure it tastes better than it looks,' Mum said in her reassuring way.

'Don't give me any of that, Tiggy,' was Dad's quick response, 'I wouldn't give that muck to the dog!'

Mum, in spite of Dad's downer on the cuisine, ladled it out around the table to be greeted with scowls from Judy, Karen and Graeme. It did really look strange and uninviting.

Reluctantly, however, all but Dad gave it a go. It tasted a little better than it looked; not much better, just marginally better, you understand.

Soon, most of it was gone, and I felt amazement, realising what sheer hunger would do to a poor soul.

At that moment, I heard a cry and looked round in the direction of the next table. A large elderly woman was standing at the table, and the other occupants were all staring at her plate.

'My God, what's that,' I heard the man next to her cry out in a rather loud, worried-sounding voice.

'It's an animal!' The lady cried out; it's a big spider, I think; my God, please take this away before I am sick!'

Her table companions all looked again, and by now, a waiter was flying over.

'It's a bloody big cockroach!' the man said. 'It's in the stew, a bloody cockroach.'

Within seconds, the waiter arrived at the table, and the woman, the victim of this crunchy disaster, was pointing at the animal lying dead on her plate.

I looked over to see Manuel heading at a brisk pace also towards the offending table. In a moment, both Manuel and the waiter stood speechless, looking at the lady's plate. We could not hear too well, but with my ears straining along with Judy, Mum and Dad, we heard the poor woman start on Manuel.

'It's disgraceful!' She said, 'a cockroach in my dinner, I feel ill now, I might be sick!'

Manuel, trying to calm her down, said quickly,

'This has never happened before in my restaurant; it's an accident, I'm so sorry I will take it away.'

With a flash of his hand, the waiter picked up the plate and scurried off into the kitchen followed closely behind by Manuel. The guests were left just staring at each other in a sort of a daze.

'I wonder what's for pudding,' Dad questioned.

As if we cared, I thought, and I looked over in the direction of our friends' table. Dennis saw me and rose to his feet and started in the direction of our table.

'What was all that carry on,' Dennis asked.

Mum replied in a quiet voice, 'I'll tell you about it when we go to the bar in a minute. Can't talk about it now!' and she gestured discretely to the other table where the dreadful event had occurred.

Dennis, however, went on, and I saw Mum cringe at thoughts of more questions about the next table.

'What did you think of that bloody dinner?' Dennis said rather loudly, looking straight at Dad.

Then, not waiting for a reply, he continued, 'I've eaten in many places in my life, but nobody has ever given me a plate of bleeding peas, fancy serving up a plate of peas; I can't believe it.'

'Neither could we,' said Dad in strong confirmation, 'It better be good tomorrow, or we will have to complain.'

Mum, in her usual optimistic way, said reassuringly,

'I'm sure it won't all be the same as this, perhaps it's just they were very busy today.'

What busy had got to do with it, I wondered, but in Mum's logic, it obviously did; she must equate crap food and dead insects in the stew as somehow time-related.

'What a strange thought, I pondered?'

Denis sauntered off back to his table just as Silvio came up smiling with little plates of ice cream for afters.

'Well, at least they can't bugger up ice cream!'

Dad commented and was promptly cautioned by Mum.

'Eat up Karen and Graeme,' Judy said, 'We can go and have a nice drink in the bar before we put you two up to bed.'

Having completed our meal, we adjourned to the bar which was quite full by now, with people waiting for the next meal sitting.

I thought, 'Please God, I hope their dishes turn out better than we were fed!' But then again, why should it!

As we entered further into the bar I looked around to see where our friends were and saw them seated at a table at the far end of the bar area.

Judy and I, kids in tow, and with our Mum and Dad following closely behind, made a beeline for the table. This, fortunately, had sufficient room to spare for us all.

I could also see Jim jostling at the bar front, waiting to order some drinks and indicating this to Dad.

'I had better get over there to help,' Dad responded.

'Mine's a beer!' I said quickly, almost feeling the taste of it in my mouth which was feeling rather dry.

'Please get a J&T for Judy and lemonade for the two Kids.' I continued eagerly in anticipation of a thirst-quenching brew.

As we got seated and comfortable, Florrie made a comment.

'It's very busy here; my goodness, this bar is very crowded!'

I could see Jim was even finding some difficulty in quickly passing back the drinks to Dad.

Dennis had also seen this and raised himself quite quickly from his seat and, in a firm voice, announced,

'I had better go over and assist before all of it gets spilt!'

He went quickly off, with a sense of some urgency in his step.

I turned to Judy and the kids to comment for a moment but paused momentarily as I could hear the sound of unfamiliar accents coming from a group nearby. I strained my ear to pick up the sound and quickly realised it was German.

'Judy,' I whispered, 'do you hear that? We've got Germans in the hotel, very cosmopolitan!'

'We met some very nice ones in Switzerland on our holiday before we got married,' she replied in a reassuring way.

Just as Judy had finished speaking, Dad returned to our table, drinks in hand and informing very firmly as if we had not seen.

It's bloody busy up there, drinks flowing everywhere!'

He was quickly followed by Jim and Dennis, similarly loaded with full trays of beer and Spanish Bacardi cocktails.

Soon, all were seated and formed our little group at the table with me sitting opposite Jim and Doris.

'It's going to be an interesting Christmas,' I advised in a matter-of-fact way.

'We've got Germans staying in the hotel; they are at the table near us.'

I was not prepared for what happened next. My remark, said in all innocence caused a sudden change in Jim's face, and he went taught and stern.

'Germans, Germans!' He blasted out in an overloud voice!

'We've got those bastards here in the hotel, have we?'

Jim said in some fury through gritted teeth.

'They had better keep out of my way!'

Dennis quickly grabbed Jim's arm, 'Now, mate,' he said in a rather consoling voice.

'I know you don't like them, but let's calm down, I'm sure their only having a few drinks in the hotel!'

Dennis continued to reassure Jim, who was looking a bit calmer after Denis's words.

Doris, overhearing what had gone on, turned to Jim and, with a worried look on her face, said,

'Jim, stay calm, we're on holiday, don't worry about them love.'

This seemed to settle Jim down further, and he grinned and, looking at us all, said,

'I'm so sorry, it's just the past, it gets to me sometimes, let's have another drink and forget about it!'

With that, he finished what was left in the glass, grabbed Dennis and led him off to the bar.

I felt so awful, 'What a stupid Dick Head!' I whispered to myself, and why did I have to mention the Germans? I should have known better. After all, Dad had told me about Jim's terrible time as a war prisoner in Germany.

I turned to the others to apologise, I said in a humble way,

'I wish I had not mentioned anything!'

Doris looked at me and said quietly,

'Don't worry, Ken; it's not your fault. Jim just gets upset sometimes at the mention of Germans; he'll be O.K now; let's just forget it and enjoy the evening.'

This made me feel a lot better, and taking Judy's hand, I said.

'Let's get the kids up to bed now and we can come back down after and relax.'

'Good idea,' she replied, and with that, I took Karen's hand, and Judy took Graeme and we marched off to the bedtime routine with surprisingly little protest from either.

Getting Karen and Graeme undressed and washed in our congested room was a feat in itself. We found it best to develop a routine, as you couldn't swing a cat around in the space.

Judy went into the small bathroom with Karen, and I proceeded to try to undress a wiggling, giggling Graeme on the bed.

This was not easy, especially as we were tired from our rather long journey and the hotel experience, but soon, goodnight kisses were suitably administered, and Judy and I were on our way downstairs for a quick nightcap with the others.

I was thinking of a little prayer on the long, weary trek down the stairs.

'Please, God, get the lift fixed for tomorrow, and please, let the sun shine bright so we can go to the beach!'

Chapter 8 – Come Dancing (Day 2)

I woke up nice and early and feeling rather good on the second day of our holiday. The sun was shining beautifully on this morning and it seemed the perfect day for a trip to the beach for a paddle with the Kids.

I nudged Judy slightly to wake her up to enjoy the wonderful new experience I was feeling; however, I just received a loud yawn followed by a light kick.

'Why have you woke me up? I was having a lovely sleep?'

'Look, the sun is shining! It's beautiful, and we can all go to the beach. We have got over the journey, so let's get in the mood to forget the travel and all the other experiences and enjoy our holiday to its maximum!'

'You're dead right on that!' Judy replied, as she turned to look at me, and continued, 'When I think of our hotel and our experiences so far with crappy food, a lift that doesn't work, and the bloody stairs, I wonder what the rest of our holiday will bring forth?'

'So God help us, she said, 'Let's get off to the beach with the kids and enjoy ourselves!'

We got ourselves removed quickly from our beds. I woke Karen and Graeme up, who, after an initial rolling about, started jumping up and down on the beds.

'Stop that!' I cried out, 'Get undressed for showers, now!' I continued with some desperation in my voice.

After our claustrophobic showers and the battle of dressing the wriggling Graeme and demanding Karen, we just managed to get downstairs at 9.00am for our first breakfast via the now working lift.

As we walked into the restaurant area we could see it set up as a buffet where it appeared you could help yourself. This looked good to me, and looking round the room, I could see Mum and Dad sat at a table. I guessed hunger after last night's dinner had prompted them to come down earlier.

As we sat the Kids down at the table, Dad rasped out.

'The eggs are just like bloody rocks!'

He further commented, rather sharply,

'It's best to have a rubber omelette like Mum's just eaten!' He continued further with a surprisingly high air of confidence.

'Go and try it for yourselves; they can't really muck up an

Omelette!'

So off we went to try our luck, armed with Dad's recommendation.

We were in high spirits that morning, all ready to take on the buffet like a pair of champions. Judy and I bravely approached the table, only to be met with a sorry sight: a selection of boiled eggs, omelettes that looked like they'd had a rough night, a sad little salad, and tomatoes so large and red they almost looked like they'd been on steroids.

We grabbed some toast, enough eggs and omelettes to feed two starving children (and ourselves, of course), then sat down to serve up our little mountain of food to our offspring, who were looking at us with wide, hungry eyes as though they hadn't eaten in days.

They dove straight in, though their faces suggested they weren't exactly thrilled about it.

I, however, had decided to ignore Dad's sage advice and picked up two boiled eggs. As I took on the larger one, first cracking the shell with a little too much enthusiasm and a faint hope of uncovering a runny yolk, I was quickly disillusioned. No such luck. My egg was as hard-boiled as a rock. If there'd been any more firmness, I'd have expected to find it in the construction section of B&Q.

I looked at Judy, grinned and said in a rather sad tone.

'These bloody hard eggs, surely I must get one that's not boiled as hard as nails?'

Mum piped up and added, 'Jim told me he had got a runny egg with his breakfast earlier; he was showing it around to Denis and the girls!'

'My God,' I looked at Judy and laughed, saying,

'Knowing Jim, I wouldn't have been surprised if he took it round tables to all the other people, but I suppose by the time he did that, it would have gone hard, which would have defeated the object. Still, I hope he enjoyed it; I bet he doesn't get another runny one!'

With that subject cleared up, we continued with our breakfasts.

We all finished quite quickly and then with a nod from Judy, drank up our juices and coffee, ready to move onwards.

I was surprisingly feeling rather satisfied, and with hunger being dealt with quickly, my thoughts went to the day's activity.

'What shall we do today?' I asked Mum in anticipation.

Mum, who was looking rather satisfied, quickly replied,

'I spoke to the others earlier and agreed that the plan was all of us going for a stroll to see what's about the place and then visit a few of the local bars.'

'Perhaps we can sit outside in the sun and have a nice drink and something to eat.'

'That sounds good to me,' said Judy.

'I've got no problem with that plan.' I replied with a smile,

'But before that, we will take the kids to the beach; perhaps I may venture into the sea for a swim; it looks like it's going to be very warm outside.'

'Mum remarked it must be 70 degrees at least, Dad and I went outside to check before we came for breakfast!'

I looked down at Karen and Graeme, whose eyes shone bright at the thought of the beach, sandcastles, etc.

'The others said they would be waiting for us in the lobby,' Mum advised in her usual reassuring manner.

Judy and I took Graeme and Karen quickly by hand and followed Mum towards Dad, who was standing by the restaurant door. For some reason, he had quietly left our table.

'How are you today, Dad?' I asked with a grin.

'I'm ok,' Dad replied, 'It's just a bit of a rumble in the tummy, but not too bad; perhaps the hardboiled egg will block things up!'

Mum quickly changed the subject to a more holiday mood.

It's beautiful outside today, just fine for a stroll.' Mum said as she turned to look at us all.

With a strong sense of self-satisfaction, we made our way to the hotel lobby, Mum leading the charge. As we entered, I spotted Florrie grinning like she'd just won the lottery, standing with Denis, Jim, and Doris. They were all gathered like a merry little gang, waiting for us to join the party.

With morning greetings suitably rendered, Jim added quickly,

'As I was coming through the Lobby, I got talking to one of the long-stay people here, and he told me about a bar called Vincents, just around the corner. He said it was really good for drinks prices, great food variety, and often has a Group playing, which is very popular with the Hotel guests.'

Doris nodded in approval and, with a laughing smile, said boldly, 'This place sounds good to me; let's all go!'

And just like that, our little band of merry wanderers set off in search of this new, thrilling spot. Within moments, we were greeted with the comforting promise of food and drinks, all in one haven of relaxation. No time was wasted—we were off to find Vincent's.

As we strolled, I couldn't help but feel lucky. The sun was shining, and this was just the first of many adventures waiting for us in the unknown.

It didn't take long to find Vincent's Bar—just a short walk downhill, a quick right around the corner, a mere few minutes from our hotel. Perfect for a leisurely stroll in the sunshine after our hearty breakfast.

The place looked a little worn from the outside as if from a long life, but as we went inside to look around, I felt that warm, pub-type atmosphere. It had a nice-looking bar and many wooden tables and chairs. Lots of clutter was around, with many ornaments and banners festooning the ceiling. Although still early in the day, many people were inside and sat down; I guessed Vincents had a good breakfast.

After our quick look at the place, Judy and I decided to leave the others for a while to go for a walk down to the beach to take the kids to play. The beach was a stiff downhill walk, which I observed was seemingly ok on the way down now but would be rough coming back up. However, on arrival we were not disappointed.

The beach was almost empty and offered an uninterrupted view of a beautiful stretch of golden sand with a panorama of many tall hotels and a sweeping seascape.

It looked just the place for us, with so much un-crowded sand for the Kids to play in.

Although it was a warm day, it was just a bit too cold for swimming, so like a dutiful father, I made sand castles and various other sand objects to the delight of Karen and Graeme.

After an hour or so on the beach, I was surprised to hear Graeme's little voice pipe up and inform us,

'Mummy, I'm thirsty. Can we have a drink at Vincent's place?'

Karen followed this request with another one for an Ice Cream.

I was happy to agree to this, not being a great beach lover and was feeling a bit thirsty myself. So we quickly packed up our things and headed back to Vincent's, where, to no surprise found the others, who were just ready to leave.

'We're just off to a new bar someone told us about a few minutes ago,' said Mum enthusiastically.

'It's just up the road and round the corner. The other people told us it's good, so we thought we would give it a try.'

'Ok by us!' said Judy enthusiastically.

It appeared she had also built up a thirst, and she, like me, was always eager to discover and try a new bar or restaurant.

Soon, we were strolling down the road to find this new watering hole and enjoying the brilliant sunshine of this day.

We turned the corner of a small, narrow street as Denis had instructed, and there it was, 'The Bodega' as shown on the small bright sign hanging on the wall outside just by the doorway. I also noticed small tables outside, which looked ideal for a pleasant hour or two with a beer or two.

Following Dennis eagerly, we entered to find a large room decorated in a really fine fashion in a typical Spanish style. A number of wine barrel ends were set into the walls, and many pictures of Spanish scenes were placed around in all sorts of order. A great atmosphere could be felt all around the room.

There were many people settled in the place, and all around seemed to be very merry and enjoying themselves, full of Christmas spirit in all senses of the word.

There were a number of wooden tables, quite sturdy looking, with thick tops and raffia mats lay neatly around. The seating looked nice and comfortable, with thick seat cushions on wooden chairs.

Dennis, in typical fashion, led us quickly to a table while Dad and I made for the bar and ordered a round of drinks and an ice cream for Karen and Graeme.

We stayed in the little bar for a while longer—what a pleasant little gem we'd stumbled upon. It was clearly popular, and by the time we arrived around 2pm, the place was buzzing with a mix of people, all rotating in and out at a steady pace.

With the events of the previous day firmly behind us, we were all in much better spirits. The joy of a fresh day, coupled with the discovery of a couple of great watering holes, made for a perfect afternoon. After downing our final drinks, we decided it was time to move on to Vincent's before heading back to the hotel.

Judy gave me a nudge and pointed to Graeme, who was already at the door, eager to get going. I glanced at my watch—it was already 4pm. How had the time flown by so quickly? We'd arrived at Vincent's bar in the early morning, and after a visit to the sea, the beach, and the Bodega Bar, it had certainly been an eventful day so far.

We waved our goodbyes to the bar and made our wobbly way back up the hill, leaving the others to head to Vincent's while we decided to put the kids to bed for a bit before our 6pm dinner sitting.

We were quickly back into our room, thankfully via the lift, which perfectly, although slowly, raised us up to the top floor.

My thoughts went to the evening as I looked towards Judy, who had quickly moved into our bathroom to get the Kids washed and into bed for a short sleep.

I wondered, what the hell would we get to eat tonight?'

I sincerely hoped the dinner, which was to be served to us soon, would be edible and without difficulties as when we first arrived.

Feeling a bit weary myself, I layed down on my small bed for a quick half-hour kip, apprehensive of the evening's events.

I finally drifted off to sleep, but after about an hour passed, I was woken abruptly by our alarm, which Judy had set before resting.

It was time to get up and spruced up for the fine evening's programme which I guessed would be a long one. It was our third time dressing ourselves in these really cramped conditions with four beds in the room, but we managed and all were quickly made ready.

We trooped out of the door with a cloud of apprehension all over us on what was waiting for us at the dinner table.

As we approached the lift my heart drooped as I could see a large piece of paper stuck to the door of the lift. Guess what, it was a sorry note of an impaired lift.

'So it's off down the stairs again!' I groaned and headed off with Judy and the kids trailing limply behind.

After the seemingly endless steps, we reached the Lobby and into the bar where we found to no surprise, Mum and Dad seated with the others.

As soon as we sat down Dennis advised us quickly, and with a kind of drawn expression on his face.

'I've overheard, while at the bar, some long-stay hotel Guests saying that the Old Time Dancing lot would be on tonight and likely be taking over the place; they had done this a few times before and just spoiled it for the other guests!'

After a few seconds of silence, Doris spoke up and, with some slight urgency in her voice, said.

'I think it may be the best plan to have our dinner and then go over to Vincent's for the evening; I guess the Old Time Dancing is not really for us!

Jim replied in a very quick response.

'I think that's what we should do as well, and just forget the dancing!'

'Let's just go in for a laugh,' I said and looked around our table, offering a rather big grin.

Dennis quickly nodded in response, always ready for fun.

'Well, I suppose it will be a new holiday experience', Mum advised. 'We can soon be over the road if it's awful!'

So, with some sort of agreement, as seen by reluctant nods around the table, the low wisdom of the plan was confirmed.

Noticing the restaurant doors opening, Florrie remarked,

'It may be best to get dinner over quickly and into the dance hall to get a decent table.

'Good idea!' said Dad, and he got up from his seat to make a start.

We all got up and moved over to the doors and were greeted by dear Manuel, who, with a smile and waving hand, directed us over to our tables.

'Perhaps it's going to be good tonight,' Judy commented with a grin while directing Karen and Graeme to their seats.

As we all sat down and prepared ourselves for what was to come, a smiling Silvio appeared. He laid down the first course of strange-looking stringy things on a small plate.

'What's this stuff?' Cried Karen, followed by a screwed-up face, with 'Ugg!' from Graeme.

I'm sure it tastes better than it looks,' said Mum as she raised the first workload to her lips. Her sour expression at first taste said it all, which mirrored the whole theme of the evening's offerings.

We finished off our meals as quickly as possible and moved on to the Bar where we could see our friends already sat down with drinks in front of them.

'We left most of ours!' said Jim as we arrived, 'It was just awful, so we all decided to have something at Vincent's after the show.

'Bloody good idea!' said Dad, 'We left lots of ours. It was just muck!'

After a few rounds at the bar, Florrie, in her usual energetic style, suggested we move into the Dance Room. With a quick, decisive motion, she sprang to her feet and headed straight for the entrance. The rest of us, drinks in hand, followed her like waddling ducks into the hall.

The room felt a bit cramped with about a hundred people inside, but we quickly found a table and settled in.

I glanced over at the stage and noticed a small table at the back, on which sat an old-fashioned gramophone. Standing beside it was an even older-looking woman—thin as a rake, with short, lightly permed, curly hair that had clearly been doused in a fair amount of blue rinse. She wore a long green dress adorned with sequins that caught the light in a way that probably hadn't been fashionable since the '50s.

Next to her stood a rather portly man, decked out to the nines in a black evening dress, sharp-creased trousers, and highly polished black patent leather shoes. His hair looked as though it had been plastered down with enough Brylcreem to grease a car engine.

It was the 1940's all in action and seemingly ready to go.

My eyes turned their attention to the rest of the room and scanned around to see many more old folks all dressed in old-fashioned gear. Sequins and Brylcream abounded. To my younger eyes this group looked so ancient, and not a single smile amongst them.

Dad nudged me and, with a stern look on his face, said quietly, like in the hushed silence of a Church.

'This lot looks like a bundle of fun. Can't see a smile anywhere!'

'Yes, I replied with a grin; I can't wait for the big show to start; I bet it's going to be a real laugh with this poker-faced lot.'

After a few minutes, when everyone had settled down, the lady on the stage, microphone in hand, announced in a rather posh voice.

'Ladies and Gentlemen, let me introduce my husband, Johnny and myself, Gloria. Tonight we have for your entertainment our Old Time Dancing group from Hornsey in South London who will be performing a number of dances from our wide repertoire.'

She continued enthusiastically and waived her hand while announcing,

'So without further ado, I call on Silvia and Harold to start the evening off.'

Almost the instant Gloria had finished her announcement, a couple arose from a table close to the stage and started walking onto the dance floor. This was obviously Silvia and Harold. What a sight for our eyes; Silvia was wearing a long blue dress covered in regulation sequins. She had blue-grey hair to match, which was neatly cropped to her head with tight curls.

Her face was all powdered up, which made her almost like a corpse, sort of a living dead look.

I felt another nudge from Dad.

'I see the perm lotion has been in full use!' He said laughingly to me.

At this, Dennis commented quickly through stifled laughter,

'This lot must have used up all Brylcream's stock for the next year!'

'Shush, you two!' Florrie rasped out, 'Everyone can hear you!'

My eyes quickly turned back to Harold and Silvia, who were standing together in front of the stage like it was some kind of religious ceremony. It was a comical sight; Harold was a good bit taller and thinner than his partner, and to make matters worse, you could see the lights from the stage and around the room reflecting off Harold's plastered-down and shining hair.

Harold's evening attire had seen better days; his jacket had wide lapels, which looked rather out of proportion to the rest of him. His trousers were a bit baggy, but to give credit they were nicely creased and looked well with his shiny shoes.

The microphone crackled into life again, and Gloria announced. 'Harold and Silvia, it's over to you.'

I could see Gloria's hand holding the arm of the gramophone and moving it onto the spinning disk below.

The gramophone crackled for an instant and from the hushed silence of the room, music then filled the air.

Harold turned to Silvia, took her hand and together they spun round the hall moving in a strange sort of step routine, occasionally performing pirouettes.

The music crackled on, giving away a secret that the track was as old and well-used as the dancers.

The record shortly came to a stop; Silvia and Harold bowed to a rather stifled applause; it seemed that most in the hall had not seen this kind of dancing before and did not know quite what to make of the spectacle.

Without pause or warning, Gloria announced the magic words, 'And again!'

This we learned was the instruction for a repeat performance.

The gramophone again burst into life, and instantly, Silvia and Harold were prancing off around the hall again. After a seemingly never-ending series of twirls and swirls, the music came to an end, and Silvia and Harold bowed again.

Gloria, obviously overjoyed with the performance, started to clap wildly; this started Johnny off in likewise fashion, and this, in turn, spread around the hall, causing Silvia and Harold to repeat the bowing for all they were worth.

Silvia flourishing her hands in a sort of wave like the Queen does from her carriage. Then, without warning, Johnny took the microphone and announced excitedly,

'Silvia and Harold will now lead the rest of the dancers in the Military Two Step!'

As he spoke, the remaining sequined and Brylcreamed members of the troupe all rose to their feet and, like a herd of Penguins, scurried onto the dance floor to take up their starting positions behind Silvia and Harold.

In a flash, Gloria had skillfully changed the record, and the gramophone instantly burst into life, first with the now familiar crackle and then again with the strains of ancient music filling the hall.

The troop lurched into life as if the sight of a group of sequinned and Brylcreamed geriatrics could be considered life.

They all looked so serious as they pranced in tight formation up and down the length of the hall. I noticed some of the men had their jaws well stuck out with teeth gritted like their very lives were at stake, the ladies likewise with faces taught like the waxwork models. Yes, this lot, I thought, was certainly no bundle of fun!

The precision of their dancing was almost too perfect to be true, with arms waving in flawless harmony and the formation and steps moving as if guided by an unseen hand. But alas, just as they pranced toward a dramatic climax, this blissful state was not meant to last.

They all swung into a coordinated move, and I quickly spotted a rather short man who had swung his partner a little too enthusiastically, sending her dangerously close to the adjacent couple. The lady's arm gracefully arced out in a turn, but instead of a neat swoop, it collided with the man's head. Something flew up, arced through the air, and landed squarely on the floor, skating a few feet before coming to an abrupt stop.

The poor man's hand shot up to his head, his face an expression of horror and disbelief at what had just happened.

A collective gasp rippled through the hall as everyone took in the scene. From the next table, a shrill voice pierced the silence, "It's a wig! He's lost his wig on the floor!"

The sound of stifled laughter rippled around the hall; I looked at Judy, which was not the wisest thing to do, as I saw the edges of her mouth quiver, which I knew could be the start of hysterics. Mum was nearly as bad, and Dennis was holding his stomach as fit to burst. The others were in various stages of suppressed convulsion.

The dancers, however, seemingly unperturbed by the event, continued with their routine, even more stone-faced than before and for an agonising few minutes, they danced round and round until, mercifully, the music slowed to its conclusion.

Gloria, again at the microphone, rallied her troupe together with even greater applause. Quickly, the audience followed suit as if to stifle the widespread laughter.

'And again!' Gloria cried out in a sort of wild excitement.

Music instantly filled the air, and the troupe lurched back into action for an encore around the room.

Judy, now slightly more composed, whispered to me.

'Where is the wig, it's not on the floor?'

I quickly looked at the place where it had been, and sure enough, it was gone. As if by magic the wig had disappeared from the floor, like an illusionist's trick.

'It's run away!' I said jokingly, looking back at Judy, who was beginning to laugh again.

It was Doris who solved the mystery and, leaning over towards Mum, whispered, not so quietly, in Mum's ear.

'It's back on the man's head again,' she confirmed, 'They must have grabbed it from the floor without anyone noticing!'

'I bet it's got a few footprints on it,' Jim said with a chuckle.

The hour continued with various other dances being performed, but after this none as funny as the Escape of the Syrup! As I now named it.

At about 9pm. Gloria announced with sighs of relief that the entertainment had finished, and there would be dancing until 11 pm.

 This, we were to learn, meant more Old Time Dancing.

Gloria just set the gramophone back into action, and all the penguins that had just finished the show got up again and started dancing the same routines again.

You could see, all around the hall, a sort of confusion on people's faces; no one else got up to dance and apart from the usual journeys to the bar, everyone remained seated. This continued for two or three more tracks from Gloria's music box until she put on a tune resembling a Quick Step.

I noticed at the far end of the room two couples from the German party getting up and then moving onto the dance floor. They were soon into action and dancing beautifully around the floor.

'Come on, Judy,' I said, 'you like a Quickstep!'

With that, I took Judy's hand, and although a bit reluctant, she followed me onto the floor and into the dance.

We had moved no further than halfway around the floor when, one by one, the Old Time Dancers started to leave the floor until only the two German couples and we were left dancing.

The record finished, and we all sat down, leaving the floor empty.

Gloria put on another record, a waltz. The troupe re-entered the floor and once again went into their formation routine. Within a minute three couples from the German contingent rose to dance, but no sooner had they started round the hall the Old Timers left the floor and sat down again?

'What's going on?' I heard Dad exclaim, 'Why are they all sitting down every time someone gets up to dance?'

'Search me,' said Dennis, 'They are all loony if you ask me; the old bag on stage said it was dancing after the show.'

'I think they mean Old Time Dancing,' said Florrie.

'That's stupid!' Judy cried out quickly in her ``Got the right needle voice! `` And continued in a strong fashion

'They don't own the floor, we are all on holiday to have a nice time, they have done their bit of dancing for the last hour or so!'

Mum, who had remained unusually silent in all this, piped up,

'I hope it's not going to be like this every night, surely people are not going to be that stupid.'

I thought to myself and replied quickly to Mum's concern.

'Don't you believe it; we have come on holiday to join a right bunch of weird people!'

The music once again slowed to a depressing halt, and the German dancers, all three couples, left the floor again, but this time, I noticed there was an air of humour about them; I wondered what to expect next!

This time, Johnny was given charge of the gramophone and we were to see full control of the microphone. I guessed Gloria wanted to go for a wee wee.

The night had not gone well so far, and although our little gang had been highly amused by the antics, I guessed the Old Time Dancers were wishing the other residents of the Flemington had never come on holiday. After all, their kind of dancing was the only possible way to enjoyment in their eyes, and all we seemed to do was spoil it for them.

I mused to myself at the stupidity of the people. Here we were at Christmas time, supposed to be enjoying ourselves, goodwill to all men and all that goes with it; yet one little group of old farts could be so mean and selfish as to want to spoil all enjoyment for the rest of us poor souls.

I quickly came back to earth, shaken out of my thinking by Gloria's enthusiastic and now unwanted voice.

'Ladies and Gentleman, we are proud to announce another dance by Silvia and Harold who will perform their championship routine as danced at the Romford Old Time Dancing Championships last year.'

There was rapturous applause from the penguins, but little from the rest of the audience, who by this time were just about pissed off with the whole boring bunch.

Dennis, who had remained surprisingly silent for some time, stood up and, with hands-on hip, looked at Dad and Jim and, with some anger in his voice, said quickly.

'Stuff this, I've had a gut load of this lot; for God's sake, let's go over the road to Vincent's Bar for a beer and some fun!'

Nothing more was said, and in that short pause, Dennis lifted himself from the table, looked round at us all and raised his thumb towards the door. Dad grinned at him in agreement as he also got up from his seat.

With Denis leading, we were quickly moving across the floor to the exit. Others must have overheard, and I noticed another group seated on the table next to us quickly following behind us.

I looked back to see others, all with the same idea, also getting up from their tables. I turned to Dad, who was just beside me and said with a laugh,

'Now those old farts can have the place to themselves, what a bunch to be on holiday with!'

Dad joked back at me with a grin, saying,

'I never realised we had booked a SAGA holiday for the senile and geriatric!'

I did not know this expression and made a strong mental note to remember the SAGA re-name joke of senile & geriatric. This, I expected, would always be good for a laugh down the Pub, at home with my mates.

'Don't worry,' I heard Judy say with a smile, 'We can have a good discussion and laugh about it when we get over to Vincent's.

As we headed towards the lobby, I could see a group of people standing around something. As we got close I could see our Hotel Manager waving his hands about.

'Stay back, please stay back!' he cried out.

I could see an elderly lady crying, with her hands on her face, being comforted by another lady by her side.

'He's dead!' she cried out, 'My Harry is dead!'

Dad, who was closest to the group, looked at me sternly and said quietly,

'Let's move out of here; they don't need a crowd of people around this sad event.'

'Quite right,' I replied, and took Judy's hand and our kids with Mum and headed towards the exit door followed by the others.

I felt the warm air as we exited the Hotel, which thankfully helped to take away the shiver which had gripped me from the previous death event in this doomed Hotel.

It seemed that I was not the only one to experience this feeling as nobody spoke as we started walking down the road until the silence was broken by Jim.

'Why don't we just go to Vincent's now and forget any other bars tonight? It's nearly 10pm now, and we have already had a bit of an eventful day today, especially with that poor man dying!'

'I agree with that!' said Florrie in a quick reply to Jim's wise suggestion.

'We have a long day tomorrow with Christmas Eve, and I bet we will all overdo it a bit!'

'Off we go then,' said Dennis, and he walked on a bit with chest forward.

'Poor sod!' Jim spoke up quickly; what a way to start a holiday; still, at least he won't have to stomach the hotel food!'

'Don't be wicked!' said Florrie, giving a severe re reprimand.

'Poor man, he's paid out all that money and had no holiday.'

The logic of this escaped me, presumably in Florrie's eyes; if the man had died at the end of the holiday, he would somehow have been more satisfied.

A thought flashed into my mind of him standing, knocking loudly on heaven's door, and just waiting for it to be opened so he could make an official complaint to God.

'Now look here, God, why have you taken me now? I've saved up months for this out of my poor meagre pension and haven't even seen the sun; it's just not fair you could have let me finish my holiday!'

Mum brought me quickly back to reality with a dose of reason.

'Perhaps he had a bed heart,' she explained,

'All that travelling about is not very good for these old folks, gallivanting about the world and getting over-excited. Some of the people in this hotel must be over eighty!'

She was right, of course, but I suppose if you're going to snuff it, you might as well be on holiday or doing your favourite hobby.

We were quickly at Vincent's door, and as we entered I could see it was quite busy. I could also see that a few larger tables were available, so I pointed one out, and we headed forward to claim it.

With the ladies suitably seated, Dennis cried out quite loudly to be heard above the general hubbub around the room.

'The bar looks very crowded, so Len and I will get the drinks, and Ken can come over and help with the trays.'

Knowing what all our little group imbibed made matters easier, so both were quickly over at the bar and jostling in through the other good patrons, who were likewise keen to purchase the various brews and cocktails on offer.

I could see Dad and Dennis had got into a good position and were being served so I went over to help, being followed by Jim, who I guess wanted to just make the numbers up.

We were having such fun, and as the evening quickly passed on, I looked at my watch to see it was 11.30pm. I realised we had better get the Kids home and in bed quickly. A big day tomorrow, I thought.

I nudged Judy to remind her of the time.

'Oh God, is it that late? We had better get off now!'

With that, she grabbed Karen and Graeme who were oblivious to the fact it was well past bedtime.

We quickly said our goodnights to all, who were clearly still in party mood, and we headed fast out of the door and back to the Flemington.

I groaned on entering the Lobby as I could see the out of service sign on still the lift door. I then considered, with a feeling of helpless, the endless steps to the summit where our room was located.

'Judy I cried out, it's up those bloody stairs again!' as I walked up to approach the first step of the many.

'Oh, that bloody lift!' she responded, 'Let's get going and get it over and all of us into bed!'

We reached our room, full of huffs and puffs, with poor old me with a sagging Graeme loaded on my shoulders for the final accent.

I must confess that our undressing and into our bedclothes routine was done with some indecent haste. Soon, the Sandman was here and doing his best on the two kids as eyelids were soon closed and sleep gently came over.

With many of the day's events to ponder over, I found myself drifting off into dreamland more slowly than usual. I could not help thinking of the poor man's death and the bereaved wife; however, coupled with the many drinks of the day, sleep was eventually and gratefully forthcoming.

Chapter 9 – Sun – Sand- Sea & The Trot's

(Day 3)

On the third day of our vacation, I woke up in a very happy mood, feeling rather less stressed than the first two days of our arrival.

The sun was shining beautifully again and it seemed another good day for a trip to the beach. Perhaps I would swim or at least do another paddle with the Kids.

I looked round to Judy to enjoy with me the new experience I was feeling, but although she was awake the response was as before, just a light kick on my leg and a scowl.

Don't be like this!' I said with a smile, 'Look! It's a beautiful day; the sun is shining, and we have got over the journey. Let's all get in the holiday mood!

Judy replied as she turned to look at me, but luckily, her face was now sporting a little smile.

She continued, 'God help us, I just worry and wonder what's in front of us?

'Come on!' I said quickly, Don't worry so much; let's get off to the beach with the kids and make some sand castles!'

Karen and Graeme suddenly woke up, triggered, I think, by the sound of me talking about the beach and sand.

In no time, they were both into the morning routine, jumping up and down on the beds.

'Stop that!' I cried out, 'Get undressed for showers, now!'

This was a phrase I had loud-voiced so many times before but had to repeat so often to achieve any result; was I to be fooled again?

To my delight and complete amassment, for once, they both did what I asked quickly and without complaint. I thought, if that's what the promise of the beach can achieve, I will try that again.

Now prepared and ready to go in the actual working lift, we just managed to get downstairs at 9.00am for our breakfast.

As we moved towards the breakfast room, almost out of nowhere, we were approached by Jim, who turned to us in a very excited manner as if he was going to impart the most important news.

Jim was so straight-faced and said quickly but in a quiet voice,

'As I was coming down the stairs, I stopped and got talking again to another one of the long-termers here.

Apparently, some poor elderly man died of a heart attack while in his sleep last night!'

Jim continued. 'Apparently, his poor wife was in a terrible state, and Carlos was called in quickly to sort it all out!'

'He learned this from one of the cleaning staff this morning, and the man's body had been put into a first-floor room, with the other dead resident as the only room available.'

Jim bowed his head towards us and, in a hushed voice as if the walls were listening, related more of his new-found knowledge.

'Apparently, a fair number of guests had dropped down dead during the man's long stay at the Hotel; it was thought by many Guests that the victims had got over-excited with the stress of travel and problems with the Hotel. Furthermore, many long stayers were worried about who among them might be next!'

Jim then continued, fortunately, on a lighter note, saying,

'The man also told me about a Spanish bar called The Cantina, just around the corner. He said it was really good for drinks prices, and great food, a visit to this place may lighten the mood!'

Mum nodded in approval and, with a laughing smile, said boldly while holding her shoulders slightly back.

'This place sounds good to me; let's all go early this evening,' and continuing with this, said in a rather sombre tone,

'It's terrible about the poor man and his wife and the other bereaved souls, but we can't do anything other than feel sorry for them and any family; let's pray God will give them comfort.'

Jim then leant back a little, gave a shrug, and related,

'Florrie is feeling very tired and a bit upset over these events, so she has decided to rest up till the afternoon; Doris has also decided to join her and just have a slow start to the day.'

Jim continued, in a rather resigned tone, and advised this plan for life without the ladies, saying something of little surprise,

'I spoke to Dennis about the ladies and we decided to have a few beers with a slow day before going out later.'

Mum nodded in agreement with this idea and added to Jim,

'We were just off for our breakfast and then off to the beach with the Kids; we can catch up later and go to the Cantina as you said; anyway, poor Len has got a bit of a bad tummy, so it's best to just have a relaxing day.'

'You've got the dreaded Trott's again!' said Jim, 'I hope you feel a bit better for later.'

Dad replied with a slight grin on his face.

'I seem to get the flipping Trott's on every holiday, but it's not so bad today, so I will see how it goes.' Dad continued with a plan; why don't we all meet up at this new place, The Cantina, at around 4pm? That will give us plenty of time on the beach with the kids and Florrie and Doris can rest up and feel a bit better.'

'Good idea!' Jim replied enthusiastically, 'You all go off and have some fun on the beach, and we will see you later at The Cantina.

Mum, Judy, and I quickly nodded in agreement, said goodbye to Jim, and moved off to have our breakfast.

Our second visit for breakfast was much as the first, with hard-boiled eggs, funny-tasting toast, and bitter coffee; however, it was food, and we all seemed to be hungry and ate it up while muffling further complaints. However, I thought, how did the long-term guests get on with this day after day, but as I looked around at some other tables, it was clear that some bought their own butter, jam, and other favourites with them.

With breakfast over, we made our way out of the Hotel and onwards to the beach, all wondering what this adventure would hold in store.

The golden beach looked so exciting with its long swept bay and rolling waves, but it was once again almost empty apart from some small groups of people, obviously enjoying the holiday break. I guessed some of them were the local Spanish people on holiday, just like us.

We soon found a good place to sit down and got ourselves settled in for good.

Although it was a beautifully warm day, I was sorely tempted to go for a swim, but as the Kids and I walked down to the sea and dipped my toes in the water, I quickly realised it was just a bit too cold for swimming. However, this did not stop Karen and Graeme who both ran into the sea and were quickly jumping up and down in the waves, which I add were pretty mild and safe.

I stood and watched them both having fun and continued resisting calls to come in and join them. I nearly did, but the chill of the water heavily overwhelmed my desire to jump in.

As I continued to paddle while keeping a good eye on the Kids, my eyes also fell on two ladies walking together along the sea edge with feet splashing the water as they walked along.

When they approached nearer, I could see their faces more clearly, and to my astonishment, they had no tops on! Both were fairly slim, good-looking, and pretty well endowed, and I could see their beautiful naked breasts bouncing up and down as they walked towards me. This I felt was quite stirring, and I blinked my eyes a few times to see if my vision was in focus. Slowly, they came nearer and then passed in front of me, as they continued their walk, I could see it was no vision.

This was certainly not something I had witnessed before and certainly not seen on visits to the beaches of Bournemouth or the Isle of Weight on earlier holidays. Perhaps this was something that would come to the UK at some time, I thought; it would certainly liven up the scenery.

However, my eyes quickly returned to the kids who were enjoying the delights of the water.

Judy gained my attention with a poke in the back; this made me jump as I had not realised she had walked down to join us. This poke was accompanied by a comment.

'I bet you enjoyed that eyeful,' She said, 'You men can't keep your eyes off that sort of thing!'

I decided to stay quiet and splashed my feet about in the water as if this could somehow take the past events away.

Judy kicked up some water at me and then gave me a wide grin. She then announced loudly while waving her arms about,

'Come on, kids, let's get out of the water and play on the sand; perhaps we can get some ice creams!'

Quickly, we were back with Mom and Dad, and as I sat down on the beach, Dad looked at me with a smile and remarked how nice the scenery was. I smiled back and then decided it may be the best plan to play the dutiful father again and make sand castles with Karen and Graeme.

We spent some time on the beach, and having found an Ice Cream Vendor, all were satisfied and enjoying life.

I looked at my watch, and to some surprise, saw it was 3pm and realised we had arranged to meet the others at the Cantina at 4pm.

'Look at the time!' I called out, 'It's 3pm, and we agreed to meet up with our friends at 4pm!'

'We better get a move on; we can clean up at the tap and shower over by the wall, I guess Judy and I can clean up the kids and get clothes on quickly.' said Mum in a confident manner.

With Judy and Mum at pace, Graeme and Karen were soon showered, dried, clothed, and ready for the afternoon fun ahead.

I was followed quickly and was soon done and dusted, helping Dad to get up from his low perch on the sandy floor.

After some hours on the beach, I was surprised how quickly the time had passed but we were soon ready and off up the road to find the Cantina.

Mum, Dad, and Judy with me on the Beach

It did not take us long to find The Cantina; it was just a little walk up the road we had taken to our Hotel, a left turn, and in a few minutes, we arrived at its door. I was first to enter and as I looked round could see clearly inside, it was just a small bar with 6 or 7 tables. I could see Jim and the others sitting at the far end by the bar, which, of course, was no surprise. It looked quite busy as most tables were taken, but Jim had seen us and was waiving us to come over having earlier found a table with ample seating for us all.

The Bar was nicely decorated in typical Spanish fashion, with lots of bottles and ornaments on shelves and pictures spread over the walls. A comfortable place for a meal or a drink was my first opinion.

There were around 30 or so people in the place and I could see some were eating, which gave a good first impression to my hungry self.

'Let's get that table with Jim!' Dad said in anticipation of his first drink of the day.

Mum eagerly responded and walked towards Jim, greeting him with,

'It looks like we have found a nice place; it was rather warm on the beach, and I, for one, am rather thirsty!'

Come and sit down here said Jim, I will go to the bar and get you all a drink.'

Jim duly got up and headed bar wards while the others soon made space for us and were all seated in perfect position for a fine afternoon.

Mum was first to start the conversation, asking Florrie and Doris,

'How was your resting? I hope all is well and you both feel better. We had a great time with the kids on the beach and also some rest to get our energy levels up scratch!'

'We both feel much better now, said Florrie, 'it's all that talk of guests falling down dead and the general moans and groans of the people at the Hotel that was getting us down; it's best we stay out of the place when we can and enjoy what's outside!'

Jim quickly arrived with some drinks and we returned to the normal conversation with our experiences of the day.

We had not been seated more than a few minutes and taking the first sips of our drinks when Dad suddenly stood up and with a strained expression on his face, looked at Mum and informed her he was off to the toilet. He moved quickly off in the direction of the Gents only to find it occupied.

After waiting for what to him must have seemed like an eternity, nature would not be held back. We watched him red-faced, hopping from one let to another. Not wishing to have an accident, Dad's eyes fell on the Senioritis just next to the Gents' door. In an instant, Dad threw all caution to the wind and made a beeline for the door, luckily to find his place of salvation unoccupied.

From our table, we would see all Dad's goings-on, and I looked around the rest of the tables in the small bar to find we were not the only onlookers. Clearly Dad's 'Trots' was becoming a focal point of attention.

Suddenly, Dennis nudged me, to which I directed my eyes from the ladies to him.

'Your Dad, he's so funny sometimes,' he said, about to break into laughter. 'You know, at work, he's a legend with his 'Trots,' he's been like that ever since I've known him.'

'That's right,' Jim added enthusiastically, 'Old Len's so funny, every time he's come back to work after a holiday abroad, we always ask him, like you do, 'How was it, Len?'

'He would always tell us what a good time he and Tiggy had on their holiday; good hotel, great swimming pool, fantastic scenery, cheap prices, wonderful people, lots of good bars, then we would all wait.'

Jim went on while sporting a grin on his face.

'After reams of Len's great explanations of a wonderful holiday, one of us would enquire about the food, tongue in cheek.

Len would always stop dead at this point and say something like.'

'Food, well, that's another thing! A lot of it was muck, all greasy and loaded with garlic! I had a big dose of the 'Trots!'

'Ken,' Dennis interrupted, bursting to add something more.

'Sometimes in the office, we did not know what to do with ourselves,' He continued, 'Your Dad made us laugh so much about his holiday problem we all used to wait for him to return from a trip to give us a good laugh.'

'Yes,' Jim quickly added, 'While he was away on his holiday, there were endless jokes going on, like, 'Well, Len's been away three days now; I wonder if he's got the 'Trots' yet?' and 'Do you think Tiggy packed enough toilet rolls for the journey?'

When he gets back, we must ask him if he could find a good Curry House!'

Judy, Mum, and I had been trying not to laugh, but on Dad's departure could not contain ourselves any longer.

I looked at Judy; she was breaking into hysterics. I, too, could not contain myself any longer and felt myself shaking hard with laughter. I remembered blurting out,

'Hope Dad's got a tissue!' and Mum quickly replied,

'You know your father with his insides; he never ventures out on holiday without a pocket full, but please don't laugh when he gets back, or you know he will get cross!'

Mum's firm comments were quickly followed by Dennis saying out loudly.

'I wonder if he's finished yet; he's been there a long time?'

But the door was still shut with no sign of Dad.

I looked anxiously towards the door in anticipation of Dad's return, wondering just how he was getting on with his predicament.

My eyes then fell onto an elderly, prim-looking woman walking into the bar, followed by a short, thin man with terrible skinny legs, which stuck out from the openings in his shorts like two matchsticks.

She had a straw hat on her head and was attired in the most awful flowered print dress. She stopped and looked around as if to be searching for something. Her eyes fell on our table, staring for some time.

'She looks like a really miserable cow!' I heard Dennis comment.

'Hush up!' said Florrie, in an angered tone, 'She can't help it!'

'No!' said Jim quickly, 'But with a face like that, she could frighten a ghost; no wonder her poor bloke was walking two steps behind!'

As the couple advanced further toward the bar, she stopped, said something to her follower, which was out of earshot, and then looked around.

'Oh my God, she wants the ladies!' I blurted out, and in an instant, her eyes fell on the large picture of a Senorita nailed onto the door. She walked forward and stretched out to take the door handle in her hand, but just in that instant, before she could grab the handle as if by magic, the handle moved on its own accord.

The door slowly opened to reveal the occupant, my father, whose face had dropped like a stone. Poor Dad just stood there, this awful woman staring straight at him.

'This is the Ladies!' she boomed out for everyone in the bar to hear. 'Can't you see the picture on the door; it's a lady in a dress!'

Everyone in the bar was looking at the scene. Dad shuffled forward, stuck out his chin, said nothing, and walked hastily towards us.

I could see people stifling laughter. Dennis and Jim were likewise trying to exercise control!

The look on Dad's face was just like a naughty boy who had been caught with a fag around the back of the school bike shed.

'Sit down, Len,' Mum said hastily, 'I hope you feel better now you have been to the toilet.'

I looked at Mum, sometimes the master of well-meaning comments, but on occasions, best left unsaid.

Dad sat down quickly, seemingly wishing the floor would swallow him up.

'Trots all right now, mate?' said Denis with a grin.

'I'll go and get you a beer,' He continued, then got straight up and went over to the bar, scarcely able to contain himself from his suppressed laughter.

Fortunately, Dad's little embarrassment was quickly put to one side by a loud banging noise; it appeared to be coming from the ladies' toilet door.

'Look, the door handle's going up and down,' said Judy.

'I bet that old cow's got locked in; that's why she's banging on the door.'

'You're right, Judy,' I replied quickly, 'This could be fun,

and she could be there from 'Monday to Saturday!' quoting part of an old song verse from past days of comedy.

Florrie piped up and continued with this play, and with a large grin on her face, sang out, 'But everyone knows she's there!'

Further laughter continued until Jim added sharply,

'Be quiet. We must see what happens next.'

In this commotion, the man with the skinny legs went hastily over to the door, grabbed the handle, and attempted to open the door. This was to no effect, and the banging continued.

'Shut up banging!' The man cried out, 'I'll get someone to open

the damn thing!'

The thought of that woman being locked in the toilet of a Spanish bar just after Dad had been in there with his little problem seemed to be a sense of rough justice for embarrassing poor Dad so much.

'She could be in there for hours.' said Denis.

'Oh, what a shame,' I replied, but quickly felt a bit sorry for her plight.

Her agony, however, was soon to be over, as in an instant, the bar owner, who had momentarily disappeared round the back of the bar, re-appeared. On seeing the commotion, he ran from behind the bar and quickly towards the toilet. I could see he had a small tool in his hand. As he approached the toilet door, he bent forward and smartly poked the tool into a small hole by the side of the door handle.

In an instant, the door was opened to release the hapless woman.

Clearly, this toilet door problem was not an uncommon event, and I wondered how many times this had occurred in the past.

The ease of replacing a door lock rather than going through this commotion with angry customers seemed hard for me to understand.

I quickly realized that my understanding of the Spanish way of doing things, or rather of not doing things, was only in its infancy.

In typical fashion, the bar owner was waving his arms about while making a frantic apology to the woman, who appeared a bit miffed about the incident. Quickly, her husband took her arm, led her to a seat near the window, and sat her down at the small table.

In a few moments, the bar owner appeared from the bar with what looked like two brandy's and placed them in front of the couple. This seemed to have a calming effect and soon they were drinking and smiling at one another.

'Thank God that's sorted out,' said Florrie, 'What a fuss about a few minutes in the toilet.'

'Yes, but it must have so been embarrassing for her,' said Doris, 'Especially after making such a commotion to get into the toilet in the first place.'

I looked at my watch to see it was 6pm already, we had downed a few drinks but there was no talk about food from anyone. Scanning around the bar, I could see a few people eating, but it looked like Spanish food, which I thought in Dad's state would not be the best for today.

I decided something must be done, and with some passion, I split out,

'What do you think of this? We have been and seen this place, which seems great., but I can't see Dad eating anything here; it's very Spanish with lots of garlic; how about going to Vincent's, where we could all have a good solid meal, like Rump Steak or Grilled Chicken!'

Doris looked at me and then turned to poor Dad, who looked a little mournful, I guessed feeling a bit guilty over the thought of everyone having to move on his account.

Don't worry, Len, it's not your fault you have a bad tummy, I quite fancy a nice steak at Vincent's; what about the rest of you?'

'It's ok with me said Jim; we can try here again on another day,' He then looked round at us for some kind of agreement.

Dennis then stood up, picked up his beer, and said,

'Come on, let's all go to Vincent's, Jim's right; we can come here again on another day when we can enjoy it better.'

So, with that announcement from Dennis, we finished our remaining drinks and moved onwards, trooping up the hill to Vincent's.

We arrived quickly as it was just a short walk to the place.

I checked the time to see it was just 6.45, which was a good time to arrive before it got too crowded; I, for one was starving after having only breakfast and a small snack on the beachfront.

We entered Vincent's to find it far busier than I had expected, so I quickly looked for an empty table to seat us all. Fortunately, I found one not too far from the Bar and beckoned our party over to seize our new feasting place.

While the ladies were seating themselves, Dad and I followed by Jim, headed to the Bar to get refreshments. The Bar was very crowded and Dad, who was in front, had to wait to get served.

Dad was soon seen, however, and with our 4 beers on order and the ladies' tipples was able to organize trays, which were soon loaded.

Dad passed the first tray of booze over to me, which, by no surprise, contained 4 large beers. I took hold of a wobbling tray, grasped it as firmly as I could, and turned in the direction of the ladies' table. I made just one step forward through a gap in the crowd and straight into a rather tall man who was crossing my path. The tray connected with his arm and left my hands in an upwards direction; its contents spilt all down the poor man and a few others around.

'Oh God,' I cried out as if that alone would give salvation.

The man and others surrounding, just looked at me in a state of shock. All I could see was beer dripping off them and a growing puddle on the floor, which was now causing some backward movement from the surrounding patrons.

It seemed an eternity for my feelings of embarrassment to last, then out of nowhere came a young lady with a mop and bucket and attacked the puddle. This had the fortunate effect of not only cleaning up the mess but also clearing away most of the wet people.

I moved slowly over to the large, tall, wet man who had been the focal point of my deluge.

'I'm so sorry!' I stammered out, It's so crowded in here I did not see you coming. So sorry,' I continued.

The man just stood there mopping some of the wetness from his jacket and arms with a handkerchief. I could see, to my horror, that the beer soaking was extensive and dripping down from him.

I thought he was going to explode, but in that instance, the lady with the mop suddenly returned with a large cloth in hand. She fronted up to the man and announced herself as Maria.

She continued, smiled, and said quietly.

'It's not so bad!' and started to wipe him down the arm and chest which in an instant appeared to take the worst of the liquid away. I had not noticed this before, but Maria was very attractive, and the man seemed to be enjoying the close attention this young lady was giving him.

After a few more wipes down all seemed to be so much better. The man's eyes returned to look at me again, and his face lit up with a big grin rather than the anger I was expecting.

'Don't worry,' he said, 'It's only beer and I'm feeling better now I've dried off a bit.'

Dad, who had moved to stand beside me, looked at the man and said in a kind of light tone.

Thanks for your great humour over this accident with my Son. Please can we buy you a drink, we certainly need to get some more beer!'

'Min's a pint of lager.' He said. 'I was on my way to buy drinks before our collision.'

He then walked towards the bar and shuffled in to gain access to order, with Dad following to re-order our lost beers.

Dad quickly returned with a tray full of beers and a broad smile on his face. He advised that he bought the man a beer and that he had told him he was from Denmark, where, apparently, the spilling of beer on one another was a regular occurrence.

I thought this strange until my short period of working in Denmark many years later, which showed this to be a fairly regular thing at the local pub on many Friday nights.

With that period of the evening, thankfully behind us, thoughts turned to food and what Vincent's could provide us with. Fortunately, Dad had brought some menus with him from the bar so these were passed round to eager hands.

'They have Rump Steak!' said Florrie in an excited voice.

'That will do me!' said Jim, followed by Dad, Judy, and Doris.

'I see they have chicken fries for the kids!' said Judy so that will be great for Karen and Graeme.

So it was steaks, two medium, one rare, and three well done, and chicken with fries.

I thought it was heaven itself coming to us after Flemington's offerings.

Jim and Dennis walked off to order while I stayed fixed to my seat in fear of bumping into anyone else on this eventful evening.

As expected the meals served were just superb, large in size, and with steaks so tender and tasty and with our two kids eating up with great relish.

We were having such fun, and as the evening quickly passed on, I looked at my watch to see it was 10.15pm. I realised we had better get the Kids home and in bed quickly. A big day tomorrow, I thought.

I nudged Judy to remind her of the time.

'Oh God, is it that late? We had better get off now!'

With that, she grabbed Karen and Graeme, who were oblivious to the fact it was well past bedtime.

We quickly said our goodnights to all, who were clearly still in party mood, and we headed fast out of the door and back to the Flemington.

I groaned on entering the Lobby as I could see the out of service sign on still the lift door. I then considered, with a feeling of helpless, the endless steps to the summit where our room was located.

'Judy, I cried, it's up those bloody stairs again!' as I walked up to approach the first step of many.

'Oh, that bloody lift!' she responded, 'Let's get going and get it over and us all into bed,'

We reached our room full of huffs and puffs, with poor old me having had Graeme loaded on my shoulders for the final accent.

As was becoming routine, undressing and into our bedclothes was done in indecent haste. So soon our two kid's eyelids were closed up as sleep gently came over them.

'That was a day!' I whispered to Judy as we both settled down at a long day's ending. Judy quickly whispered back to me.

'I can't help feeling sorry for the two men who had died and the poor wives; what a terrible blow, especially at this special time.

'So do I,' I replied with some feelings of concern.

'It's just so awful, and what a place to die in!'

I sighed a little and turned over onto my side while continuing in thoughts of both the grim and funny sides of the day. I soon realised I still had some last strains of humour left in me on the thoughts of Dad's Trott's incident and how this news would resonate around ''The Firm;'' however, in some tiredness, I quickly found myself in sleep's good hands.

Chapter 10 – Awaiting Christmas Eve

(Day 4)

I woke up after having had a really good night's sleep and once again to another beautiful sunshiny morning. It was our fourth day in Benidorm; Christmas Eve was upon us with all the new day could hold.

Yesterday had started off with a bit of a bang, to say the least.

Finding The Cantina and Flamenco Bars, then a late night in Vincent's Pub had left me with a slightly fizzy head. After all the trials and tribulations of our journey to Spain and the events of the previous day, we really needed a well-deserved rest today. However, I feared that would not be the case!

I reflected on last night's evening meal at Vincent's with our scrumptious steak and chips, so good with a still imagined taste lingering in my mouth.

I quickly put this away from my mind as too much for a morning's awakening and rolled over to speak to Judy, who had just stirred, moaning quietly.

I quickly put this away from my mind as too much for a morning awakening and rolled over to speak to Judy, who had just stirred, moaning quietly.

"Good morning, Judy,' I said quietly, being respectful of possible fuzzy head pain. 'Did you sleep well, Graeme and Karen are still sound out! We should be thankful they have given us such a wonderfully uninterrupted night.'

On hearing my voice, our peace was soon interrupted by Karen's little voice merrily chirping,

'What are we doing today, Daddy? Are we going to the beach?' I replied it was Christmas Eve today, and we had decided with Mum and Dad that after breakfast, we would definitely take you kids down to the beach.

It took us a short while to get up, and the kids showered and dressed. We were soon out of our room and walking towards the lift.

Today, the dammed thing was working well, and with some pleasure on our part, whisking us smoothly down to the lobby for breakfast.

Mum and Dad were seated with our friends, and all seemed to be in good spirits. We waived and then went over to the buffet bar, which had the expected selection of hard-boiled eggs, omelette, toast, and tomatoes, which Judy scooped up for herself and the kids. I just grabbed a couple of eggs and toast slices then we walked over to join our group.

During breakfast, general discussion fell onto the breakfast and more jokes about the eggs and moved on to what today's events would be. I advised that we were off to the beach with Mum, Dad, and the kids and would join our friends later at Vincent's.

In a happy mood, we departed from Flemington, and after a walk down the hill, we arrived at the beach. It was 11am, and it was getting quite warm in the sun.

At a request from Karen and to the amusement of all concerned, I had agreed to venture into the sea for a swim.

Cold or what! My gonads were quickly frozen like ice cubes, and after ten minutes, I decided it was time to get back on shore before hypothermia set in or, even worse, my balls dropped off!

The Kids, of course, were jumping about in the sea like it was a warm bath and moaned at me for getting out of the water so soon.

After some resuscitation from the cold and the building of numerous sand castles to the delight of the kids, we moved off to Vincent's Bar and spent a few happy hours before returning to the infamous Flemington Hotel for the kids, 'going to bed!' routine for a little afternoon sleep before preparation for the long evening ahead.

Christmas Eve had come so quickly, and we were all so looking forward to it with some dancing and fun in the hotel.

Judy decided to take the kids up to bed for their nap while I stayed in the bar with Dad, Mum, and the others. After about twenty minutes, I thought I would go up to the room and give Judy a hand with the kids.

I duly announced to Mum I would go upstairs to see if Judy was ready.

I walked out of the bar and into the reception to take the lift only to find a crowd of people collected around the doors of the lift.

The Manager was in the centre of the people, waving his arms around, as we learned the Spanish were prone to do this when excited.

'It's the lift!' I heard someone cry out. 'Someone's trapped in the lift!'

'Oh my God,' I said to myself, not the sodding lift again!'

I walked over to the crowd, eager to find out more, and I questioned a man next to me who seemed to be in a high state of agitation.

'My wife's in there!' he said, 'With someone else, another lady, I think from the top floor like us.'

'Oh shit,' I muttered. 'I hope to God it's not Judy inside; there will be hell to pay when she gets out!'

I decided the best plan was to climb the stairs and check the room to see if Judy was present. I scaled the never-ending flights as quickly as my poor, unfit body would let me, wishing like hell I had taken more exercise and fewer pints in my life.

Wheezing and puffing like a clapped-out old nag, I made my way along the corridor to our room, only to find it locked.

'Oh Shit, where the hell is Judy?' I said out loud.

I was in a sort of panic mode by now and, turning quickly round, headed back for the stairs and down to reception. The crowd was still gathered around the lift door, and as I arrived. A man in a brown boiler suit, who I quickly recognised as the maintenance man, was standing by the lift.

I noticed he had a panel removed from the side of the lift entrance and was poking about with a screwdriver.

As if by magic, the lift door suddenly opened to reveal four people, two men and two women, looking very pale. The four quickly bolted out of the lift. Instantly, a rather large lady, all done up to the nines, confronted the poor, helpless manager, Julio.

'We've been locked in there fifteen bloody minutes!' she blurted out loudly. 'Yes, fifteen bloody minutes!' her companion confirmed with equal venom.

Julio continued to wave his arms about. 'I'm so sorry,' he said, so sorry.

The crowd gathered around in support of the four victims of entombment.

'What sort of hotel are you running?' The lady continued,

We could have died in there.'

One of the ladies from the lift was quite old and looked in a terrible state of shock.

'Look at my wife!' the man rasped out. 'She has a bad heart; she could have died in there!'

Poor Julio didn't know what to say; he just rocked from side to side, still waving his arms and stammering out, 'I'm sorry, I'm sorry,' over and over again.

Suddenly, I woke up from the sort of dazed disbelief I had slipped into and realised that Judy was not one of the lift victims.

'Where the hell is she?' I thought, 'If she's not in her room and not in the lift, what has happened to her?'

I decided to go back to the bar and quickly turned in that direction and sped off. To my surprise and relief, there she was, talking to Dennis, Dad and Jim as though nothing had happened. The Kids were seated quietly next to her.

'How did you get in here?' I asked urgently.

'Down the stairs, she replied. The lift wasn't working when I tried, so I had to walk down the stairs, but I'm alright now; Dad got me a Martini.'

'But I thought you were locked in the lift,' I said in a worried sort of voice.

'In the lift, why in the lift?' Judy asked with both shoulders, shrugged, clearly unaware of what had happened.

I explained to everyone the events of the last fifteen minutes or so.

Dennis started laughing. 'What a bloody place!' he continued,

'I'm surprised more have not died here; if the food doesn't get you, the lift will.'

He went on, 'I wonder what the bloody hell is next!'

'A fire like that film on TV last week,' Jim retorted.

'Shut up!' said Doris firmly, 'we are in enough trouble here already; don't you start tempting fate!'

Mum hastily changed the subject by inquiring,

'Did Karen and Graeme get off to sleep, ok? I bet they were excited as Father Christmas comes tomorrow?'

'My God, I had some explaining to do,' Judy said, 'Karen was full of questions, but I managed to get them answered and off to sleep for a while, which allowed me to get dressed and ready for tonight.'

Judy continued with the story while we listened in silence,

'We are so lucky the Hotel has a Father Christmas coming tomorrow morning around 11.30; I told the kids that he is stopping off especially at the hotel tomorrow for all the English children on his way back to Snow Land.'

We all laughed when Judy went on to explain further,

'Graeme was so excited he was wiggling all the time I was trying to put on his clothes.'

'Goodness knows what this Father Christmas is going to be like?' said Dennis with a large grin across his face.

'Probably got a big black moustache instead of a long white beard,' Jim replied with a laugh.

'In the morning we are going to give some presents to Father Christmas so he can give them to the children,' Judy said, with an air of confidence that somehow seemed unadvised when I considered the events of the last days. All the cock-up's and confusion that's happened. 'Still, I thought, what can go wrong with Father Christmas giving out a few presents?'

In our enthusiasm for all this talk of Father Christmas we had not noticed the bar beginning to empty. Meal time had crept up on us like a heavy morning mist.

'Into the Frey,' cried out Florrie in an unusually loud voice.

'Let's see what they have got for us tonight; it may be special as its Christmas Eve!'

'Special, my arse!' Dennis grunted out rather loudly and was quickly reprimanded by Florrie with a rather heavy nudge.

As we approached the restaurant doors were greeted once again by Manuel, who, with a smile and waving hand, smoothly directed us over our tables.

'Perhaps it's going to be good tonight,' Judy commented as last night and sorted out Karen and Graeme to their now familiar seats.

As we prepared ourselves for what was to come a smiling Silvio appeared. He laid down the first course of a new strain of strange-looking bean things spread on a small plate. Further courses of unclear description continued until the Ice cream finality.

The meal this evening, to be fair, was a little better than before and, with a few exceptions, actually tasted quite reasonable. This could be a one-off, but it may give a good indication of Christmas Dinner to come, I wondered?

We departed the restaurant quickly and soon found the others waiting for us in the lobby.

'Not too bad a Dinner this evening!' Denis grunted, not sure what it all was, but some of it was tasty!'

So let's get off to Vincent's and hope we can find a seat. It's nearly 7.30.'

We trouped steadily down the road and arrived at Vincent's door in a few minutes.

We had fortunately found Vincent's Bar first on our travels, and having popped in for a view and a few, we learned it was a bar well known all over Benidorm, being in operation for many years.

The bar was run by a friendly guy called Jose. We later learned of his long and enjoyable employment during some discussion at the bar. We found out he knew just about every drink you could name and, more importantly, did not hold back when serving Bacardi and other spirits in your drinks. We became bar friends very quickly, as shown in the chapter lead picture taken with me, Ken, the author.

The Bar was quite crowded with people, and we could see all were in great spirits awaiting the Christmas arrival at midnight. We were so grateful for our new found venue full of fun and laughter.

As we moved further into the room, it was a great relief to see a group of people just getting up and leaving one large empty table.

This was luckily near the bar, which was a big bonus.

We headed quickly over to commandeer it and duly secured it firmly with the ladies seated with Karen and Graeme beside them.

'Let's get the drinks; the time must be getting on!' I heard Jim call out. I quickly checked my watch and was surprised to see that the time had marched well on, and it was already 8.15pm.

With a sense of some urgency, I proceeded towards the bar, being followed close behind by Jim, Dad and Denis. Although it was very crowded, the bar staff worked so fast, and within a short time we were walking back to our table armed with enough drinks for all and more!

We soon hit the magic time of midnight and the whole place was in uproar as Christmas was enthusiastically welcomed in!

Everyone was hugging and kissing rather more like a New Year's Eve than Christmas, but like all good things coming to an end, we were all out of Vincent's and marching up the road.

It seemed like just a few steps and we were back to the Flemington, saying goodnight to all and off to our beds.

Judy and I were quickly into our rooms and feeling so lucky that the lift was working again. We soon tucked the Kids up and crawled into our bed, having had a very long day.

The kids drifted off so quickly, and when out for the count, Judy spoke quietly in my ear.

'Don't forget the presents; we must put some on the kids' beds before they wake up and the rest in reception for Father Christmas in the morning.'

As I drifted off to sleep my thoughts went to the morning and the arrival of Father Christmas to the Flemington.

'God help us!' I cried as I felt my body shiver with the sudden premonition of something unnerving about to happen.

Chapter 11 – Father Christmas Ho Ho Hic!

(Day 5)

The big day had finally arrived. I realized this quickly as Judy and I were abruptly woken up by Karen and Graeme, who were bounding on our beds.

'Mummy, Daddy.' Karen's voice shrilled. 'It's Christmas, It's Christmas!'

Graeme, was at this point, was looking at the end of his bed where a small sack was lying.

'Father Christmas has been,' he said excitedly and pointed to the sacks which Judy had left at each of their beds the night before. I sat up in bed to notice wrapping paper everywhere; it was as though a gang of marauding squirrels had attacked their beds. How four sheets or so of wrapping paper combined with the box debris from the presents could reach such a level of mess was beyond my simple understanding.

I was interrupted from my observations by Judy, who gave me her usual nudge. 'Merry Christmas,' she said and leant over to give me a kiss on the cheek.

'Graeme,' I said quickly and continued,

'Let's see your presents from Father Christmas!'

Judy and I had bought the presents in a local Spanish shop the day before, as it was not very practical to bring too much from England in the cases. We had bought some small-sized presents from home, which would fit in and with the idea of handing these over to Father Christmas on his visit to the Hotel later on in the day.

Karen's Spanish presents were a nice doll and a pretty dress, while Graeme had a wooden soldier and a new pair of shorts for the beach.

The next hours passed quickly, but when it was time to get up, trying to get the kids ready for breakfast proved to be a bit of a trial. Both wanted to play with their new toys, but with sheer perseverance, Judy and I managed to get them washed and dressed. In no time, and full of excitement, we headed off to knock up Mum and Dad to wish them Merry Christmas and go off to breakfast.

Mum and Dad were awake and dressed when I knocked on their door, and after Christmas greetings were fully completed, we were on our way down the stairs for breakfast.

My thoughts went to last evening when our second visit for an evening meal was not as bad as our first. I hoped in my heart that Christmas dinner would not be a big disappointment.

On a good point, our head waiter had sorted our family with a table together, which was a great hurdle to overcome.

My mind quickly drifted back to matters in hand and moved on to our breakfast.

We quickly followed Mum into the breakfast area, where Dad was busy sorting out some tables.

Breakfast at the hotel was a daily buffet affair, and while the spread was generous, it never failed to serve up a surprise or two.

Take the hard-boiled eggs, for instance. Here, "hard-boiled" was taken to a whole new level—truly the fifteen-minute egg. They reminded me of the china eggs my Uncle Horace used to place under his broody hens when they'd stopped laying. Those porcelain stand-ins were meant to nudge the hens back into productivity, but I reckon they were no harder than these Flemington specials. I half-expected the waiter to hand out chisels alongside the cutlery!

We completed the breakfast routine quickly as the kids were getting a bit twitchy with over excitement at the thought of the arrival of Father Christmas at the Hotel. We had already given Sharon the children's presents to give to Father Christmas the previous day, so all was in hand and well organized to perfection.

Mum, the master of these situations, said with a warm smile,

'Let's go down to the beach for an hour or so, and we can come back at around twelve to meet up with our friends, who should be enjoying an hour or two in Vincent's.'

I quickly replied, thinking of the possibility of a Christmas swim with the Kids.

'That's a good idea, Mum; what do you think, Judy?'

Judy paused for a moment, then answered enthusiastically,

'Yes, that will keep Karen and Graeme occupied for a while; they are both a bit excited and a run down to the beach will give them something to do, although the thought of you swimming again after last time and your complaints with your frozen Gonads, maybe not such a good idea!'

I pondered on that for a brief while but then thought, what can a man do when his kids want you to join them so much? What's frozen Gonads against this?

We strolled into the Hotel lobby, and I could see Jim standing with Doris and Florrie, but I noticed Dennis was a few steps away in a serious-looking conversation with a tall lady well into her seventies. She was thin and slender and had a rather strange appearance, dressed in a kind of tapestry dress, with all gold flowers woven into the fabric. Her hair was long and grey in colour, and it was secured in place with a Victorian-looking silver slide.

She reminded me of someone from the Hampstead Heath set who I had seen so often in my earlier days when Rick and I had gone to Hampstead to down pints in Jack Straws Castle, the famous local Pub.

We walked over to the others, and as we approached the lady turned her attention from Dennis and onto us.

'This is Mrs Fortesque,' Dennis informed us and said that she was from Hampstead, which, of course, was no surprise for me!

Dennis continued, 'Mrs. Fortesque is putting a big letter of complaint together about Sunrise Holidays and all the problems.'

But before he had time to relate any other information, Mrs. Fortesque announced in a very firm and quite excited voice,

'I have been staying here with friends for about three months!'

'It's a disgrace!' she said,

'The food is awful every day, many of us have complained, but to no effect, and being Christmas time, we all have to pay extra for everything.

She continued, with more revelations, saying in a strong voice,

'Most of the elderly people here are staying for two or three months or more on a special package!'

'Thank God we've only got eight days,' Jim piped up quickly while moving forward into a better listening position.

I thought, in a happy belief, that we had now reached the end and could go onwards to the beach, but that was apparently not enough for Mrs. Fortesque.

She then went into a long dialogue about all the events that had happened since her unhappy arrival at The Flemington.

My poor brain was fogged, but after a full ten minutes, she had only gotten past the first two weeks of her holiday and well into the third week to tell us more.

Almost without a stop, she went on and on to tell us about the dreadful experiences she and her friends had endured, ranging from the terrible food, awful room service, problems with the lift, and finally, in exhaustion, the Old Time Dancing. She paused for breath.

As my befuddled brain came back to my surroundings, Mrs Fortesque repeated once again her mission plan.,

'I'm organizing a petition to Sunrise Holidays about all the problems, so would you like to put down your names?'

She then paused in anticipation while gesturing with her right hand and pointing to a large pad of paper she had in her other hand.

'That sounds a good idea,' said Dad. 'That bloody Sunrise Holidays wants a good sorting out, sending us to a place like this!'

Dad continued, saying with some urgency in his voice,

'Just give me a pen!'

'And me,' said Florrie,' quickly followed by Doris.

The petition was duly signed, and without waiting for the ink to dry, Mrs Fortesque said a quick thank you and moved swiftly over to another group of guests waiting by the reception desk.

'Thank the Lord she's gone,' said Dennis in his usual manner,

'She's been giving me earache for about fifteen minutes before you came, all about the Hotel, the food, and just about everything else imaginable!'

'Were off down to the beach with the kids before Father Christmas comes,' Dad said in expectation to Denis and the others,

'Fancy coming. It's such a beautiful day?'

'I'm game for that,' said Florie, 'A bit of sunshine will do us all good, and then we can come back for Father Christmas and the Children's Show afterwards.'

I laughed and said out loud, without thinking,

'I bet even Father Christmas will kill himself, and the thought of coming in here!'

Judy nudged me quite hard and scowled as only she could.

'You berk,' she whispered, 'Shut up, you'll upset the children!'

Dad, seizing the opportunity, marched off towards the Hotel doors and out into the street and brilliant sunshine.

He was quickly followed closely behind by the rest of our gang, all eager to get onto the beach and have a quick paddle in the sea.

As we strolled down to the beach, the sky was so blue and unbroken by any clouds. The sun was streaming down and reflecting off the little white shops and cafés that ran along the road and along the seafront.

'What a Christmas!' I thought, 'To be here in the sunshine away from the cold English winter, it's just heaven.'

For that short moment, I had forgotten all about our previous dramas and was just happy to be here with my family.

The kids, on seeing the sea, made a beeline for it, and in seconds, shoes and socks, which had taken so much pain and struggle to get on, were off! They were both straight into the water and splashing about, yelling and giggling without a care in the world.

Mum and Dad were keen to sit down while the kids were in the sea and were soon seated as shown!

Both settled in a typical UK holidaymaker fashion without a major bit of skin in sight and not a care in the world.

Dear Mum and Dad - The good English on holiday

We stayed on the beach for about an hour when Jim reminded us of the time and the fact that he was getting thirsty in all this heat. It needed no further requests, and shortly, we were off back up the hill towards the hotel and our little Spanish Bar and Restaurant nearby, Called Maria's, which we had discovered to our delight on our previous walkabouts.

The bar was owned by Alberto and his wife Maria they were really nice and friendly and had both made us so welcome the first time we had gone in for a drink.

They had made a big fuss of the children and kept them amused with little games and regular supplies of sweets.

As we walked into the bar, we were welcomed warmly again, this time with a warm Merry Christmas.

Karen and Graeme immediately went up to Alberto, who they had quickly learned was always good for a sweet or two.

He greeted them, picked up each in turn, and placed them on a barstool. He went quickly behind the bar and rummaged into the little box at the back shelf where the sweets were kept. His hand reappeared, holding two candy bars, which immediately brought a beam on the faces of our two eager children.

We seated ourselves at a table and I contemplated the cold drinks about to arrive. Shortly the lovely Maria came to the table with a tray loaded with cold beer for us men and gin and tonics for the *girls*.

I had hardly gotten into quenching my thirst when Dennis cried out.

'Look outside, there's Sharon coming up the hill, I'll go outside and invite her in for a Christmas drink.'

With that, Dennis got up from the table and went outside to greet Sharon.

As Dennis stood outside, Sharon came up to him and stopped.

I noticed she had a very worried look on her face, and as she talked to Dennis I could see she was agitated and was waving her hands about as she talked. After a few minutes, she walked off, at a fast pace, towards the Flemington.

Dennis returned quickly to the bar; he had a terrible, worried frown on his face. He looked furtively over at the children who were still being amused by Alberto, then sat down at our table.

He blurted out, 'It's Father Christmas; Sharon said he's pissed as a fart, he's a bloke from England who lives here permanently, and he volunteered to do it this year but has a drinking problem!'

Dennis continued, still with a frowned expression.

'Sharon said he promised not to drink today, but apparently, some of his friends came round earlier, and they got into drinking; after an hour or so, he was drunk. Apparently, they had a heavy Christmas Eve in the pub, and all the drinking caught up with him.

'It's better we want to go back to the Hotel and check what's happening,' said Judy, 'She said he was supposed to be here at 3pm; it's now 2.45. Karen & Graeme are waiting for their presents.'

The four of us walked over to Mum & Dad, and the other still seated at the table. Judy said

'We must hurry down for the children's entertainment; God knows what is going to happen.'

'We should go back now,' I announced, 'We had better see what's happening.'

Mum replied nervously, 'Yes, it's 2.45 we should go back.'

I looked at Doris, Florrie, Jim & Denis; all had concerned looks on their faces.

The prospect of disappointed children, not seeing Father Christmas as promised, was all too much. Not just our kids but all the others in our hotel, all looking forward to their presents and seeing Father Christmas.

With heavy hearts, we moved towards the door, said our goodbyes, and proceeded up the hill and back to the Hotel.

As we approached, dear Karen, who was slightly in front, reached the hotel and, with a shrill announced

'Father Christmas is here, I can see him in the hotel.'

'I can see him too,' said Judy, peering franticly through the glass door at the entrance.

'It's a miracle. Let's get inside,' I said in a very urgent tone, 'Please let us get this over quickly before anything else happens.'

We went into the Hotel dance room and there he was, Father Christmas, sitting on a large chair, dressed in the usual magnificent red robe and complete with a long white beard. He was with about a dozen children and on the floor as a number of parcels. The children's faces were all filled with excitement and looks of anticipation.

His outfit, his white beard, black boots, and big red hat all matched well with his over-red face.

We approached, but not as fast as Karen and Graeme, who were already, as if by magic, seated on the floor with the other kids.

Carlos, the Manager, was standing next to Father Christmas. He looked extremely worried and stuttered.

'Come and get your presents, children, as Father Christmas calls out your names.'

Father Christmas remained silent, his eyes glazed as if in a trance, and it was from the lips of Carlos that the first child was called.

Carlos picked up one of the parcels from the small pile on the floor in front of him; with a slight shaking of his hands, he nervously read out from the label on the parcel. 'Feda,' he called out.

A small girl got up from the floor and ran over to face Father Christmas and Carlos. Father Christmas remained silent, managing only a small sort of screwed-up smile. Carlos handed over the small parcel to Feda, who took it, held it close to her, said a loud thank you, and, with a big smile, went back to sit with the other children.

Carlos continued to call out more names and quickly got through about ten more children's presents. Father Christmas remained in a state of trance, just managing to make the occasional nod as the children approached.

Judy and I waited in anticipation, trying to recognize our kid's parcels from the others on the floor. Carlos bent down to pick up the next present, and as he raised it, we recognized it as the one for Karen. Carlos read out the label,

'Karen Birch,' he called out in a sound voice!

Karen leapt to her feet and almost flew over to Father Christmas and Carlos.

This time, Carlos had passed over the present to Father Christmas; he must have somehow thought the man had recovered sufficiently to perform this simple task.

We held our breath as Father Christmas, somehow realizing that he was required to do something, handed the present out into Karen's eager hands.

Karen grabbed it with a sense of urgency as though she anticipated it could be taken back. Clutching it close, she came back to us at a fast pace.

'Look, Mum,' she cried out, 'Father Christmas has given me a present.'

And with that, she sat down on the floor quickly to open the box. I leant towards Judy and whispered in her ear.

'This Father Christmas is strange; why has Carlos been handing out most of the presents so far? He has only passed a few over to Father Christmas to give to the kids so far,'

Judy replied quickly, 'Well, Sharon did say Father Christmas was a bit the worse for a drink; perhaps that's all he can manage.'

Our brief conversation was interrupted by Karen's unwrapping of her present, a Spanish Doll. She got up from the floor to slow us her present.

As she did, we heard Carlos call out, 'Graeme Birch.'

In a flash, Graeme was up on his feet and ran over to Father Christmas, who had already been handed the present by Carlos. Graeme quickly took the present from Father Christmas and came running back with a wide grin on his face.

Graeme quickly unwrapped his present and announced.

'It's a car!' Father Christmas has given me a really super car!'

Judy and I sighed in relief at the completion of the presents.

I thought to myself, 'Thank God that's over!'

I turned to look again at Father Christmas and Carlos and paused to watch them for a minute or two. Father Christmas continued to remain silent throughout the present giving and Carlos just carried on reading out the names on the presents.

My longer look at Father Christmas gave me no confidence that the proceedings would improve. I observed that the large white beard did not sit well on his big, round red face, and his large, bloodshot eyes were still glazed over, which seemed to be exaggerated by the large red hat sitting awkwardly on his head.

The last child ran over to collect her present, and with great relief, I could see that all the presents had now been given out.

Suddenly, Carlos walked forward and waved the children to move forward to sit round Father Christmas. He did this with some urgency and with more hand waving, while trying to get them all positioned.

As if by magic, a short and portly man appeared from behind us carrying a rather large camera. After some more manoeuvring of the children, who were in no mood to sit still while being separated from their presents, it appeared that the scene was now set.

The photos with Father Christmas were duly taken for a while amid much fidgeting around until the camera was lowered, and the short and portly man turned and drifted off and out of sight.

The children's group moved quickly away like a small storm, moving back with their new presents to eagerly waiting parents.

I continued to look around and towards Carlos, who was still standing next to Father Christmas. I saw he was leaning towards him and then put his hand on his shoulder.

Suddenly, Father Christmas let out a loud snore, followed

quickly by another.

'He's asleep!' I heard Judy cry out.'Father Christmas is asleep!'

'Must be all that work he's just done, handing out presents!' Dad replied with a sarcastic laugh in his voice.

Suddenly, Sharon, who had been standing to the side of the lobby, walked quickly to join Carlos. She seemed to confront Carlos then she leaned forward and shook Father Christmas hard by his shoulders. Father Christmas sat bolt upright, his left arm raised as though in salute. Carlos put his arm around the back of him and assisted him to his feet.

Father Christmas wobbled slightly and lurched over, only to be held from falling by the aid of Sharon, who now had a real look of rage on her face.

Fortunately, all but a few people were left in the hall to see the latest antics, and I guessed the kids would not have realized what had really gone on.

Carlos and Sharon hustled Father Christmas towards the lobby, each gripping an arm and steering him toward the lift like two determined reindeer wrangling a sleigh gone rogue.

I followed, naturally, curious to see how this festive fiasco would unfold. Poor Father Christmas, his feet sliding limply along the polished floor, eventually made it to the lift. Carlos jabbed the button, and by some Christmas miracle, the doors opened on cue. The pair bundled their wobbly charge inside, and with a soft *ding*, the trio vanished from sight.

Mum, who'd been watching the entire spectacle in appalled silence, suddenly whirled around to face me.

"How dare they have a drunken Father Christmas for all these dear little children!" she huffed, her outrage as sharp as tinsel caught in a vacuum cleaner.

'Still, look on the bright side; at least he wasn't sick on any of them,' Dennis replied in very bad taste.

I shuddered at the thought of a drunken Father Christmas throwing up everywhere. It was too horrible to contemplate.

I went back into the hall to get Judy and the kids, and as I entered, I looked over towards Graeme, who was sitting on the floor playing with his new car. I could also see Karen seated next to him with her new doll in hand; both kids seemed oblivious to the mad events of the last hour.

'Come on, it's all over in here,' I said to Judy,

'Let's move into the bar and have a drink before the children's rest time, Mum and Dad are going to take them for a lay down in their room so we can get ourselves dressed and ready for the big evening.

After about an hour, Judy and I went up to our room as planned to get ready for Dinner. Both of us were feeling very light-hearted and happy in the expectation of the evening's events.

I got myself ready fairly quickly to give time for Judy to get her Christmas outfit sorted out in peace, and bidding goodbye, I strolled off to collect the dear little souls from Mum's room.

Mum and Dad seemed OK and smiled as they let me in.

'Karen and Graeme have been very good with us,' Mum was quick to tell me. Then, slightly paused and continued,

'The kids have both had a good sleep and after we played eye spy.'

I looked towards both Mum and Dad, who seemed to have enjoyed their babysitting, and said thankfully,

'I'm off with the kids to get them changed for tonight. It should be a really good evening, but I hope there's no Old Time Dancing!'

Dad replied firmly, 'I don't think they will after what Dennis had said to Sharon the other night!'

Dad continued, 'He told her good and proper that all the old farts were trying to take over the dancing and entertainment.'

Sharon told him that a band was definitely coming and we would get some good music played on Christmas night.'

'Not Disco?' I said excitedly.

'No, you daft sort,' Mum quickly responded,

'We are having a band!'

With happy thoughts of a great Christmas I made my exit from the room, towing Karen and Graeme, one in each hand. We strode quickly off to see Judy, who I hoped was now dressed and ready for us to get the kids into their outfits.

After sliding through the dreaded door gap for the umpteen times, I got into the bedroom to see Judy sitting on the bed doing something with her new Christmas dress. She looked at me as though relieved from something, saying harshly.

'That bloody dress, the zip was stuck; it's taken me all this time to get it working, but I have fixed it now, thank God!'

She continued, although now a bit more calm, having fixed the zip problem.

Let's get the Kids and yourself dressed, then all go to Mum's while I get dressed.'

She continued to instruct in a manner that I had learned over the years was best to be strictly followed.

'You all go down to the Bar with them and wait for me, I won't be too long.'

Judy set into firm action, and the battle to get a wriggling Graeme dressed into his special Christmas outfit was quickly commenced. Judy, offering up long trousers to Graeme's unwilling legs and me, holding his other end, offering some mild restraint.

Soon, the battle was won with long trousers and a shirt neatly set. Graeme was now looking the part, but for how long, I thought.

I quickly got into my clobber and, after combing my hair, looked over at Judy.

What do you think, said I, in hopeful thought.

'Yeah, you look very dapper, hair looks ok; now let me get on with Karen, please!'

With that small approval, I sat down on the bed with Graeme and let Judy do her best.

Karen was soon dressed and looked really pretty in her party dress, lemon coloured with shoes to match. She smiled at me and held up her arms like small girls do when they want your approval.

I was quick to comment on seeing how lovely she looked.

'You are very beautiful in that pretty dress, Karen, I said with a smile, and you look great too, my handsome boy Graeme!'

Let's go and show Nanny and let Mum get herself ready.'

We quickly left Judy in peace, leaving the room via the ever-aggravating small gap in the door opening.

It seemed to me that each time we went through that bloody door, the gap got smaller and smaller.

Was I becoming a little paranoid, I wondered?

We quickly went back down the short corridor to Mum and Dad's room. Seeing her two Grandchildren looking so spruced up promptly caused Mum to get rather tearful.

'Oh Karen, you look lovely, Graeme, what a smart outfit!'

Mum went on and on until Dad, in his wisdom, suggested we go down to the bar and meet up with the others.

I quickly confirmed that this was just what Judy had previously instructed.

I walked over to the lift to see to my great relief, it was now working. I called over to Dad, and we all quickly boarded as though in some fear it might not move down, but with all luck, it slowly moved down to the Hotel lobby and into the bar.

As we walked in, we were able to see that the bar room was very crowded and I could feel the atmosphere built up all around.

Everyone was in high spirits, judging by the noise, all seemingly with a joint intent to get a fair share of booze down their necks before dinner.

Dad noticed Dennis and the others, and we made our way over to join them.

'Want a pint?' Jim asked us, with an air of expectation.

'Not half,' said Dad in a flash of ferocity,

'I've got a thirst like a bloody camel tonight!'

'Coke for you two, I guess,' said Dad, looking at the kids,

'But not too much, as you've got a big dinner to eat.'

I nodded in agreement, not wishing to have requests for the toilet halfway through my turkey breast.

With that firm response from Dad, poor Jim hurried off to the bar to get us all our refreshments.

'We were all talking about the dinner and what it might be like before you come in,' Dennis said with a wink of his eye.

'It had better be a special effort tonight,' said Dad, looking for support from Florrie and Doris.

'Sure, it will be ok,' Dennis piped up in his reassuring way while Florrie and Doris nodded in approval.

However, I questioned to myself the basis on which they felt so optimistic, given the first night's questionable servings.

Jim, after what seemed like ages, returned with drinks loaded onto a large tray and, as approaching, commented loudly,

'Bloody loads of people trying to get served up there!'

I chuckled knowingly as if we couldn't see for ourselves.

'Still, you've done a great job,' I told him and helped to pass the drinks around the table.

Dad lifted his glass up to Jim and, with a grin on his face, said,

'Cheers to all, and have a great evening, I'm really looking forward to our dinner!'

I eagerly took hold of my pint and followed suit, then supped

it with relish, soon feeling considerably more refreshed.

I looked around towards Karen and Graeme, who I noticed, to my alarm, were rather preoccupied poking cocktail sticks into things in the ashtray on the adjacent table.

'Don't do that,' I said, and they both jumped back.

'Come here, you two,' I continued, 'Dinner will be served soon; it's going to be a long night!'

Almost as I finished my sentence my eyes fell on Judy, as I saw her walking towards us. She looked so beautiful in her new dress, with her hair set up high and a big smile on her face.

Within seconds, she was at our table; I stood up to greet her.

'Judy, you just look perfect,' I said in an almost hushed breath.

'Well, it took a lot of effort,' She replied with a grin.

So get yourself off and get me a large Gin and Tonic; I'm as thirsty as can be after getting all dressed up!'

I quickly stepped to her command and scurried off to the bar.

It was certainly busy all around me as I moved forward, and it took some effort to get served. Just as I started to order, I felt a tap on my back and the voice of Dennis, now stating the obvious.

I've come over to help you get the drinks; everyone wants the same as last time.

As I started the order, with Dennis firing instructions to me on what seemed the endless number of drinks, I could also hear some others at the bar voicing, first quiet and then becoming louder and more clearly in German. Oh God!

I heard my inner self exclaim, please, no stress with Jim tonight, please God! I further felt a coldness of fear strike me as somehow I felt that tonight would be something to be remembered in dark thoughts.

Chapter 12 – Christmas Fare –
The Bird Has Flown

As soon as Judy mentioned dinner as if summoned by some culinary incantation, the doors to the restaurant creaked open in slow motion. There stood Manuel, chest puffed out like he was auditioning for the role of head waiter at the Ritz. The only snag? This place was about as far from the Ritz as a greasy spoon is from a Michelin star.

"I bet their customers don't get cockroaches in their food," I thought to myself, the notion sending a chill down my spine. With that cheery thought, I considered what horrors we might soon be served, silently praying, "May God make us truly thankful."

As people began drifting into the restaurant, I nudged Judy's arm gently.

"Shall we dine, my dear?" I said, adopting a lofty tone. "Yes, I'm starving," Judy replied, clearly unfazed by the potential risks ahead.

"Karen, Graeme, Mum, Dad—the restaurant's open. Let's eat!" I announced boldly, taking Karen and Graeme's hands and leading the way to our supposed culinary extravaganza.

We stepped inside and took our seats at the table. Silvio, our waiter, spotted us almost immediately. With a determined expression plastered on his face, he charged towards us like a man on a mission. What that mission was, I couldn't yet say, but it seemed we were about to find out.

I noticed he briefly stopped and welcomed Jim, Florrie, Doris, and Dennis on his way over to us; they had followed my lead and were just behind us in the scramble for the feast.

When all were seated and settled down, I picked up the menu from the table and ran my eyes over it. I could not make what it was as it was all in Spanish, as usual. All I did know was that we were having turkey.

Silvio arrived and, with his usual smile, greeted us with,

'Merry Christmas to you all!'

We all replied, 'Merry Christmas,' and then, with a flourish, Silvio placed our first course in front of us, which was given to him by a young waitress nearby. This was a plate of something that I could not make out quite what it was, a sort of paste crossed between some mashed potato and spam.

I looked at Judy, Mum, and Dad, who were also staring at the strange stuff.

'What is this muck?' said Dad; 'looks like plastic padding to me,' he went on.

'I'm going to taste mine,' said Mum, and so she did.

'It's not too bad,' she exclaimed and looked at us in turn. So with that, we all got stuck in with the exception of Dad, of course, who had his nasty foreign muck look on his face.

I looked around the restaurant and could see most people with either their heads down, staring at what was on their plates or poking it with forks. Others appeared to be discussing it. Hardly any were munching.

With a resigned note in my voice, I said quietly.

'Well, let's finish this and get on with the soup; I think it's soup next anyway.'

'Yes, it is soup next,' said Judy. She liked soup and, with a smile on her face, pushed her bowl around in anticipation.

By this time, most of the other folks had discovered that the H'or d'oeuv was not quite as bad as it looked and had resumed talking, and the whole atmosphere seemed to have regained the Christmas fever.

Silvio appeared again and whisked away our plates only to return as if in an instant with the soup tureen, which he placed in the centre of the table. Dad, who had only just recovered from the sight of his starter, stretched out his hand and lifted the lid of the tureen.

'Suppose this is some sort of stew stuff,' he said in a resigned sort of way.

'Now Len, I bet it's nice,' said Mum, 'I'm going to try it.'

With that, she picked up the soup ladle and spooned it onto her bowl with some gusto, I noticed.

Mum always liked her food, and being denied 'Foreign muck' for most of her life by Dad, who was always plain and simple English cooking only, she took every opportunity to try the food abroad.

I remembered fondly how she used to tuck into Rick's Mum Paulina's Italian lasagna and ravioli. She often made it for her family and always made a good portion as extra for Mum.

Happy days, I thought as that small part of my childhood flashed across my mind.

'Wake Up!' I heard Judy cry out at me. I jerked into reality again.

'How's about my soup?' Judy asked a bit impatiently.

'Sorry,' I said quickly,' and picked up the ladle to dish out her puddle of stuff.

The soup was pale—too pale—like washing up water with delusions of grandeur. Floating in it was a generous helping of pasta shapes, but, to my surprise, not a single suspicious bit of egg in sight.

"It's got worms in it!" Karen announced, her face contorted in that classic kid expression reserved for things they're convinced belong in a medicine cabinet, like cod liver oil or cough syrup.

"No, it's not worms," Judy replied patiently. "It's pasta. It's made from flour. It's nice soup—try it," she added with the kind of confidence usually reserved for convincing someone to adopt a stray cat.

With the "worm" issue diplomatically resolved, I ladled some into Karen's dish, then into Graeme's, all the while silently wondering if Judy's sales pitch was even remotely accurate.

'Now try the nice soup,' I said. It will fill you up.

They looked at me, still unsure, but then, staring strangely at one another, picked up their spoons and dipped in.

Karen tried it first and, to surprise us all, said, 'It's nice soup, Daddy, you try some,'

'Thank God,' I thought and got stuck in.

It wasn't bad at all, and soon every bowl was empty, even Dad's, whose "Foreign muck" expression had been replaced by a smile or two.

'It's Turkey next,' said Judy, with a big grin on her face.

Silvio was quickly over to take our soup bowls away and, with his usual smile, whisked off to get our Turkey feast.

'Hope it's nice,' said Mum.

'Well, they can't do much wrong to a Turkey, can they, 'Dad replied confidently.

Don't you bet on it, I thought to myself? I then worriedly looked around to see Silvio hurrying over to us with a large, round, bright dish in his hand, vision of Turkey breast, neatly sliced went through my mind. My mouth watered in anticipation.

My eyes drifted over to Judy, who was obviously thinking the same as me as I could see by the look on her face.

Silvio arrived and, with a grin, held the dish slightly towards us to show us proudly the fine display.

'Turkey,' he said. 'Just like English Christmas.'

I quickly looked at the dish, which was tilted a little in our direction. It was full of round disc-like things, some immersed in a clear-looking gluey-like fluid.

'It's Spam,' I said as I poked it a bit to investigate further.

'Spam,' said Judy, in a very hushed voice, 'It's spam, but it's supposed to be Turkey!'

All of us sat quietly as if it suspended in time whilst Silvio dished out the stuff onto the plates. It was round like Spam, and as Silvio went off to get the vegetables, Mum dug her fork in a bit on her plate and put it into her mouth,

'Ugh,' she quickly uttered, 'it's like tinned meat; I don't know if it's Turkey, it doesn't taste much like it.'

I quickly tried a bit, and as I lifted it off the plate, all this gravy-like goo dripped off like rain.

'Oh God,' I said, as I tasted my piece, 'It's like a greasy sausage!'

'Turkey sausage,' Dad exclaimed with a cross look on his face.

'How can they give us turkey sausage and running in bloody gravy.'

So engrossed with viewing our plates, we all failed to see Silvio arrive with the vegetables, and he gave us all quite a start as he started dishing out the potatoes onto Dad's plate.

Dad scowled at him, and sensing something was wrong, he quickly moved onto Mum and round to the rest of us. Soon, our plates were awash with carrots, peas, and potatoes, all swimming in the clear liquid.

Resigned to our fate, and without speaking we started to eat. Even Karen and Graeme, for whom I guess, the meat looked like a burger and therefore could not be too bad.

'Oh dear,' said Judy. 'I was so looking forward to a proper piece of Turkey.'

'Still, let's tuck in, I'm still hungry!' I said, hoping to give some encouragement to the proceedings.

I turned round to look towards Dennis at the end of the table as they were being served with their turkey. I could see by the stern expression on their faces that they were about as impressed as us.

Further views around the restaurant confirmed the general displeasure with what they had received; not many looked truly grateful.

In my eagerness to monitor everyone else's dining experience—or survival—I had completely lost track of the kids. A rookie mistake. My eyes landed on Karen, whose face was a picture of pale, tight-lipped discomfort.

"What's the matter, Karen?" I asked, lowering my voice like I was afraid of spooking her.

"I feel a bit sick, Daddy," she replied slowly and ominously.

"Hell!" I hissed, panic bubbling up as I turned to Judy. "Judy, look at Karen!"

But Judy was already on it, her motherly instincts in overdrive. She shot up from her chair like she'd been launched from a spring.

"Ken, get round!" she barked. "I think she's going to be sick."

We converged on Karen like a crisis team. I scooped her up off the chair while Judy grabbed her hand, her voice now urgent.
"Let's go to the toilets, Karen—please don't be sick yet!" she pleaded.

With that, Judy took off like a heat-seeking missile, Karen in tow, weaving through tables in a desperate dash toward the exit. I followed close behind, only to see our escape blocked by a waiter with a tureen the size of a small bathtub.

We skidded to a halt next to a table, but it was too late. In an instant, Karen became a human geyser, unleashing a cascade of vomit. It poured onto the restaurant floor, with a sizeable detour down the grey jacket of some unfortunate diner who had the misfortune of sitting with his back to us.

"Oh God," I muttered, wishing with every fibre of my being for the ground to open up and swallow us whole. But, of course, it didn't. Because life, as I was learning, isn't that kind.

The seated man, or victim, as better described, turned round

, not realising what was on his jacket. The others on his table did as they had a full view of the proceedings.

'The little girls have been sick,' I heard someone say.

'I'm sorry,' Judy said. 'I better go to the toilet quickly!'

She sped off, leaving me standing there, dumbfounded, in the middle of the restaurant, so with a hankie quickly in hand, I started to wipe the man's jacket, saying sorry as I did this; he just stared at me in silence.

I felt like everyone in the place was looking at me, and of course, they were, but thankfully, I saw Manuel rushing over, followed by a waitress carrying a bucket and mop.

I thought they were quick and wondered if this happened on a regular basis?

I made my quick apologies to the guests at the table and then to Manuel and continued, 'I must go to my wife and see if Karen is ok.

I quickly scurried off, red-faced, to the exit and out of further embarrassment.

It seemed to take a lifetime to reach the restaurant door, but I made it, and as I crossed the threshold, I felt such a relief, like I had walked into Shangri-La.

Knowing Judy, I realized that she would have taken poor Karen up to the room for a wash and change of clothes.

I quickly went into the Lobby only for my poor heart to drop to see the lift door, in the open position with red tape across one side to the other.

I reluctantly scaled the stairs once again, at my best hurry-up speed, with every step feeling like a trek up Everest!

I finally reached the summit, panting like an old dog just getting off his girlfriend, and sped towards our room. Sure enough, Judy was in there, Karen smiled at me and seemed ok but Judy was staring at her dress.

'She's sicked all down me, all over my new dress!' She quickly rattled out, looking furtively at me for sympathy.

'I'm sure it will clean up and look like new again, perhaps the Hotel has a cleaning service, I will ask in the morning,' offering a quick solution with the hope of bringing Judy some comfort.

'Is Karen ok now?' I quickly followed, trying to move on.

'Yes, she is, I think it's out of her system now. Perhaps it was the soup!'

'You had better put on your other dress now, I'm sure we can get this one cleaned up ok, and the other dress you bought is very nice.' I said, trying my hardest to cheer her up

'Ok, you sort out Karen while I get ready again, I'm not really bothered about missing any more of that bloody awful food,' Judy said with a strong, determined look on her face.

After a short time, Judy emerged from the bathroom wearing her second dress of the evening, which was actually better than the first in my eyes.

'You look lovely, Darling,' I said, 'Let's go and enjoy the rest of the evening.'

'Come on, Karen, you look better now; let's go down and have a dance.'

Judy, Karen, and I left our room and prepared ourselves for the journey down those bloody stairs again.

So, with the best feet forward, we started the long descent.

We reached the lobby, with the great relief of the numerous steps now completed, and turned into the bar to see if Mum and Dad were there.

Sure enough, they were, Dad and Mum sitting at a table with their friends, all looking furtively in our direction.

We walked over to them, Kids going quickly in front.

Dad waved us over, bearing a big smile and seemingly pleased it appeared we had gotten over our sick incident.

'How are you now, Karen?' Mum asked quickly, with a worried sort of look on her face.

'I'm ok now, Nanny,' Karen replied with a smile.

'Yes, she is much better after being sick,' Judy said with some relief, 'I think it must have been the soup or her lunch, but she seems ok now!'

Dennis looked at us and grinned, and with a laugh in his voice, said rather loudly.

'You didn't miss much of that bloody awful Christmas Dinner; I'm surprised we aren't all sick after that!' and continued with some level of displeasure in his voice, 'I've never seen anything like that turkey.'

'It was all floating in gravy!' said Florrie firmly and repeated,

'All floating in gravy,' wanting to emphasize the point for all to hear.

'It looked like turkey roll to me,' said Doris, with Jim joining in, both trying to talk at once.

Doris continued, 'If I gave Jim that muck for dinner, he would divorce me!' she said while looking at Jim.

'Yes, that's true enough,' Jim firmly replied, 'I wouldn't give that bloody muck to the dog.'

Turning to look at Judy and me, he continued the story.

'You didn't miss much to eat after you left! The pudding was supposed to be Christmas pudding, but it was like a tart covered in white sauce! It didn't taste too bad, but it wasn't anything like proper Christmas pud.'

I was dying for a drink after our ordeal, so I asked everyone what they wanted and scurried off to the bar.

'I'll come with you,' said Dennis, 'Why don't the rest of you go into the dance hall and get a good table? We can bring the drinks in.'

So, while we queued to get served, the rest of our gang made their way into the hall, as Dennis suggested.

'I hope we get a good place,' Dennis said, 'Better not be near the Germans!'

'Oh, Shit!' I said, having forgotten about our previous incident with Jim.

'When we get back in the hall, I had better talk to Dad in the quiet,' I said.

As I walked back into the hall, drinks held firmly in a large tray, I felt a slow shudder down my spine. How the hell was this evening to go? I was sure feeling another premonition of bad things to come.

Chapter 13 – The Battle Of Flemington

As we entered the dance hall, balancing trays of drinks like a synchronized act, the first thing that struck me was how well the place had been decorated. Tinsel shimmered on the walls and ceiling, and there was something that could've passed for holly draped along the edges. Whoever had been in charge of decorations had really done their homework, I thought, nodding in quiet approval.

In the far corner of the room, however, things got a bit peculiar. A cluster of unfamiliar decorations stood out, along with a banner featuring writing that looked foreign but definitely not Spanish. For a moment, I wondered if these were tied to the German guests, but then I glanced at the people seated at the tables nearby. They couldn't have looked more English if they'd tried. Tweed jackets, pearls, and that unmistakable air of small talk over sherry—these were definitely not the Germans. A couple of them, I realised, had even been on our coach earlier.

I scanned the room for Judy and the rest of our group and quickly spotted them in a prime spot on the opposite side. Their table was tucked just far enough away from the stage to escape the brunt of the speakers but close enough to enjoy the show. The band on stage was busy setting up for what I could only assume would be a "musical extravaganza," as the poster outside had promised. Whether it would live up to that billing, however, was anyone's guess.

The hall was a nice size, with many tables set all around the dance floor with plenty of room for dancing.

Dennis had also seen the others seated and headed over, with me following carefully behind. As I continued over and reached the table, I suddenly became aware of a raising of voices; I turned in its direction towards the group of people seated by the strange decorations and banners I had observed earlier.

'Oh shit!' I said quickly, realising some English people had sat at the German's table.

It's the beach towels on the sunbed scenario all over again.

I couldn't hear too much of the language, but from the noise they were generating and the waving of arms, the Germans were somewhat pissed off about this.

Suddenly, a large fat woman walked forward from the group of about ten angry Germans, said something to an elderly man seated at the table, then put out her hand and tore down the banner from the wall. Next, she went on like something possessed and proceeded to tear down the remaining decorations from the corner.

I noticed everyone in the hall was looking around at this scene; that's the Christmas spirit, I thought.

The fat lady, having scooped up all her decorations, turned round and confronted the English group seated and said something loud in German, which I sensed was the equivalent to 'Fuck You' or words to that effect.

She then bundled the contents of her arm into the arms of a rather small, balding, thin man standing motionless behind her; she grabbed him by the sleeve and pulled him off in the direction of some empty tables a few yards away.

The rest of her entourage followed and, within seconds, had commandeered the adjacent tables. They sat down together to claim their new territory.

I looked at Judy and saw anger on her face.

'What an old cow,' Judy said, with a snarl in her voice.

I noticed Jim, all red-faced, faced with Doris, looking at him and with her hand on his shoulder as if to restrain him.

'How rude,' Mum piped up; it's supposed to be Christmas, fancy taking down the decorations, what an awful woman.'

'Typical of that lot,' said Dad in support. 'You know what they are like around the swimming pool, with towels on all the sun beds!'

I had forgotten one of the kids' drinks and reluctantly had to go back to the bar. As I walked across the dance floor towards the bar, I could see everyone engaged in conversation, pointing at the incident.

I thought, what a bloody Christmas, shit dinner, Karen sick, and now a squabble with the Germans on where you can sit! It can't get any worse.'

I had only just got to the point of being served when, to my surprise, Dennis and Dad joined me. They had decided to follow me to get another round in before the dancing started.

We got served eventually and picked up our drinks to head for the dance hall. I heard the band start up as I walked into the hall. Little did I know the events to come!

The music sounded good from what seemed to be a decent little group now getting into its stride.

We stopped momentarily at Dad's request to discuss quietly just what had happened with the German party.

Dad looked at Dennis and said in a hushed tone,

'Luckily, we are sat down at the opposite corner to the German group, but we must keep Jim in check; we don't want any upset on Christmas night!'

Dennis exclaimed, 'Good grief, don't let Jim get dragged into that mess,' he said, clearly on edge. 'You know how he gets about Germans.'

We all exchanged knowing looks and silently resolved to keep Jim as far from any German-related topics as physically possible that evening.

The hall had got quite full I could see as we walked in. People were dancing, and I could feel the atmosphere, which previously you could have cut with a knife, had changed, and a more happy sort of feeling was around. Christmas had at last come.

We continued over to our table and served out the drinks.

I sat down next to Judy, who was in some deep conversation with Doris and Florrie.

'That's bloody welcome,' said Jim as he saw the beer glass put in front of him.

'I was dying for a pint after all that carry one over there,' he said quietly while pointing in the direction of the Germans.

However, to my surprise, he did not appear affected by this at all and was really cheerful!

By this time, many people were up dancing, and a carefree feeling filled the hall. Judy told me that while we were at the bar, Sharon had got many people up dancing and was promising all sorts of fun for the night ahead.

I looked over to the stage and at Sharon. She had a really nice blue dress on, fairly low cut and revealing her superb form blossoming to superb effect. After the Airport incident, I guessed she was beyond embarrassment, but what a beauty, I thought, with such a nice figure. Being accustomed only to seeing Sharon in her Miss Sunrise clobber, I failed to realize just what a fine lady she was.

I felt a sudden pain in the side and turned to see Judy's taught face, her elbow just withdrawn.

'Had a good look?' she rasped.

'Look, look at what?' I replied in an innocent way.

'You know what, you dirty sod, it's anything with big tits for you, isn't it?' She went on.

Doris added, 'You men are all the same. My Dennis is always looking at the girls, aren't you?' She responded.

She gestured at Dennis, who quickly replied, 'But none so nice as you, dear, shall we dance?'

Dennis immediately held out his hand and took Doris in tow to the dance floor. Jim and Florrie, seeing this seemed a good idea and followed.

'Shall we dance too?' I said to Judy, who just grinned at me in a forgiving sort of way.

'Ok, after you,' she said and took my outstretched hand to lead her onto the floor.

The band was playing a waltz, and we were soon scooting around. We had completed around four laps of the floor when I noticed the big German woman who had torn down the Christmas decorations walking to the dance floor centre with a chair. People were dancing around her as she continued to the centre of the floor, placed the chair down, and sat on it.

'What the hell is she doing,' said Judy.

'Beats me; perhaps it's a German game, a version of musical chairs!' I replied in an unsure sort of way.

The woman just sat there, and everyone was dancing around her, looking and, in some cases, laughing.

The short man, who I guessed was her husband, went to her and said something. She got up from the chair and started to wave her arms about. After a few seconds, I saw her old man head back to his table.

At this very moment in time, Jim and Doris, who had traversed the floor for a couple of laps, arrived at the point where the lady had got up from her chair. As Jim passed by he moved out his hand and swung it out, skillfully pulling the chair away. My hand went to my mouth in expectation of the impending event.

The woman stepped back, unaware that the chair she intended to sit on had vanished. With an almighty crash, she landed on the floor, legs flailing in the air as she tumbled over.

She let out a loud cry in German—a string of words I couldn't decipher but sounded equal parts shock and indignation. The music stopped, and the dancers froze mid-move, turning as one to stare at the scene unfolding before them.

Her massive frame rocked and rolled on the floor like a ship caught in a storm as she tried, without much success, to right herself. The more she flailed, the more impossible it seemed for her to get up, and the more people stared, wide-eyed.

I glanced towards the German table and saw her husband rise abruptly. His chair scraped back, and he moved towards her with determined strides, his face carved in a stern, granite-like expression that would've stopped most people in their tracks. It was clear he wasn't approaching to help her up—he was marching over like a man with a mission.

He reached the lady who was still in her ungainly predicament, being totally unable to rise from the floor. He stretched out his hand and quickly grabbed her to pull her large bulk up to her feet, which, believe me, was no mean feat for a little bloke like him.

He then turned to face Jim's direction and faced Jim with a raised hand and clenched fists.

Jim did no more but started to take off his jacket.

'Oh God, not a bloody fight,' I said, but saw Dennis quickly heading towards Jim.

The band had stopped and Sharon was also hurrying towards the scene. Jim and the German man were squaring up to one another both waving arms. Jim was clearly about to clock him one when Dennis quickly got in between them.

'Come on, Jim,' Dennis said,

'No fighting; it's Christmas, mate!'

A friend of the German man had also arrived, and one put his arm around the 'little bloke' and tried to pull him back. Sharon ran over and immediately, in an angry but firm tone, said,

'You men! It's Christmas, and no time to get angry; now shake hands and let's have no more of this behaviour!'

I couldn't believe to this day what happened next.

Sharon was only a small young lady, but within a second, Jim and the little German bloke were hands outstretched and apologizing.

'What a gas,' I thought; they were as meek as mild as could be, just putty in Sharon's hands.

At that moment, I had a fleeting thought of being putty in Sharon's hands, but it was all too much for a young man like me and I diverted my eyes and turned to Judy.

'Shall we sit down and have a drink?' I said, feeling rather exasperated with the evening's events, 'I hope nothing else happens tonight; what a Christmas!'

Judy nodded firmly in agreement.

The band started up again with a waltz and people were once again dancing. I looked over at Sharon again who had done such a wonderful job in defusing the situation. She was being chatted up by some bald-headed man.

I continued to follow Judy to our table, where Jim, Dad, and Dennis were deep in conversation.

'You did the right thing, Jim,' I heard Dad say as I approached the table. 'Best to walk away from that German lot and let them get on with it!'

'That right' said Florrie strongly, no time for this at Christmas, let's not all forget what this day is all about?'

'Yes, this day is special,' said Mum in firm agreement, but just as she finished, Karen piped up.

'Why did Uncle Jim get cross with that German man?'

Karen, being only small, had not seen much of what had been going on, hearing only the aftermath conversation.

'Nothing,' said Judy in quick reply,

'A man from Germany and his wife fell over dancing, but she is ok now.'

'I bet she has a sore arse!' I whispered to Judy.

She giggled, saying, 'With an arse that size, I'm surprised she felt a thing, and I don't know how her poor little husband got her onto her feet again; she must weigh a ton!'

I instinctively turned round to look in the direction of the Germans only to find that the woman and her husband were whizzing around the dance floor like nothing had even happened.

Many other couples had also returned to the floor, seemingly bent on getting back into the Christmas spirit as quickly as possible. Judy nudged me.

'Do you hear what they are playing?'

I looked at her to see a huge grin on her face as my ears tuned to hear the strains of a 'Walk through the Black Forest.'

'My God,' I said, laughing out, 'No sense of tact with this band, what's next, I wonder?'

I noticed Sharon had now escaped from the earlier problems and returned to the stage where she was bending over with her hands in a box on the floor, seemingly sorting out some packages.

The bending over had not escaped the attention of a small group of old men lurking by the side of the stage, who all seemed intent on feasting their eyes on what was before them.

The thoughts of her heaving breasts, defying gravity, bulging out of the top of her skimpy dress must have been racing through their minds. But this joyous spectacle was only for a brief moment as she arose and walked to the centre stage and reached out for the microphone.

She waited a short moment as the band finished the final notes of their music and then spoke.

'As it's Christmas, tonight we have arranged some great party games!' She went on, 'While everyone is dancing, just when the music stops, you must change partners with the next couple. I've got prizes to give out, so let's have some fun.'

The band struck up, and dancing commenced. This went on for about ten minutes stopping and starting until all the dancers were well jumbled up with one another.

'Look who's dancing with Jim,' Mum piped up. It was the rather attractive woman we had met a few days ago in the bar, and Judy and I had been talking to her and her husband, June, and Matt.

They were a pleasant couple from Hatfield, a town not far from ours. She'd mentioned she worked as a secretary for a book company while he—well, he was *something* in ladies' underwear. That got the predictable grin, though nothing compared to what we all noticed perched on his head.

It was a wig.

'He's got syrup,' I thought immediately. The kind of NHS-issued masterpiece that the old music hall jokes made famous—"can't see the join." Except, you absolutely *could*.

Honestly, even a Davy Crockett hat, complete with its ridiculous tail, would have been an upgrade. This wig looked like some unfortunate furry creature had crash-landed onto his shiny dome and decided to take a nap.

While we were chatting at the bar, I found my eyes magnetically drawn to it. No matter how hard I tried, I couldn't stop staring at the thing. The longer we talked, the more certain I became that it was about to wake up, stretch its legs, and make a dash for freedom.

My thoughts were interrupted by a nudge from Judy, who said quietly to me.

'Look, Ken, the big German woman is still dancing,

"Oh, God!' I blurted out; I hope she doesn't get Jim when they change partners!'

'That would be terrible!' I replied and then turned to Dad to tell him of the impending possibility.

'I've already noticed,' Dad said, looking a bit serious, 'There are only about ten or twelve couples on the floor, so I don't fancy the odds.'

Jim seemed to be enjoying himself as the music carried on and sped in close embrace with June around the floor, chatting away as Jim could do well.

Miraculously, the dance came to an end without Jim and the German lady meeting.

Sharon gave out some prizes for the best dancing couple, which caused a laugh as she picked a very tall man with a short partner and a very fat lady with a short, thin partner. It seemed to further break the ice with everyone and the previous Anglo-German incident had been forgotten.

I looked at my watch and remarked to Judy, 'My goodness, it's 10.45 already!'

But as I did this I saw from the corner of my eye a few people stopped on the dance floor.

I turned to investigate, and at the far end of the dance floor, I could see people standing around staring. Quickly, people stopped dancing, followed almost in an instant by the band. I noticed Sharon jump from the stage and walk quickly through the stationary dancers and over to the group at the end of the dance floor.

'What's happened?' Judy said.

'I don't know, perhaps someone's fallen over on something,' I replied.

Sharon reached the group quickly and parted two men to get into the thick of it. We could see no more for a few minutes then Sharon came running out from the group and in the direction of the exit to Reception.

'What's happened?' said Karen.

'We don't know,' Mum replied, 'perhaps someone's sick!'

'Not something else this evening,' said Florrie, who had got up from her seat for a better view.

Within seconds, the Manager, Julio, came darting through the door followed by Sharon in close pursuit and forward into the onlookers, then out of sight. Another ten minutes passed and then through the door arrived two uniformed men carrying a stretcher.

'Someone's ill,' said Mum in a loud voice.

'Top marks for observation,' said Dad, 'no wonder you got your school certificate!'

The two men took the stretcher forward and beckoned the people around to move back. Soon, we could see the figure of a man lying on the floor. I could make out it was one of the men who was staring at Sharon's boobs earlier when she was bending over on the stage. Perhaps it's too much excitement, I thought!

The medical men soon had the poor man on the stretcher and proceeded to march off with him towards the door. They had covered over his face, so we knew the worst.

'Poor sod,' I heard Dennis say; 'I thought the food tonight would get some poor Bastard.'

'I think it was all too much for him looking at Sharon earlier.'

I replied, 'I saw him when she was bending over on the stage, got my heart going, never mind an old boy like him; the strain of it all may have been too much.'

'This is the third one to pop off since we have been here,' Dad remarked.

'What with the bloke at Reception, one dying in his sleep, and now this poor sod, God only knows who's next?'

The hall was hushed, and I looked around; people were in small groups, some staring and some talking in whispers. Most are old and probably wondering whose next, I thought.

I noticed Sharon talking to an elderly lady, and after a few minutes she returned and walked towards the stage and then onto the platform and up to the microphone.

'Ladies and Gentlemen,' she said in a shaky voice, 'poor Mr. John Brooks has just passed away. I have spoken to his widow, Margaret, who doesn't want this sad death to cloud the Christmas evening,' Sharon paused to compose herself briefly, then continued, 'Margaret has requested two minutes silence as a sign of respect, then wants us to continue the evening as would have been John's wishes. So I ask you to pause now for two minutes.'

The two minutes seemed like an hour, and you could have heard a pin drop, never mind an OAP. But quickly over, Sharon spoke to the band, and they struck up rather appropriately with, 'Fly me to the moon.'

I turned to Dad and Dennis, who were standing transfixed next to me, and said quietly, 'I think knocking on heaven's door would be more like it, don't you?'

'You're bang on,' Dennis replied, looking at me with a grin on his face, 'what the hell can happen next?'

'Fire in the Hotel,' Dad mused, 'Mass food poisoning, plane crashing into the roof! We have got five more days here, and anything can happen.'

Mum piped up sharply. 'You two, pipe down and think of that poor lady whose husband has just died; it must be terrible for her!'

'Yes, your right, dear,' said Dad, sounding very apologetic now,

'We were not thinking, with too much Christmas spirit.'

It wasn't long before the guests were up dancing again, and the evening lurched onwards to the finale.

'Let's get a beer,' I said!

'A large G&T for me, please,' replied Judy.' What a shocking night,'

A large number of guests seemed to have the same idea, and the bar was packed.

The remainder of the evening passed without further incident. I pondered on where the body had been taken. The kitchen flashed in and then quickly out of my mind.

I could now believe that anything could happen at the Hotel Flemington.

Suitably filled with ale I gathered up Judy and the Kids, who were still in high spirits at 1.00am, and wished everyone a good night.

 Off we went, Kids in hand, and journeyed back up the bloody stairs to bed.

With the kids settled down and eyes closing fast, it was our turn to rest.

As I laid down quietly in my bed with Judy close at my side, my thoughts moved through the day's events and I wondered just how this could all have happened in such a short space of time.

Truly, this place where we are staying must be cursed!

Was the Grim Reaper on every corner, hiding in the shadows and awaiting the next victim?

A shiver went down my spine at the thought of all this! Whatever would the next few days bring forth?

Chapter 14 – Life Balloons On Boxing Day
(Day 6)

I woke up feeling like I'd been hit by a freight train—courtesy of yesterday's disaster of a day. As my brain slowly defogged, I turned to Judy with what could generously be called a morning smile.

"Let's drag the kids down to the beach after breakfast for an hour or two, shall we? With any luck, today won't be the raging bin fire that was yesterday."

"Good idea," Judy said, ever the optimist. "They'll burn off some energy."

"Right, let's suffer through breakfast, then hit the beach for a bit. We'll come back, change, and pretend we're excited for the Magic Show at 3 pm."

So, another glorious morning began in this haunted excuse for a hotel—where the only real magic trick was how they kept getting away with serving food that looked like it had already been digested once.

By now, we'd all come to terms with the daily offerings of the bizarre, and in some twisted way, a few of us were even starting to enjoy the culinary roulette. Even Dad was managing to stomach some of the meals, which, as Mum so eloquently put it in private, was nothing short of a miracle.

"He must be absolutely *bloody starving* to eat this rubbish," Mum muttered under her breath, eyeing Dad as he bravely tackled whatever monstrosity had landed on his plate.

After crashing out from the chaos of Christmas festivities—topped off with a late night that probably shaved a few years off my life—I was expecting to wake up feeling like roadkill. But surprisingly, I felt... decent. Maybe my body had finally just given up on protesting.

The morning kicked off as usual: dragging ourselves out of bed, wrestling the kids into clothes like some kind of Olympic sport, and then attempting to escape our room in one piece. The plan was simple—take the lift. The reality? Not so much.

Predictably, Graeme and Karen had bolted ahead, leaving us no choice but to trudge after them on what felt like an *endless* trek to Reception.

"I'm *sick to death* of these bloody stairs!" Judy snapped, clearly one step away from staging a full-blown protest. "We've been up and down so many times on this holiday, I feel like a *mountain goat*."

"Billy Goat Gruff," I shot back, smirking.

She turned to me, unimpressed. "You *do* like to have a moan, don't you?"

"This bloody place could make a *saint* moan!" she huffed. "And knock it off with the goat jokes while you're at it!"

Before I could offer another wisecrack, she playfully elbowed me in the arm—though with the force of someone who'd clearly had a few years of pent-up stair-induced rage.

"Oi!" I yelped. "Steady on! Just because your family's got a few boxers in it, don't start thinking you're Henry Cooper!"

Judy just rolled her eyes, but I swear, if we had to climb those stairs *one more time*, I was about to start demanding a knighthood for endurance.

At this point, we were only one flight from the bottom and, as such, greatly relieved. We soon found the kids waiting by the restaurant door.

'Let's go to the restaurant and find the others, I said,

'Come on, Karen and Graeme.'

I led the family into the restaurant and paused to see where our little group were.

'There they are!' cried Judy excitedly, 'I can see Mum and Dad with the others sitting down.'

We quickly stepped over in their direction with some pace and were soon greeted by everyone. But suddenly, I heard Florrie say quite loudly to us.

'We were all talking about Spanish Tummy; all you ever hear about is that Jim was talking to someone about it, and it appears many people are getting it here!'

'Don't mention that!' said Mum abruptly.

'You know what Len is like; just a whisper of those two words is enough to start him off with a dose of that!'

'Don't worry!' said I with a grin, 'Dad can have a few of those boiled eggs for breakfast; that will bind him up!'

'I've never known anything like it. The bloody place is filled up with geriatric old dears, the food crap, the rooms are like bloody rabbit hutches, the swimming pool stinks, the lifts don't work very often, and we have to climb those bloody stairs four times a day, now Spanish Tummy!'

'Enough of that talk from you lot!' Dad quickly spoke up and looked at me with a kind of daggered expression.

Hoping to have averted further attention from Dad, I quickly advised everyone that we were off to the beach after breakfast and would meet up for the Kids' show at 2.30.

We quickly moved away and found a suitable table. Breakfast was completed quickly without further comments on the medical benefits of eggs or the quality of yolks.

With Breakfast endured, Mum, Dad, the Kids, and I headed off for the beach, walking slowly through Reception.

Outside, the sun was doing its best impersonation of a spotlight, blasting down on us as we wandered through the maze of narrow streets towards the seafront. Cafés, bars, and shops lined the way, all practically screaming *tourist trap*, but at least the weather was playing nice.

It actually felt good—warmth on my skin, a light breeze coming off the sea and the promise of a half-decent morning. All that was left was to find somewhere to sit, soak up the view, and pretend we were in some sun-drenched paradise rather than just a few bad decisions away from sunburn and dehydration.

Mission accomplished. We claimed a spot, and as I glanced around, it became apparent that the beach was absolutely *heaving*—mostly with Spanish families making the most of the holiday period. Fair play to them. If you live in a country where the weather actually behaves itself, you may as well enjoy it.

Finally, the long-awaited *holiday mode* kicked in. The kids were busy engineering some kind of sandcastle empire, and I even braved the water with them. Cold? Absolutely. But after the past few days of chaos, I was just happy to be bobbing about instead of refereeing another family squabble.

An hour or so of bliss passed before Dad shattered the peace with a loud, snort-like snore, jolting himself awake in a panic. Classic. He had drifted off mid-basking, as he often did, and now, suddenly re-entering the land of the living, he announced with great urgency that time was slipping away— we had places to be. The *Kids Show* awaited.

With that, the great exodus began. Beach towels, buckets, and half-built sand structures were abandoned as we gathered our belongings and braced ourselves for the dreaded uphill slog back to base.

The kids, of course, had somehow found an extra burst of energy, sprinting ahead, giggling and shrieking like tiny, sun-kissed maniacs. At least someone was enjoying this.

Back at the hotel, we approached the *notoriously unreliable* lift, bracing for disappointment—but against all odds, it actually worked. Miraculously, it whisked us up to our floor without a single jolt, stall, or emergency evacuation.

After parting from Mum and Dad, with the plan of meeting at 2.30pm in the bar, we entered our small room, and all just flopped on the beds. Judy set the alarm just to allow us all a short nap, which we all seemed to need after late nights and our unaccustomed display of the strength of the sun.

As I started to drift into sleep, my thoughts went onto Karen's chicken pox, which was now fortunately becoming lost in the past. Graeme certainly exhibited no symptoms of going down with it, thank God!

I awoke to the dreadful sound of the alarm clock,

My God, it could wake the dead, I thought as I jumped up at its command. But then further thought, perhaps not quite appropriate for the current situation at Flemington.

Judy got up from the bed quickly, straight into the bathroom, and soon I heard the sound of running water heralding the start of the dreaded washtime routine.

After the trial of getting the kids and ourselves scrubbed and dressed in our small room, we all headed downstairs to the bar.

Guess what! The bloody lift was out of order, so back down the stairs, we reluctantly descended.

We journeyed into the bar to see the others already sat down and with a goodly portion of drinks around the table.

Jim stepped up, offered a welcome, and asked me to join him at the bar. This met no opposition from me, and I quickly followed him to order.

With the job done, we returned to the others; I, drinks in hand and Jim bearing a trayful.

As I sat down I noticed the lovely Sharon walk into the bar. She was followed by Georgio, who we had learned earlier was the much-derided Flemington Maintenance Man. A poor soul, I thought.

It quickly became apparent that our Georgio was also the Children's entertainer.

Georgio was carrying a rather large red and blue striped box with both hands firmly in grip. It looked rather heavy and seemed to dwarf him, being a rather small man.

'What's in that box, Daddy?' said Graeme.

'That's the magic box,' I replied in earnest, as if I had some special knowledge of its contents, and continued as if foretold.

'You will see later when the show starts!'

People started to go into the hall, and I was surprised by the number of children; then I realised from the sound of the language some of the kids made that a number were Spanish. I guessed that their parents had brought them in from outside to see the show.

We got another round of drinks in and went into the hall and started looking to find a table near the stage. The man who played the organ was up on the stage setting up, and as we sat down, he started to play soft and pleasant music. Soon, the place started to fill up, and Georgio put his box up on the stage and then disappeared to go behind the curtain, presumably to get ready.

Within minutes, Sharon was up on the stage, microphone in hand. She looked really nice today with tight-fitting blue jeans and a red cotton top, sized just correctly in my view, showing more than ample contents.

She picked up the large microphone, paused slightly, and, with a big smile, commenced her opening presentation.

'Ladies and Gentlemen, and of course all you Children.

This afternoon we are proud to present Georgio to entertain you with his special and magical Balloon Show.'

With a clap of her hands, Gorgio walked proudly out on stage. Although he was a little man, thin-faced with a pencil moustache, he looked somewhat bigger on stage and looked magnificent dressed in a Clown's top with tight black trousers.

He had a red nose, his face was painted in true clown fashion, and on top of his head, he wore a red and white pointed hat.

The kids all clapped wildly as he bowed to the audience and raised his hands into the air. As he did this the front of his trousers opened slightly to reveal something white behind.

I nudged Judy quickly and whispered close into her ear.

'His flies are undone; look, they are, aren't they?'

Judy put her hand to her mouth and swiftly hissed out.

'Oh God, Yes, when he moves, they open and close; he must have got dressed in too much of a hurry.'

Gorgio bent down to the box and got out the first of his exhibition; three small balloons, and started to blow them up in turn. Each time he waved his arms to flourish the balloons as he prepared to construct his first animal his flies opened and closed in unison.

The sight of poor Gorgio prancing about on stage in complete oblivion to his predicament made it all the more funny.

He made his first animal; it was a dog, a sort of sausage dog, and as he waved it into the air, his flies popped open more. People clapped and laughed. Like us, they were waiting for the laughter point to relieve the tension. I was nearly wetting myself, holding back laughter while the poor unsuspecting Clown was performing.

The applause and laughter only spurred him on to greater things involving more prancing about on the stage, waving his arms like a matador enticing the bull and, of course, increasing the opening and closing of his flies to an alarming rate.

'God knows what will happen if his Willie comes out!' I whispered to Judy

'Perhaps the Kids will all think it's another little red balloon?' She replied, stifling her laughter.

But God was on his side that day, and Georgio pranced about for another full 20 minutes, making all sorts of wonderful balloon animals for the kids' delight, so many and each so different.

I thought kindly and surely we could now forgive him for the poor Hotel maintenance, perhaps the poor soul was not allowed funding for repairs?

When he took his final bow, the applause was beyond his wildest dreams. Who, I thought, would have the heart to tell him about his flies?

Judy and I got up from our seats, still grinning at each other. Judy took Karen's hand and led her and Graeme out of the hall and towards the bar. I followed behind and turned round to Dad, who was also grinning.

'What did you think of Georgio?' I said with a beam on my face.

'Good God!' Dad replied, 'I thought any minute he would have a nasty surprise; I can't understand why he did not sense something was odd?' Dad continued, 'Lots of people were laughing, and he must have realised it was not just his balloon animals that were funny!'

'God knows what would have happened if his Willie had popped out!' I replied quickly, laughing somewhat as I did so.

'I guess Sharon would have leapt to the rescue to stand in front of him; I think I will go and ask her.'

Sharon was still on stage; Georgio had rushed off, obviously now in full knowledge of his embarrassing predicament.

Sharon quickly stepped down from the stage and started to head away from our direction towards an outside door.

'I bet she could do with a drink now,' I said to Dad, who nodded firmly in agreement.

I continued, looking at Dad with a grin, and said with a wave of my hand,

'Let's get a few drinks in and join all the others in the Bar.'

We continued into the Bar, which, to my surprise, was fairly clear. Then I thought it was 4.30 p.m., and all the people with kids would be off to either change them or put them to bed for a while. The local people would have gone home or to outside hostels.

Not all kids were able to stay up like Karen and Graeme, who were both impossible to persuade it was bedtime when they were on holiday or weekends.

The phrases are known well to all persevering Mums and Dads, 'Just another five minutes, please, and then we will go to bed,'

These were heard often in our family.

We promised them on this night, they could stay up later for the party providing they had a little nap first. So, given the rest earlier, they were clearly 'Good to go for tonight,' which Judy confirmed with a waving gesture and then said!

'Let's go up to the room now and get changed for tonight, we can be quick as the kids have had a good sleep before the dancing.'

Mum and Dad nodded in approval, with Mum quickly saying.

'Karen and Graeme have been very good all day,'

And then continued, 'The kids have both had a good sleep earlier, so all should be good with them tonight.

Judy looked over at Mum and Dad and said thankfully,

'I'm off with the kids to get them changed for tonight; it should be a really good evening as long as we don't have any problems with the German party.'

Dad replied in agreement and continued quite firmly.

'I don't think they will after what happened with the near fight and the poor man dropping down dead on the dance floor last night.

Dad continued adding further information he had gotten from Jim.

'Jim overheard some of the other Guests talking about last night and had complained strongly about the Old Time Dancing and the German people who made the trouble last night.'

Dad continued, 'Sharon apparently told them she had spoken to them all about the problems. Also, she told them that tonight a good band was definitely coming, so we should have some good music and dancing tonight.'

'Not Disco?' I said jokingly.'

'No, you daft man!' Mum quickly responded, 'Looks like we are definitely having a band!'

'Joe Loss or Dead Loss,' Dad joked.

With that, I made my exit with Judy towing Karen and Graeme one in each hand.

The battle to get a wriggling Graeme dressed into his special Christmas outfit again was quickly commenced with Judy trying to restrain me offering up long trousers to Graeme's unwilling legs.

Once again, the battle was won and Graeme was now looking just right!

Karen was soon dressed and looked really pretty again in her new red party dress, with shoes to match. She smiled at me and held up her arms like small girls do when they want your approval.

I took hold of her for a quick cuddle, then grabbed Graeme and left the room with them to leave Judy to herself to get ready. We then went back down the corridor to Mum and Dad's room. Once again, Mum gets tearful on seeing her two Grandchildren looking so nice.

'Oh Karen, Graeme, you both look super,' and on and on again.

Dad quickly suggested we go down to the bar and meet up with the others.

I speedily concurred and soon we were into the lift, which miraculously was now working, and down to the bowels of the hotel and to the bar.

As we walked into the bar, it was clear that the atmosphere was building up. Everyone seemed in high spirits; I looked round to see Denis and Jim at the bar. Fortunately, Jim saw us and raised his thumb which indicated a few extra drinks would be set in hand.

We saw Florrie and Doris sitting at a table and moved forward to join them. In no time, I saw Jim, followed by Denis, both with large trays in hand and moving towards us. Well, I thought this was a damn good way to start the evening, a fair share of refreshment down to be followed with a hopefully good dinner.

I stopped and thought again; well, at least the beer is ok, thank God, and I hope we can eat the culinary offerings.

My thought was soon turned into reality when, like magic the restaurant doors swung open, and there was Carlos standing in place to invite us in.

A lot of the Guests must have been very hungry as, like a swarm they headed for the open doorway. What did they know that we did not? Who would hurry for the food within, going on our previous day's experience!

Florrie piped up, noticing the rush to the restaurant.

'What do you think we have for dinner tonight?'

'God knows,' said Jim,' It's got to be better than last night's offerings, I hope!'

'Don't you count on it!' Dennis rasped, 'With what we have had before, it's likely to be yesterday's Christmas left over!'

Dad's eyes rolled over in agreement.

'Well, at least we have got to try it,' said Doris firmly,

'It may be better tonight; anyway, I'm getting a bit hungry now, so at least it will fill a hole even if it's no better than usual.'

'Florrie reassured us we could always take refuge in Vincent's later if the meal or the Band was naff."

So, with some reluctance but with the strong pangs of hunger starting to be felt, our small party braced itself and moved onward towards the restaurant doors and a promise of uncharted delights.

We walked into the room, which had become quite full, and over to our tables. When quite near, I caught sight of Silvio, who saw us and raised his hand to us in a gesture for us to become seated. He walked up quickly and, with a big smile, announced.

'We have another very special main course dish for you today; I think you call it trotters.'

'What the hell is that?' Dad whispered softly in Mum's ear?'

'I think its pig trotters,' Mum commented through a tense face, but I expect it may be very nice!'

'Good God!' Dad harshly whispered under his breath,

'Pigs trotters, we can't eat that muck!'

In oblivion to Dad's comments, Silvio served out the first course to an anxious-looking Mum.

This, I observed, had the appearance of a sort of spam-looking stuff. Mum advised us, on quickly tasting the morsel, that it was a sausage of some kind with garlic.

For Dad, this was again almost beyond description and not for a good Englishman's palate. The evening meal progressed, and the spam stuff was followed by a soup with bits of egg and meaty lumps inside.

A little later, I looked around and could see Silvio, who was just on his way over to us; I guessed to clear away before the main event.

Silvio emptied our table quietly, with just a smile as he did so.

He quickly returned with a large serving tray in his hands, and as he lowered the tray to our table, I could see a number of these Trotters surrounded by potato and green beans. Dad was also quick to see this, and I witnessed his screwed-up face and realised it was all too much; a breaking point had clearly been reached.

He slowly turned towards Mum and, with a look of resignation, just sighed and, in a low voice, announced.

'Sorry, but I'm off to Vincent's, I just can't eat this muck!'

With those few words, Dad rose from his seat and headed onwards, only to be followed just a few minutes later by Jim, Dennis, Doris, and Florrie, who had been served just before us.

Without any comment as to Dad's departure, Mum just looked at me and Judy, then said quietly, and almost enthusiastically.

'Let's all try this Trotter; it may be nice!' Mum advised in a strange expectance of a new and exciting dish.

She tucked in with some excitement and, after a while, gave a culinary comment. She had not even noticed our companions leaving the room earlier in Dad's direction.

Mum just continued her culinary adventure advising.

'It's got a funny taste to me, and it's a bit dry and tough; it's also got a strange sort of smell, also the beans are stringy.'

She continued. 'I don't think I will be serving this at home!'

Well, I plucked up courage and tried a bit; it was not as bad as it looked but I agreed fully with Mum's vivid description.

I could see the expressions of frown all over both Karen and Graeme's faces as Mum related her view on the meal.

Karen looked at me and announced, 'It's horrible, Daddy, I can't eat this muck!' Graeme quickly followed his Sister, announcing,

'I can't eat it, Daddy. It looks nasty, and it's very smelly!'

Judy, surprisingly, just stared silently at her plate and then, after a short pause, looked at me and cried out with her opinion.

'Ugg! This stuff is just awful, I can't eat this!

With those conclusions, we just waited for Silvio to take it all away.

In clearing the table, his look was of some surprise, almost hurt in finding us not enjoying the delicacy, but he said nothing, just smiled as he took our plates away.

Mum decided it was best to hold on for the Ice Cream dessert, which the kids scoffed eagerly down and then shared Dads between them.

With the kids finishing, we got onto our feet and scurried out of the restaurant. Mum and I were certainly eager to get out of the Hotel as quickly as possible.

Suffice it to say that the strange meal fed us enough to survive and the strength to pop down the road to Vincents to meet Dad and the others for a drink or two.

Chapter 15 – Men In Black –
Back On Track (Day 7)

Waking up to a brand-new day, my brain and I had a little debate about whether opening my eyes to the blinding light was a good idea. I compromised, one eye open first, just to ease into it. Surprisingly, my head felt relatively fine, considering yesterday's marathon of merriment. Might as well rip off the band-aid, I thought and opened the other eye to get the full shock over with.

As the fog in my mind lifted, the harsh realisation set in: six glorious days of holiday down, just today and tomorrow left, and then—oh joy—back to the dark grey skies of England and that lovely, bone-chilling cold. Reality hits harder than the sun on a hangover.

I further contemplated the joys of England's winter greeting us with snow, sleet, and death-defying slippery roads—it was enough to make anyone want to crawl under the duvet and weep. Despite the trials of this holiday, my earlier grumbles suddenly faded, replaced by a desperate wish to extend our stay. I could even tolerate the dodgy food and our less-than-stellar hotel. That's how serious this had become.

In just six days, Judy and I had experienced a world completely foreign to us. Sure, there had been plenty of moments I'd rather forget; deaths, questionable meals, fights, and sharing space with peculiar strangers—but the highlights had been worth it. We'd found a gem in Vincent's, where the food was surprisingly good, and the nights were even better. The kids had fallen in love with Benidorm's golden beaches, and despite the sea being bloody freezing, swimming in it had been an oddly satisfying achievement.

On the bright side, the Germans had proven to be a decent lot. After the chaos of Christmas night, things had settled down to a peaceful coexistence. Not that we'd become best mates—we barely exchanged more than a polite "hello" or "good morning"—but the atmosphere was light and cheerful. Even poor old Jim, who had been rather wound up about the German guests, had mellowed out and reached a truce of sorts.

Then it hit me; we had something to look forward to today: a trip on the famous Lemon Express, one of Benidorm's iconic adventures. Suddenly, the gloom lifted. At least for today, reality could wait.

Jim had picked up this information from another Guest.

Jim, I learned over our holiday days, was certainly great at finding out all this stuff by reason of his inquisitive and chatty nature. Jim told us that the Lemon Express was a little yellow train that ran from Benidorm to Gata-de-Gorgos, with programmed stops along the route. There was also a visit to the guitar factory and to the wicker and cane shops in Gata, then on the return journey clients were served champagne.

This trip sounded like a great day out, and the Kids would love the train ride. With us and the others all keen on this outing; Jim had dutifully found Sharon and made arrangements for all of us to join in.

On this new day, the Kids had got up so excited with the prospect of the train trip; both had woken up quite early and feeling hungry, so we planned to go downstairs quickly for our breakfast.

After the dreadful squeeze into the bathroom and its minuscule shower and the usual battle of dressing a wriggling Graeme, we all managed to get dressed and ready. We now just awaited Judy who was finally in the bathroom, putting her face on.

Graeme and Karen were providing some amusement while waiting for Mum, chatting away while jumping on the beds; the kids sure were in a buoyant mood on this bright, warm morning.

Judy appeared from the bathroom unusually quickly.

'Let's get a move on!' I heard Judy cry out. 'We said early, so let's get downstairs!'

This shook me into prompt movement, and we quickly left the room and off to the lift, which thankfully was in operation. We jumped inside and off to the Lobby and quickly into the restaurant.

As we entered to find a table, I looked around, and young Karen piped up,

'Daddy, there's Nanny and Granddad!'

Judy and I looked round to see Mum with a big smile on her face as she walked towards us, leaving Dad standing by the door looking like a spare part.

Mum quickly arrived and, in a rather loud voice, pronounced.

'Good morning, isn't it a lovely day outside! I spoke to the others and agreed we are all going for a stroll before we get picked up at the Hotel for our trip on the Lemon Express today. We may have time to sit outside in the sun and have a nice drink.'

She continued, 'Dad and I will go off to the Bar to meet the others and wait while you finish your breakfasts.'

Mum then looked at me a little strangely for some reason and grabbed my hand as I sat down. She leaned towards me quickly and spoke in a low whisper into my ear.

'There's just one problem!' She hissed, 'Dad's still got the Trots, He's been on the toilet this morning, three times before breakfast!'

She continued the story quickly while still holding my hand.

'He seems a bit better now after eating three eggs for breakfast, so I'm sure he will be alright for the rest of the day; I've put lots of paper in my bag just in case!'

Mum paused slightly as if to take a breath, then announced.

'I have discussed with Dad and he thinks he will still be ok for the Lemon Express trip this afternoon. It's at 1.30pm, so he thinks he will be much better by then.'

While hearing the news, I humoured inside, realising that Mum once again showed how she would overcome all of life's adversities, taking it all in her stride.

Typically, Mum, the eternal life optimist, would always believe a toilet would be just around the corner; Dad would plan on the likelihood that the nearest one would probably be miles away, and in the event there was one nearby, it would be closed anyway, or at minimum would have no paper.

'Don't worry, Mum!' I offered in support, 'I'm sure the train has a toilet on board.'

With that, she smiled, turned, and walked away to meet Dad, who had been patiently waiting by the door.

Feeling rather hungry, I alerted Judy, and we walked towards the buffet, leaving the kids waiting at the table. The buffet looked ok this morning, so with trays ready, we took our collection of boiled eggs, croissants, juice, and tea and went over to join our brood.

We sat down, and Judy started to dole out the meagre meals to me, Karen, and Graeme.

Having got settled, I picked up my spoon and gave my first egg a whack on the top. Nothing moved, so I started to attack my obviously very hard-boiled egg once again, and now just breaking the shell. I tried the second egg with the now-fading expectation of ever finding a runny yolk inside.

My expectation was correct; the egg was the same as the first one!

I looked at Judy with a sad sort of face and announced.'

'These bloody eggs!' I said in resignation, 'Surely I must get one that's not boiled as hard as nails. Have they never heard of egg timers?'

We continued our breakfasts quickly and in an unusual silence before heading off to join the rest of the gang waiting in the Lobby.

I looked at the clock to note it was still only 10am; Dad and Mum were just at the Lobby entrance looking at the Lemon Express poster on the wall.

Dad saw us approach and said in confirmation,

'We leave the Hotel at 1.30pm, so we have plenty of time to go out for a stroll and maybe visit a bar or two.

'That sounds good to me,' I said, 'It's such a nice day. Let's go out and enjoy it,

Given Mum's earlier information on Dad's problem, with slight concern, I turned to Dad and gently inquired.

'How are you today, Dad,' I proceeded with a little grin.

'I'm ok,' Dad replied, 'It's just a bit of the Trots, but not too bad, so I should be alright for the day's trip.

As we entered the Lobby, I looked around to see that it was filled with an unusual number of people all milling about. My eyes luckily found Florrie, Dennis, Jim, and Doris standing together by the wall and talking away as usual.

As we advanced towards them, I just saw Carlos, the Manager, standing by the entrance doors to the hotel and was, to all appearances, trying to usher people away from the door and back into the lobby.

'What's going on now?' I heard Denis say.

'I don't see what the holdup is?' I replied and walked over through the gathering to a position where I could see outside. I noticed that the narrow street, which ran slightly upwards along the side of the hotel, was full of people; furthermore, many were dressed in black. I strained to view further up along the street and could just see two black horses with a large black carriage in tow.

I looked round at Judy, who had just given me a nudge.

'Ken, look, look at Carlos, he's in a panic again!' she said.

Hotel guests had gathered around poor Carlos and realising answers were necessary, turned to face the rest of the crowd he had imprisoned in the lobby. He stammered out,

'Ladies and Gentlemen, sorry, please, we have a man who died across the road, and the funeral men must now collect the deceased.

Everyone looked outside in the direction of the horses. Four men were carrying a coffin, which they quickly loaded into the Hurst. They then moved to a position alongside the carriage and stood still. They seemed to be doing their best to cover the coffin from the gaze of the multitude of the hotel guests now trapped in the lobby.

'Christ Almighty,' Jim blurted out quickly. 'I don't believe this is really happening'.

'It is!' said Dennis quickly,' It's a flipping nightmare!'

'We have stiff outside in a horse-drawn carriage and three more in the hotel!'

Florie replied in a rather sarcastic tone.

'I can't see the Co-op doing it like this!'

'Still, think of the Members Dividend,' I said, looking at Dennis and Jim with a bit of a grin on my face.

'That's enough,' Mum quickly intervened, it's all a bit sad with the deaths over Christmas; we will just have to wait while it's all done!'

'Great!' said Dad and continued with dry humour,

'Perhaps the hotel has done a deal with the undertaker and will take them in the carriage together!'

'Don't joke about that,' said Mum in her cross voice,

'They don't do that sort of thing, I'm sure!'

I looked out into the street again to see the coffin, now covered with flowers, which had been quickly loaded into the horse-drawn carriage.

After a few minutes, the Hearse started to make its way forward and towards the hotel.

'I think it's coming here now,' I heard Judy say. She had followed me the few steps to the hotel door, looked, and come to Dad's conclusion.

The carriage advanced slowly and was soon at the hotel but continued onward without stopping to take its poor occupant to his final resting place.

My attention was now drawn to the lift, where I could hear the hubbub of raised voices. While we had been looking out to the street I had failed to notice what had been going on behind me in the lobby.

I could see four men in the lift, which by God's grace was working, and could now plainly see they were struggling to get a rather large-looking coffin out of the lift and into the lobby.

It appeared to be no mean task; I could see three of the men at one end of the coffin, which was resting on the lift floor. The other two were holding the end, which was leaning slightly up against the wall of the lift at a slight angle. I was, to my eye, a bit too long to fit across the width of the lift.

Carlos moved over to assist, but I could see they were having some difficulty in dislodging their cargo from the clutches of the lift.

'That bloody lift got a real life of its own!' I heard Dennis comment in the usual loud fashion, 'Look at the poor sods trying to get the coffin out!'

Now, the Spanish are not noted for their calm in a situation, and I could see the undertakers and Carlos, now assisted by another member of staff, all talking at once on how best to dislodge the item. After an eternity of groaning and wailing, pulling and shoving, the lift finally gave up its grip on its sad occupant. The coffin was quickly lifted aloft and onto the shoulders of the bearers, who made a dignified but slightly hasty move in the direction of the door.

'Where's the hearse,' said Mum,

'Perhaps they have to wait until the other one comes back!' replied Dad, and that could take all day!'

But as if by magic, from the other street to the right-hand side of the hotel, a horse appeared, towing a large black carriage. It stopped outside the hotel, and the coffin was then carried outside by the four men and placed gently inside.

The undertakers returned to the lobby and, at a slow pace, walked over to the lift. One pressed the door button, and the doors opened to reveal a second coffin, leaning slightly up in an identical manner to the first.

'Oh, not again,' said Jim, 'Not another one jammed in the lift!'

I looked around; you could sense the feeling in the air; everyone had their eyes on the open lift, wondering if the same thing would happen again.

The five good men, followed by Carlos, walked into the lift and, in the same manner as before, attempted to relieve its contents.

Who said practice makes perfect, I thought as I watched the struggle repeated? But quickly, the fight was over, and the coffin was being carried out and put into the carriage.

Within moments, the carriage started to move, a man walking at each corner slowly until it turned into the street and out of sight.

The aftermath of the Christmas chaos had left us all wandering around Benidorm in a bit of a daze, nursing a mix of exhaustion, amusement, and mild regret. Poor Dad's infamous bout of the Trots turned every outside excursion into a strategic mission, with routes carefully planned around the nearest toilet, preferably no more than 50 yards away. Thankfully, given that most of our "sightseeing" involved hopping from one bar to another, this wasn't exactly a logistical nightmare. Still, his sudden pale-faced exits mid-conversation became a source of endless entertainment. One moment, he'd be laughing along; the next, he'd turn ghostly white, excuse himself, and sprint for the nearest bog. Poor Dad!

The departure of the Hearse brought a wave of relief to the sizeable crowd loitering in the hotel lobby. With that unsettling chapter behind us, we eagerly stepped outside to breathe in the fresh air and continue our adventure. Dennis, ever the fearless leader, guided us past the other guests and down the road in search of our next watering hole.

Mum's directions led us into a narrow street, and there it was: *The Cantina,* marked by a modest sign dangling on the wall. We entered to find a cosy, Spanish-style room, the kind you'd imagine from a postcard. The walls were adorned with traditional paintings and charming little ornaments perched on shelves. The tables, dressed in bright tablecloths, were paired with wooden chairs sporting raffia seats, rustic but inviting.

The place had a lively buzz, the kind of atmosphere that instantly puts you in a good mood. Dennis wasted no time weaving through the tables and claiming one for our crew. As everyone settled in, I noticed Dad's predictable dash to the loo. No surprises there. Meanwhile, I headed to the bar and ordered drinks for the group, along with ice creams for Karen and Graeme.

We stayed in the little bar for a while longer, enjoying its hospitality. But time was marching on, and an urgent exit from this nice little place was now necessary if we were to catch the Hotel transport for the Lemon Express.

Fortunately, we arrived back at the Hotel a bit early, which gave Judy and me some time to go back to our room and get us and the Kids toileted and cleaned up.

We were quickly sorted out and back down in the lift, which was still ok, thank God. On reaching the Lobby, and as the lift doors opened I could see Dennis and Jim chatting to a small group and Florrie and Doris chatting together. Please, not more Hotel problems or some poor soul dropping down dead again; I shuddered to think but was surprised to hear Doris and the word train as we approached.

Doris explained, as we got close, that the nearby Guests had been on the trip before and said it was really a great day out.

They loved the fact that the train travelled through the centre of the villages, and the people waved and cheered at the carriages as they passed by. They also said they had a commentary along the route until it arrived in **Gata-de-Gorgos.** Apparently, the idea belonged to an English businessman, and he made it a great success among the English and other tourists.

So armed with this information, I happily thought we were all in for a great day.

Suddenly, I heard a voice cry out, which I recognised was Sharon's.

'All people for the Lemon Express trip, please go outside to the coach!'

'Let's get off now and onto the coach. As Sharon just said, we can get a good seat!' I said to Judy rather firmly, and with Karen and Graeme in hand, we set foot out of the Lobby and onto the street outside, where a small coach was standing by. I looked around as we climbed up the steps and claimed our four seats; I could see Mum and Dad behind, followed by the others.

Soon, everyone was seated, and we moved off; I could sense a feeling of excitement around the coach as we travelled the short journey to the Train Station. As the coach arrived, we were met by the sight of a bright lemon engine connected to just three small carriages.

There was almost a scramble to get off the coach as Sharon stepped down and guided us with a waiving hand along to the platform.

I was slightly in front of our friends and holding Karen and Graeme with both hands for safety; bearing in mind platforms had sharp drops onto railway lines.

From behind me, I could hear Dennis, in a rather loud voice, utter the not unexpected words.

'I'm going to find the carriage with the Bar and sort out some seats!'

With that, he sped forwards and around us, then briskly walked along the platform carriages, peering through the windows like a crowd member at a Harrods January sale. At the second carriage, he stopped, pointed, and waived to us to come quickly to his newly discovered sanctuary.

I realised Denis certainly found the right spot and as we stepped up and entered the carriage. I could see the beautiful old world decor and all in perfect condition as if preserved for posterity.

Dennis had quickly found good seats right by the Bar, and beckoned us over to join him, which we did in smart order.

The little carriage was quickly filled with people, and very soon, all were seated and ready for the off! The feeling of excitement was still flowing all around.

After a short time, I heard the train whistle loudly sounding; this was followed by a shudder and then by slight forward movement building up slowly. I looked through the carriage window to see us moving along the platform, and then the view soon changed to one of countryside and flat plains of trees and vegetation.

Through the clatter and clicking sounds of the train on track I heard the man at the Bar shouting out.

'The Lemon Express is now open; refreshments will be served soon!'

'That sounds good to me,' said Dad quietly, turning round to face me with a pleased look on his face.

Florrie quickly spoke up with a strange reprimand,

That's all you Men think about are boozing; look out at the nice scenery, it's very beautiful!'

Suddenly, I felt a pang of guilt, but it quickly passed as I thought of the Man behind the Bar announcing its opening.

Dennis shot upwards out of his seat as if assisted by a giant spring in his arse and, at the same time, saying loudly,

'I'll go over and see what's on offer!'

Dennis said nothing more but I could see some beer bottles being put on the Bar top and some glasses of what looked like wine.

I stepped up to join him, and surely we had beer, white wine, and kids' coke served, which I quickly carried back to our tables, followed by Dennis.

'That's all they have on the train; it's just a small Bar, so I guess they have to be a bit limited, but no problem, I guess?'

'I like wine, what about you girls?' Mum said with a shrug.

As Mum spoke, I could not help to see Doris and Florrie, both with glasses up to their lips, must be ok I thought.

Our little train chugged faithfully along the tracks, its wheels creating that comforting, rhythmic clickety-clack as we were pulled through a breathtaking panorama of rolling hills and quaint countryside. The view through the carriage windows felt like something out of a travel brochure, just enough to keep us mesmerized without lulling us to sleep.

We arrived at Gata-de-Gorgos after a few brief stops, hopping off the train with the excitement of explorers but keeping a cautious eye on the time—there were no more trains that day, and we had exactly two hours to explore. The town, a charming little Spanish gem, was easy to navigate. While the Girls and Kids busied themselves wandering through basket shops and souvenir stalls, we Men decided on a more culturally enriching experience. After a quick peek inside the Guitar Factory, we discovered a small bar with sunny outdoor seating, where we indulged in a well-earned beer—or two.

Our blissful lounging was abruptly interrupted by the Girls, who arrived like a whirlwind, warning us about missing the train. Forced to abandon our beers and dignity, we drank up quickly and made a hasty retreat. But much to my surprise, we were among the first back on the train, managing to reclaim our seats near the Bar, which—thankfully—remained unoccupied.

When we had all settled down, Mum, who looked bursting to say something, said almost in a whisper,

'When we were in a shop, a group of very noisy British Girls came in, they were all dressed in very tarty clothes with boobs bursting out and faces covered in war paint and big cheap earrings; they all seemed to have been drinking a lot!'

I thought quickly; I did not see them on our train; perhaps they came on the morning train, and it looked like it may be a rather lively trip.

Almost as I thought this I heard a loud woman's voice.

'Come on in here, you lot, there's some free seats near the Bar, we can get a drink when the train moves off!'

I looked round to see, as all on our tables did, almost in unison.

Then Florrie said, gesturing with her hand to her mouth as if surprised.

That's the lot we saw in the shop. You remember Tiggy? They spoke to you, and one called Gloria said they were all from Wigan, up in the North of England!'

Just as Florrie finished, a hubbub descended on us. The Wigan crew arrived and sat down on the few seats near us; then, in no time, the train whistle blew, and we were off.

We had hardly travelled a few minutes when the Barman announced the Bar was open and champagne was being served.

This caused Dennis to rise again and move to the Bar, which was now laden with glasses, which the barman was quickly filling.

One of the Wigan women got up, stepped up to us, and said directly to Mum.

'Hello, you remember me from the shop? It's Gloria; we had a quick chat about Benidorm and your Hotel.'

She bent over me towards Mum, who looked quite horrified; all I could see was an enormous pair of knockers billowing out of her overstretched top and opposite the look on Dad's face, mouth almost half open.

Gloria looked round at her friends, voiced and gestured,

'Come over here, it's the lady we met in the shop with her family!'

She continued in a rather loud voice,

'The Bar's open, and champagne's served!'

Almost in a rush, her companions moved over to us and round the Bar. Gloria stood up a bit and I could now see more of her friends, now with glasses in their hands and all looking at us.

Gloria, announced loudly this is Pat, Joan, Deirdre, Alice and Debbie. All were just as Mum described, a bit Tarty, with lots of billowing busts and short skirts showing plenty of legs.

The Bar area was quite large for a small train and Gloria and her mates still left some room for others to get served. However, they seemed to like our bit of area and soon they were chatting away with Dennis and Dad as well as Mum.

I heard I cry from Karen,

'Can we have a drink, Daddy? You forgot us, and Graeme and I are thirsty!'

I dreaded to get up and go over to the Bar with that lot of dangerous women around it. But I must I feared and raised myself to do my duty.

I found myself being quickly pressed between Joan and Deirdre, who were quite being friendly, as I got the Kids' drinks and handed them over to Dad, now behind me.

'More Champagne for Mum and the others he requested!'

I did my best to get more glasses and duly handed over to Dad and got one for myself. Gloria had now sat in my seat, which left me no escape from Joan and Deirdre, who were asking me lots of questions about Benidormas if I could know much after just seven days. I told them about Vincent's and then realised this may be a bad idea.

The Lemon Express bounced along for many more miles while Judy looked at me, not angry, but occasionally trying not to laugh at my predicament. My new companions were getting more tipsy and wiggling their boobs about right under my nose. I could smell the strong, cheap perfume as they closed up on me.

Deirdre spoke up in a rather slurred voice, pressing ever closer.

'You should come up to Wigan, Lad; we could show you a thing or two!'

I shuddered at the thought but decided to give up at this point, being somewhat trapped, surrounded by others on the train, all trying to get at more booze.

It seemed just best to stay marooned between the girls, join them in more Champers's, and wait until the train stopped.

Dad, Dennis and Jim were no help as they had parked themselves at the other part of the Bar so they could giggle at my predicament.

Mercifully, the end of our journey happened soon and we were quickly onto the platform and being collected by our dear Sharon.

Gloria collected her lot, who were now well into happy land and disappeared over to another coach, waving to us and away.

I felt so relieved as now we were all grouped together; moving off on our coach, back to our Hotel.

'You had a good eyeful with those two at the Bar!' Dennis remarked out loud. This comment caused Judy to reply with a laugh.

I thought that if the train rocked a bit, Ken would fall into one of those slapper's tits; God help him if he enjoyed it!'

She then burst out laughing, which started the rest of us off, and a few on the coach who must have overheard.

Things fortunately quietened down a bit, and we soon approached the Flemington.

The coach came to a halt right outside the hotel, and soon, we were down on the road and wondering what to do. The time was 7.30pm and too late for the Hotel restaurant.

I was feeling quite famished now, so I remarked out loud,

'I guess we are all hungry; what do you all think?'

I'm hungry; Florrie commented and was followed by Jim in agreement.

Dad, who had remained a bit quiet on the coach, suggested.

'What about that small Bar called Maria's, run by Alberto and his wife Maria, we went to the other day, that looked quite good for food; lots of people were in there; it's only a five-minute walk!'

'Good idea!' said Florrie, and then Mum followed with 'I'm in for that!'

'So it's Maria's, then!' Dennis remarked, 'Let's get off and grab some nosh, no hanging about!'

So that's where we finished the long day, enjoying a great meal of Maria's Paella as highly recommended by Alberto.

Even Dad loved it and thanked Alberto and Maria for the first Spanish meal he had enjoyed.

So, with the ending of a long and rather strange day, we all were soon into Flemington and away to our rooms.

Chapter 16 – Our Bavarian Saviour (Day 8)

I dragged myself back to consciousness at the speed of a dying Wi-Fi connection. The sun had no mercy, blasting through the curtains like it had something to prove. Reality hit: just one day left of our so-called holiday before the grim fate of going home slapped us in the face tomorrow. Brilliant.

I sat up, groggy, only to see that Judy—clearly some kind of overachiever—was already up and prodding Karen awake like she was conducting an important mission. Graeme, ever the morning enthusiast, grunted, rolled over like a sack of potatoes, and finally managed to sit up. After a bit of reluctant shuffling, he stumbled out of bed while Karen followed, furiously scrubbing her eyes like she could wipe away the fact that morning had arrived.

With Judy and me up early—because clearly, we're gluttons for punishment—we dove headfirst into the daily chaos. First, sorting ourselves out like a couple of overworked stagehands, then wrangling a squirming Graeme into something that resembled "washed and dressed."

Thankfully, Karen, the little miracle worker, had evolved into someone self-sufficient and managed her routine without needing a full production team.

The morning was disgustingly cheerful: bright skies, kids giggling, everyone buzzing with excitement for our last hurrah. By the time we'd wrangled clothes, shoes, and sanity into place, hunger kicked in like an uninvited guest, so we bolted out of our closet-sized room—tripping over each other, naturally—and made for breakfast.

Ah, the lift. That clunky relic was usually more temperamental than a moody cat, but today? It was shockingly cooperative. As it quietly lowered us to the lobby, I figured it must have been in a rare good mood. Or maybe it just wanted us gone. Either way, we weren't complaining. The breakfast treat in the restaurant was as usual, still no runny eggs, but enough of the rest to fill our hungry Kids and us.

While quietly seated, attacking my eggshell, I felt a quick nudge from Judy, who advised of my promise to take the kids to the beach.

Given that today was our last day, it seemed the appropriate thing to do, especially as just the mention of beaches and sand set Karen and Graeme into a frenzy of kid-like excitement.

It was another beautiful day, though cold enough to kill any hope of a beach swim unless hypothermia was your thing. So, I settled on the next best option: paddling in the sea and constructing the world's least impressive sandcastles. Judy, ever the beach queen, was happily snoozing away, clocking in a solid 40 winks like she was getting paid for it.

After an hour of sandy chaos, it was only a matter of time before Karen's familiar plea echoed through the air. *"Dad, I want a drink, please, I'm thirsty. May we go soon?"* Classic. Right on cue, Graeme chimed in with his daily agenda item: *'Daddy, can we go and find the Bar where the man gives out sweets?'* I was happy to agree to this, as I have done so on the past few days of beach duties. After an hour or so of the bright sun reflecting off the sand would always make me feel a bit thirsty.

I checked the time, it was 2pm, and I gave Judy a little nudge to wake her from her slumber.

This was not taken well as she lurched up and uttered.

'Why did you wake me up? I was having a really nice sleep; sometimes you make me mad!'

It's 2pm, I replied in haste; the Kids were moaning and wanted a drink and ice cream; what was I supposed to do?'

Judy looked at me in silence, then quickly packed up our things.

We headed back to Vincent's, with Judy remaining fairly quiet; I realized that waking her from her dreams had not been a great idea.

As previously arranged, we found the others set up at Vincent's. I could see they were obviously enjoying themselves, judging by the array of gasses and bottles on the table.

'Glad you are here, 'said Dennis, 'Were just planning to go to another Bar someone told us about, 'It's a Spanish Bar called The Bodega, not far away, just down the road; they said it good, and the drinks were cheap so let's give it a try.'

'Ok by us,' said Judy, eager as me to discover a new Bar.

With Dennis leading the way, we were quickly strolling down the road to find this new Bodega spot. We turned the corner into a small, narrow street as Dennis had instructed, and right in front of us was the large sign, 'The Bodega,' as brightly shown on the wall outside. From the outside, the Bar looked very smart, with a multi-glass door and bright little windows in small square frames set into the walls on either side.

We entered to find a larger-than-expected room decorated with pictures on the walls and many beer barrels and ends protruding from the walls with names, I guessed as wine formally within, hence the name of Bodega.

There were quite a few places to sit and plenty of tables, all with thick tops and rather strong-looking chairs and bench seats.

There were quite a few people in the place and laughter coming from many directions. It looked like a very popular place to be. Dennis, in typical fashion, led us quickly to a free table, and Florie, Doris, Mum, Judy, and the Kids spread around to comfortable positions.

Jim, who was standing at the table end, spoke up and, with a hint of sarcasm, commented in a slightly raised voice.

'Well! I see you ladies have got yourselves all sat down and comfy; I suppose, as usual, us men will have to get the drinks in?'

'Of course!' Doris replied with a laugh, 'Go get them!'

Dad looked at Jim and me while simultaneously pointing his finger at the Bar, which, to no surprise, set Dennis in motion in that direction, quickly followed by us as willing servants.

We settled in the friendly Bar for a good while, which was another nice little find. It was certainly popular, and when we arrived at around 2.30pm had quite a mixture of people, which seemed to go up and down in numbers as the patrons came and went.

You could feel a good atmosphere all around.

I suddenly felt a nudge in the arm from Judy, who pointed to Graeme. My eyes fell on my son, once again, sound asleep in his pushchair, as though without a care in the world. I looked at my watch; it was 4.00pm. I had no idea that the time had marched on so much. We had arrived at Vincent's bar mid-morning, done the beach, and then to The Bodega; all told, it had been another typical holiday day. We waved our goodbyes towards the bar and trooped out to make our unsteady way back up the hill to rest and get ready for the evening's feast of surprises.

Judy and I had moved a little in front of the others. Karen and Graeme, for some reason were showing no signs of being weary and were still full of fun, laughing and giggling at everything as excited children are inclined to do.

The others were not far behind us on our long climb up the hill. I could hear Dennis beaming out loudly, still joking about the day's events and whether the Flemington would claim any residents this week; would it be the shock of the journey, the place, or the food?

Judy and I turned round to look at the others and, in our distraction had failed to notice Graeme, who had seen Sharon with a group of other residents standing outside the hotel entrance now only a stone's throw away. I turned forward again only to see, to my horror, Graeme starting to run towards Sharon. In front was a car speeding down the hill, just by the hotel, and in an instant, Graeme was on the road, completely unaware of the car, now only yards away, his eyes fixed only on Sharon.

'Graeme,' Judy shouted, but too late. The car braked hard; the tyres were squealing, but it was still going too fast.

Suddenly, in an instant forever frozen in my head, a man leapt out from the group of people at the side of the road.

He was running right into the path of the car, then diving headlong at Graeme. His hands locked around Graeme's small frame, and together, they travelled some feet and sprawled onto the side of the small road, escaping just only inches out of the path of the car.

The car just sped on into the darkness, leaving Graeme and his saviour lying on the road.

Judy and I ran the few yards to Graeme, and the man both just sprawled on the floor. Judy picked up Graeme and held him close to her; he burst out crying with fright and shock but was obviously undamaged by the experience. The man, still on the floor, was starting to compose himself. I stretched out my hand to help him up, which he took eagerly.

'Thank you,' I blurted out, 'Thank you so much,' finding it for once difficult to speak.

As the man started to get up from the road, he was silent; I could see his face in the lights from the hotel. As he stood up, he looked at me and grinned. 'Thank you,' I said again, you saved our son's life.' I will remember his words all my life.

'It vas nozing,' he said, 'I vas very near him, is he ok?'

'Thanks to you, yes,' I replied. I quickly recognised him as one of the German guests in the hotel, but we had not spoken before.

By this time, Mum and Dad, the others, and a bit of a crowd had gathered around us; the air of relief was everywhere. Mum started shaking the man's hand; Dad was patting him on the back in quite uncharacteristic fashion. Sharon, with such a worried look on her face, had now come up to us. She stammered out,

'Graeme was running across the road to see me, I thought he would be run over when I saw the car,'

She continued, 'Thank God he is alright!'

I turned to face the man and, with my hand out, nervously requested,

'Please, I want to know your name and at least buy you a drink.'

'It's Manfred, Manfred Leutoff,' he replied.

'Well, Manfred, I am Ken, my wife is Judy, please come with us to the Hotel bar if you have time.

'Of course, we will be delighted,' Manfred replied, 'I think I need a drink after zis experience.'

By this time, Judy, Mum, and most of the congregation that had gathered around had suitably comforted Graeme; Karen gave Graeme a big hug, which produced a rather big grin on Graeme's face.

'Let's go with Daddy and Mr Manfred now, and we can have a nice drink of lemonade,' Karen said enthusiastically.

I suspected this was a tactic designed to put off bedtime a bit longer. It was 5.30pm now, but I thought, what the hell! Graeme just survived near death.

'Come on!' I gestured to our newfound saviour, 'Let's get that drink; I think we all need one after this!'

We spent the next half hour talking to Manfred about so many things. We discovered he came from the German province of Bavaria and was living with his wife in Munich. He talked about the superb beer that Bavaria was famous for and made me feel rather envious and keen to try these famous brews.

.We talked for some time about the awful Hotel

We joked at length about the unbearable dancers to the point that Judy reminded me we had to get the kids ready for tonight at Vincent's.

This brought things to a bit of a halt, and then I had an idea and turned to Manfred said.

'Manfred, why don't you and your friends join us at Vincent's bar tonight for a drink, that's if you can at this short notice?'

Manfred was quick to reply,

'My wife and I would love to join you, and I will speak with my other friends. I'm sure they will come as we all hate the Hotel food and the dancing group!' Manfred continued,

It will be a happy time to visit a new place, somewhere else from the awful Flemington, and have some fun outside!'

With that done, we parted and agreed to meet up around 8pm at Vincent's. 'How would this pan out, I wondered?'

Life's just like a run across a busy road. You never know what may knock.

Chapter 17 – The December Fest

Having thoroughly enjoyed our little rendezvous with Manfred at the hotel bar, Judy wasted no time in rounding up the kids and herding them towards the lift.

Oh, what a shock—press the button all you like, but the lift remained as elusive as a competent politician.

"Right then, the long trek it is," I declared with the enthusiasm of a man about to climb Everest in loafers.

Up we went, once again braving the arduous ascent, clinging to what little dignity remained. By some miracle, we reached the summit with our limbs intact, only to barrel into the room and immediately agree that the best course of action was to vacate it as swiftly as humanly possible.

With a mere 30 minutes to transform from bedraggled travellers into presentable human beings, speed was of the essence. I grabbed a fresh set of clothes and bolted to Mum's room to wash and change—partly to save time, partly to grant Judy a moment's peace in what was rapidly becoming a war zone. A stroke of genius, really, as Mum and Dad were just about to head downstairs to join the others for pre-Vincent's drinks. Perfect timing, if I do say so myself.

I got ready really fast and was soon cleaned up, clothed, and off back to my room. I opened the door, with some reservations about the state of readiness but was so happy to see Judy and the kids all looking finished. As they filed out of the room and into the hallway, I could see them properly, and sure enough, a shining Graeme and a beautifully dressed Karen appeared. Judy was just behind, and as she came out of the room, I could see she looked so lovely. She turned to face me, standing in a fine new dress, shoes, and handbag. Judy, once again, had performed a miracle.

'Wow, I exclaimed, you look fantastic, the Kids look great too!'

Judy grinned, smiled in a wry sort of way, and confirmed that I looked ok, and continued, saying with a laugh!

'Let's get off and enjoy our last night in Benidorm with our saviour, Manfred, and his friends.'

By good fortune, the bloody lift was actually working, as witnessed by the vision of a lady who was just stepping out. As she moved away, we could see the lift doors were still open as if to welcome us in. Without stopping, we quickly jumped inside before it took a mind to default.

I cried out to Judy, desperate to move downwards.

'Quick, press the flipping down button; that bloody lift has been a major curse we have experienced during our stay!'

'I really hope it's ok tomorrow, when we have to lug the luggage around and down to the lobby.' I said quickly as I watched Judy's finger press the button down hard.

With some surprise, with a tremble from the lift, we happily descended down to reception and onto the bar.

We entered, and as expected, we found Mum and Dad sitting around a table with the others.

All were clearly in good spirits and I felt the warm glow of Christmas inside me and was now ready for anything.

We sat down to join the others. Jim quickly jumped up, as if spring powered, and advised he was off to get us a drink. Then ran off quickly to the bar as if on a serious mission,

After some time and deep discussion about Graeme's accident, his salvation, getting the children ready, and the other general events of the day, Dennis piped up,

'I guess it's time for us to go to Vincent's Bar and meet Manfred and friends.'

With that, we drank up and proceeded out of the hotel and into the early evening, full of high expectations of a great night before us.

As we strolled along the short path to Vincent's, I had the distinct feeling that tonight was about to unfold into yet another chapter of unexpected events—because, let's be honest, when do they not?

Upon arrival, we were greeted by a sea of cheerful faces; clearly, we weren't the only ones bidding farewell to Ben's dorm. The place was heaving, yet, against all odds, we managed to find a table. A minor miracle, really, though it seemed most of the crowd had taken a particular liking to standing—fine by us.

Dennis wasted no time marching up to the bar, masterfully orchestrating the drinks order like a man on a mission. Moments later, he returned, arms laden with beverages, closely followed by Dad and Jim, who had evidently decided that playing the role of his eager assistants was a worthwhile pursuit.

We had been seated only moments when the door of the Pub, which was close to us, opened, and a small, large, rounded woman entered quickly, followed by another, then another, till the number was up to six, all seemingly full of the Christmas spirit, giggling and laughing rather loudly. They pushed their way to the crowded bar, shuffled in quickly, and ordered their drinks.

Oh! My Goodness, I thought, the only spare table left in Vincent's was next to us, we had been saving it for Manfred.

I leaned over to Dad and said quietly in a worried tone,

Have you noticed? I think that lot are the ones from the train trip; look, see Gloria, followed by her mates, Pat, Joan, Deirdre, Alice, and Debbie. Í hope that lot don't sit over here; they look a bit sloshed to me.'

'Yes, I think you are not far wrong on that point,' Dad replied with a grin, 'I bet they could be a bit lively!'

We were soon to find out just how lively when one of the ladies saw the empty table next to us and shrieked,

'Girls, over here, there's a free table!'

She quickly wobbled her way over, and as she got close, I could see the full horror of it all.

Gloria's rather large knockers billowed out of a low-cut top, which was only just keeping the lot in place. The other girls were similarly dressed, all boobs and short dresses.

Suddenly, she looked over at our table, turned to her mates then pointed at us and started coming over in some haste.

I thought to myself, don't sit next to me, but within seconds, she, now followed by the other girls, stood around us.

Fancy seeing you lot from yesterday on the train? We have been round the town's bar today, and you said this place was great!'

I quickly realised my stupidity in recommending Vincent's and felt that I was going to quickly suffer for my folly.

Gloria was looking a bit wobbly, firmly holding at our table for support and, on the other hand, sporting a cocktail of some sort. She put the cocktail down right next to me and then sat down on the little space left on my bench seat.

Pat, Joan, Deirdre, and Alice unceremoniously plonked themselves—and their drinks—onto the table beside ours, which was uncomfortably close. Our little party had been well and truly invaded.

I glanced across the table and spotted poor Jim, who had somehow acquired the undivided attention of the well-rounded Debbie. She stood beside him, dressed to kill in a tight-fitting blue number, cut so dangerously low it was a miracle her boobs remained contained at all. One wrong move and physics would take its revenge.

With a grand sweep of her hand and a voice that teetered between flirtation and outright inebriation, she reintroduced herself as *Debbie*—as if Jim had any chance of forgetting. He, on the other hand, wore the expression of a man who had just realised he was the prey, not the predator.

'We had a bit of fun on that train, Jim,'

She paused and then sat heavily down right next to Jim on the next table, far too close for comfort. I cringed, looking on in horror at the rest of the troupe; not one looked sober.

They were all dressed to the nines, and boobs lifted out to the hilt. The make-up shop in their town must have done roaring business before their holiday.

Debbie went on, in some earnest.

'My mates and I have left their husbands at home and come over for a good time; I'm divorced and fancy-free.'

'Well looks like you are well into that good time mode!' Florrie said in a rather disapproving but hushed voice and then looked at Jim like he could be in deep shit if he continued further conversations with his new table mate.

The music in Vincent's was playing quite loudly, but mostly slow sort of stuff, and a few of the other people in the bar were dancing.

Without warning, Gloria looked at me and announced.

'I fancy a dance!' She then got up and grabbed my hand.

'Fancy a dance?' She slurred out at me again.

I was too shocked to speak at first, and then she bent down towards me, boobs billowing out of her top, and repeated the request.

'Well, I'm no good at dancing,' I quickly stammered out.

'Don't be daft, love!' She laughed and pulled me up towards her, almost thrusting me into herself.

We were in the small dance area just a few steps away, and almost before I realised her arms were around me, dancing had begun.

Gloria was so well into the booze, and as we went round in small steps, dancing slowly to the music. I could feel her heavy on me as if I was now part of her support system.

Her hands were round my neck, and her head planted on my chest.

As the music played on, she clung to me ever more tightly, and I cast a desperate glance toward our table. Judy caught my eye, and I braced myself for a spectacular telling-off—only to find her stifling laughter instead. A miracle, truly. I had fully expected a row of biblical proportions.

Dennis, Dad, and the rest of them, however, weren't nearly as discreet; they were openly enjoying the spectacle, caught in various stages of barely contained hilarity. Meanwhile, Karen and Graeme, blissfully unaware of my predicament, were far too engrossed in fiddling with Christmas toys on the table to pay me any mind.

Then, mercifully, the music came to an end. Wasting no time, I extricated myself from her grasp with the urgency of a man escaping quicksand.

'Thanks, Love,' she slurred out and turned towards our table, which was only a few feet away. Her state was such that the next step towards her table was her last, and as she moved forward, her right leg gave way, and she stumbled forward and sort of collapsed slowly in a surprisingly graceful way onto poor Jim, landing on his lap.

Jim's face went to horror. His arms were outstretched as if this thing that had landed on him was not to be touched by the pain of death.

Two of the lady's friends, Alice and Debbie, I believe, got up quickly from the table and went to her aid. They tried to lift her off poor Jim's lap but to no effect.

Dennis, who was still trying to compose himself managed to get up and assisted with the ladies' removal.

After some pushing and shoving, Gloria was finally raised to her feet, and Joan provided further assistance.

'We better go after this and put Gloria to bed; perhaps we will come back later.'

The ladies all quickly got up and wobbled off towards the door and out into the night.

What a relief, I thought, but almost as I was composing myself from my earlier experience, I saw Manfred walk into Vincent's, followed by his friends. I counted six in all. They must have just passed the ladies as they came in and I wondered if they had witnessed any further shenanigans?

Manfred was looking around, so I waved over to him to catch his attention. He smiled as he saw me and the others and gestured for his friends to follow and head the few steps to meet us.

'Hi,' said Manfred, with a broad smile, let me introduce you to my wife Ingrid and friends Marcus and Yvette and Gunter and Helga.'

We all shook hands and introduced ourselves to Ingrid and friends.

Dad gestured and asked in his usual quiet manner,

'Please be seated,' indicating to the empty table just vacated by the 'Women from Wigan.'

I thought with some horror, thank the Lord the ladies had moved on, and we had been spared the prospect of more of their overflowing company!

'What would you all like to drink?' Dad asked?

Manfred stood up and replied, 'Thanks, I will come to the bar with you as I know what we all like to drink.'

Dad, Manfred, and joined by Dennis moved forward to Vincent's large bar; I quickly followed to help.

Dad ordered everyone a drink, and considering the bar was so full, Dad got served quickly. We were soon seated round the table with our new guests and I raised my glass to Manfred.

'Your good health,' I said with a grin, 'and once again, our thanks for saving Graeme.'

'And to you,' Manfred replied, 'I'm just happy Graeme is ok.'

I had noticed that Manfred was limping slightly as we had walked to the bar.

'Did you hurt your leg when you dived into the road?' I asked.

'No,' Manfred replied, smiling. 'I did this in the war; I was a young pilot on my first mission over Kent in England. I was flying my ME109 aircraft when a Hurricane came out of nowhere and shot at me; one of the bullets went into my leg, and my plane was on fire, so I bailed out and was captured as soon as I landed.'

'I was sent to a hospital for three weeks until my leg was better, then spent the next three years as a prisoner of war; that's how I learned to speak English!'

'Oh, not the war,' I said to myself in horror, 'Don't start Jim off, please God.' But to no avail.

'I was in the war,' Jim blurted out; he continued,

'I got captured in France and was held prisoner for six months till I managed to escape.'

Manfred quickly interrupted, 'I could not escape, unfortunately, as I was fed too much of your Yorkshire pudding to be able to run away.'

Everyone laughed, 'What an icebreaker,' I thought; who said Germans don't have a sense of humour!'

Jim replied, 'You were lucky; I had to live on sour crout for six months!'

The laughter continued until tears were streaming down our eyes. I guess the nights of drinking, Graeme's salvation, and the relief at getting over potential war problems were all too much.

We were all enjoying ourselves greatly, with stories being exchanged about the hotel, our homelands, holiday experiences and customs. Certainly, our new German friends were having a great time as we all were, and copious quantities of Bacardi drinks, beer, and strange cocktails were being downed.

At this point, it was about 10.30, and I felt Judy give me a quick poke in the arm to dislodge me from my enjoyable and humorous conversation with Marcus and Gunter.

'Ken!' Judy said in an urgent sort of tone.

'We better get the kids up to bed. It's getting late and we leave tomorrow; we can come down to the Hotel bar again after.'

'Great!' I replied, 'That's a good idea; we will just put the kids to bed and come down for a little while.'

Manfred looked over at his friends, waived his hand, and questioned,

'Shall we move to the Hotel bar soon and join Ken, Judy and the others?'

Manfred received a round of eager-looking nods confirming the promising plan.

We set about rounding up our two, who were happily engrossed in play with a boy and girl at the next table. Graeme, looking a little worse for wear, offered no resistance to leaving, while Karen—though reluctant—was just about ready to call it a night.

With a final, somewhat melancholic wave to dear Vincent, we left the others to finish their drinks, knowing full well this was likely a farewell rather than a *see you next time.*

Hand in hand with the kids, we made haste back to the hotel, bracing ourselves for yet another encounter with the dreaded lift. But lo and behold—this time, as if recognising our suffering, the doors slid open on cue, almost welcoming us in. A rare victory.

'Thank the Lord!' said Judy as we slowly ascended upwards. I pinched myself as we rose, realizing that I was sort of losing it, almost believing the lift had something of a life and soul!

It took us no time to settle Karen and Graeme down for the night. Graeme had quietly got into his bed, and I went round to tuck him in.

'You caused a bit of trouble today, young lad! I said quietly,

'You must be careful of the road in the future; we don't want you to get run over.'

Graeme looked up at me with a bit of sadness in his eyes,

'Sorry Daddy, I will be good next time and be more careful.'

I kissed him goodnight, and then Karen, and said quietly.

'We won't be long downstairs, just a few drinks and a chat,'

I closed the bedroom door and gently took Judy's hand to rejoin the others down in the bar.

Many more drinks went down that evening, and we learned that despite earlier reservations, our newfound friends were really nice people, full of fun, and were just as able to make jokes at the Flemington's strange modus of operation as us.

We all had such a good laugh that last holiday night. Some other Germans came over, and we were soon laughing with them about the strange antics of our Old Time Dancers, prancing about in their 'Get-ups,' as Dad called their glittering strange outfits.

Manfred, who was one of the more jovial of his group kept us in stitches that night doing impressions of the dancing, all Poe faced and spinning about like he was in some vital Come Dancing competition.

Time had passed on, and with this hectic and rather eventful day coming to a close we unfortunately had to part.

I thought in a sad sort of way, we had all enjoyed each other's company so much it was a bit sad we had not talked together earlier in our holiday. However, it was not to have been so we said our goodnights to all and started off once again to the lift for our final upward journey.

Did the lift work? No, the bloody thing was static again. I pressed the buttons in frustration again and again and then just gave up.

''It's the bloody lift not working again.' I said to Judy as if she could not see for herself!

So it was up those shitty stairs with hundreds of steps, each one creaking with a different noise as if wanting to torture us poor sods even more.

'What a night,' I said to Judy as I unlocked the door to our little room. We moved inside and prepared to get undressed for bed when suddenly Judy burst into tears,

'I thought Graeme was going to be run over,' she said, sobbing at the terrible thought, so I quickly put my arms around her for comfort and said with a sigh,

'Let's get to bed and be thankful that Graeme is safe and sound!'

I got into my bed and pulled up the cover to my chin as if to hide from the terrible incident.

'Good night, my love,' I said wearily, 'let's see what tomorrow brings. It's our last day and we go home.'

As I lay quietly, it seemed difficult to get to sleep; my mind kept drifting onto today's events and what could have happened if Manfred had not intervened so quickly. I thought of Graeme and how dear he is to us. Thank God he was safe and now tucked up in bed.

I said a small prayer of thanks and tried to go off to sleep.

Our party, and like residents, had all become players in a kind of horror show mixed with comedy that our Hotel was staging.

I pondered on with thoughts of the fragility of our daily lives and what tomorrow could bring till I drifted mercifully off to sleep.

(Graeme and Karen – both safe and sound)

Chapter 18 – Going Home (Day 8)

As I emerged from what felt like a coma, the symphony of sledgehammers in my skull kicked off in full force. Clearly, divine intervention—or at the very least, some Headache Potion—was needed to save me from my suffering. Thankfully, Judy, in all her wisdom, had packed some for our holiday, a decision that had already secured her a spot in my personal Hall of Heroes.

Dragging myself out of bed with the grace of a zombie on its last legs, I staggered to the bathroom where the sacred tablets were kept. With the urgency of a man on a mission, I ripped two from their packet, chucked them into my mouth, and reached for the nearest glass. In my desperation, I poured in some good old *Aqua*—or, as we mere mortals call it, water—and downed it like my life depended on it. Which, to be fair, it probably did.

"I really hope this does the trick," I thought, clinging to a sliver of optimism with the kind of desperation usually reserved for sinking ships.

I lay there for about half an hour, staring at the ceiling and waiting for my brain to reboot. Eventually, my senses stumbled back into place, and like a slow, painful slideshow, the events of the previous night began to replay themselves. Our marathon day exploring the town, the long evening at Vincent's, bumping into the *Ladies from Wigan* again, and somehow ending up in the company of Manfred's friends— it had all added up to one hell of a night.

And then, like an unwelcome guest, the memory of my *fatal miscalculations* arrived. A reckless mix of copious amounts of beer, followed by Bacardi, then Gin, and— because apparently, I have the restraint of a Labrador at a buffet—whatever else had seemed like a *good idea at the time*.

I turned over to Judy, who was quite still. I gave her a slight nudge, which seemed to bring forth life.

'Are you awake?' I said as if I didn't already know.

'Oh!' she groaned at me, 'I've got a terrible headache!'

I went on, 'Suppose it can't have been the ten gin and tonics?'

I replied in a sort of superior tone.'

'Get knotted!' was all I got in response.

After a few minutes of lying in a self-pitying haze, I dragged myself up and glanced over at Karen and Graeme, who, mercifully, were still fast asleep. It had been a *rather* late night—highly eventful, I thought, as a shudder ran down my spine at the memory of Graeme's near escape.

Both kids had been up well past their bedtime, but considering it was our last night, I figured we'd let it slide. Besides, *apart from the incident*, they'd had a great time and would soon be back home, forced into the cruel reality of normal routines and reasonable bedtimes.

'Fancy breakfast?' I said to Judy with a grin, trying to appear far more enthusiastic than I felt. 'Nice fried egg and bacon?'

The response was unfit for print, but it was swiftly followed by a rather firm request for tea.

'Let's get up!' I suggested, though it was more of a plea than anything. 'At least a nice cup of tea or coffee would go down well under the current circumstances.' *The current circumstances* being a desperate need to rejoin the living.

Getting ourselves, plus Karen and Graeme, washed and dressed took an ungodly amount of time—seriously, it felt like we were preparing for an expedition rather than breakfast—but after what felt like an eternity, we finally made it out the door.

As we passed Mum and Dad's room, I banged on the door in what I thought was a fairly considerate manner. No reply. I could only assume they'd already made their way downstairs and were currently wrestling with something lukewarm, rubbery, and suspiciously greasy in that *classic* Flemington style.

We walked into the restaurant, and sure enough, there were Mum and Dad seated with Denis, Florrie, Jim, and Doris.

'Good night last night!' said Denis as we arrived at their table.

'How is Graeme this morning?' Mum inquired, looking at her small grandson. 'We were all so frightened last night,' she went on.

'I'm ok, Nana,' Graeme replied in his squeaky voice, seemingly having forgotten all about the car incident.

Everyone on the table was looking at Graeme.

I guessed in the relative sobriety of the new day all were thanking the good Lord that the little lad was safe and sound.

'How are you feeling, Judy?' Dad inquired.

'Not too bad,' she replied, 'I had a bit of a headache earlier, but it's starting to go now!'

I looked at poor Judy, who still had a rather pale expression on her face.

'Come on, love,' I said in sympathy, 'Let's get you a cup of tea.'

After what felt like an entire lifetime of queuing—long enough to question all my life choices up to this point—I finally emerged victorious, balancing a large tray loaded with enough food to sustain a small army, or in this case, the four of us on the long homeward journey ahead.

As I approached the table, I noticed that, miraculously, a good amount of space had been cleared—undoubtedly a result of sheer desperation rather than courtesy. Wasting no time, I began dishing out the contents with the precision of a seasoned caterer, doing my best to divide everything in a way that might prevent squabbles (an impossible task, but one can dream).

The sheer volume of food made me feel momentarily proud, as though I'd somehow *achieved something significant* before the day had even properly started. In reality, all I had done was survive the breakfast queue—a feat in itself, to be fair.

'Oh my Goodness,' said Judy, as she observed her boiled egg as it rolled across the plate and came to a halt against the tomato slice I had just served.

'Come on!' I said with a laugh, 'Eat it up. It will do you good!'

These famous words had no meaning for Judy at this point in time, as I realised the headache tablets were not doing so well for her as for me.

'Just the tea will do!' She replied and then looked up at me and repeated slowly, 'Just the tea!'

It was now left for me and the eager-looking kids to eat it all up. Fortunately, I was now feeling better than I should have done and Karen and Graeme seemed to have got no ill effects from the long night's adventures.

After a few cups of tea, which I eagerly served, Judy came around a little and announced it was time to finish the packing.

We were all due to leave the Hotel mid-day, and we still had a few things to put in the cases.

'See you all downstairs,' I said to Mum and Dad, who had already packed much earlier and had left their cases in the lobby.

Mum advised it was fortunate that Carlos had seen poor Dad struggling with the cases and had got another staff to help him down with the luggage. Carlos had apologised to Dad for the lift breakdown and said convincingly that Giorgio, the Maintenance Man and part-time entertainer, was coming quickly to fix it.

'Leave Karen and Graeme with us while you finish packing,' said Mum, to our great relief.

'Oh! Thanks,' said Judy, 'That's a big help!'

We both quickly got up from our seats, as if we feared dear Mum would change her mind, and headed back up towards the stairs for the final sort out.

By some miracle of engineering (or perhaps sheer luck), the lift was finally working—a true parting gift from the universe, sparing us the agony of yet another gruelling stair descent, which had haunted us for our entire stay. Had it been operational earlier, it might have saved us days of unnecessary cardio, but at this point, I wasn't going to dwell on past injustices.

As we ascended, I felt a twinge of melancholy creeping in. In spite of all the *dramas, near-catastrophes, and questionable decision-making*, the holiday had been a brilliant blur of adventure. It was hard to believe it was already over. The thought of returning to normal life and work felt almost surreal—like stepping off a rollercoaster straight into a queue for the post office.

With packing done, I took on the final boss battle— hauling our cases to the lift, praying it wouldn't change its mind and break down *one last time*. Miraculously, the doors opened smoothly, as if the lift had finally decided to show us some respect. Wasting no time, I hurried Judy inside before it could reconsider its newfound generosity.

With a mildly ridiculous amount of effort, I crammed all our belongings into its gaping jaws, silently wondering if we'd accumulated extra luggage purely through the weight of souvenirs and bad decisions. With Judy at my side and a suspicious clunk from somewhere within the lift, we were soon gliding downward toward the lobby, one step closer to the journey home.

As I composed myself from the task of dragging our overlarge and heavy cases out of the lift I could see Mum and Dad were downstairs in the lobby with the kids beside them. They were standing over at the far end of the Lobby close to the Hotel entrance doors.

Of course, I was duly left to carry the bags over, but after all, I thought sarcastically, that's what we men are for.

Judy had headed fast towards Mum, Dad, and the kids, who were looking at me and grinning broadly at my poor efforts.

As I reached Mum and Dad, I could see they were both quite cheerful and seemed to be enjoying my struggle.

Almost as I put the cases down, I heard Mum announce,

'Look, there's Dennis and Florrie!'

I turned to see Dennis struggling down the stairway's last few steps, carrying some enormous bags. He had one in each hand and another smaller one tucked under his arm. Florrie was close behind, carrying her handbag and a small carrier bag.

Seeing us, Dennis marched forward clearly relieved at reaching the Lobby. Momentarily, he turned round to see Florrie but failed to see Carlos, who, with a determined look on his face, was carrying a tray of something across his path. At the last minute, Carlos saw Dennis lurching in his direction and diverted quickly to avoid him.

However, as Carlos turned in a new direction, the tray in his hands caught the front of a poor, unsuspecting lady standing just to his right.

Carlos jumped, being caught sharply by surprise at the lady's presence, and the small tray fell forward. As if seen in slow motion, the contents cascaded down the front of the lady's dress.

The tray fell to the floor with a clatter, the soup bowl, bread rolls, and cutlery all following.

Dennis turned forward to face this; he stopped dead, cases in hand and mouth wide open.

Carlos had his hands in the air and was waving them about frantically.

The poor lady stood there, silent and shocked, looking down at the front of her dress soaked in soup and pasta. Bits of pasta were clinging to her dress like the sequins on our Old Time Dancers. The rest of the contents of the soup bowl were distributed in a large puddle on the floor and mixed with the rest of the meal.

Angrily, the lady faced poor Carlos, who went into a frozen state of shock and embarrassment.

'You stupid man!' she rasped out. 'Look what you have done to my new dress!'

Carlos, now with hands clasped out in front like in prayer, could do nothing but stammer. The lady's husband turned onto poor Carlos in full battle stations, red in the face as if to explode.

'You idiot, can't you look where you are going?' he shouted out,

'I've had enough of this Hotel and everyone in it!'

His anger was interrupted by the Manager, Julio, followed behind by the little maid we knew as Maria. She had a bucket and mop in hand and judging by the speed of their appearance, this sort of event was not so new to them.

While Carlos was trying to comfort the angry couple, the man continued to berate him. Julio joined in to assist him, but apparently without much success, as much noise was still coming out of the group.

Dennis seized the opportunity. He quickly composed himself and, making a diversion around Maria and the contents on the floor, he scurried over to where we were standing, neatly followed by Florrie,

'Not again!' Dad blurted out at Dennis.

'It wasn't my fault this time!' Dennis replied, like a scolded kid, 'That Carlos did it, not me!'

His pain was momentarily interrupted by the arrival of Jim and Doris into our group. They were both laughing, having just caught sight of the events.

Jim, still grinning, sharply announced,

'What about that, Dennis? Are you in big trouble again?'

'That poor woman!' said Mum, 'Look at her nice new dress, all covered in soup!'

'Still, at least the soup wasn't hot!' said Jim, 'We know this from experience!'

He continued, still laughing, and despite this ably spurted out,

'Mrs Fortesque grabbed us as we were coming down the stairs; it was about the food again.

Doris took up the story in the most seamless way, continuing.

'I had a more than long conversation with the woman and realised she was trying to rope us all into writing off to Sunrise Holidays with endless complaints.'

Doris continued and, seemingly weary of the whole saga, said,

'In desperation to get away I suggested she got prepared for the next lot of guests who would soon be here after we had gone to the airport.'

That did the trick, and Mrs Fortesque scurried off, pen and paper in hand, and gave us the chance to escape.'

'Judy and I got a good ear bashing from Mrs Fortesque early yesterday,' I said in a sympathetic tone.

'She told us she was organising a fight with 'Sunrise Holidays' for compensation.

'Some chance!' Doris quickly replied, 'That firm will not be bothered about us, I bet!'

Florrie replied, nodding in agreement, and continued,

'Just think, after we all leave, today will be the next poor mugs, blissfully unaware of what they are about to receive.'

I thought to myself, thank God for them. It was not Christmas.

'The coach is here!' I heard someone call out as if it was a lifeline thrown down to people on a sinking ship.

This interrupted further laughter at Dennis and Mrs. Fortescue's expense and I looked outside to see the arrival of our coach, which stopped just outside the hotel entrance.

I could see Sharon at the open door of the coach door, ready to get off. She was wearing her Sunrise outfit with a red jacket and a snug-fitting white blouse. She bounded down the steps of the coach, those ample adornments thrusting out before her.

Jim nudged me and said quietly for only me to hear.

'Look at young Sharon, their bouncing beautifully as if having a life of their own. Let's try to keep Dennis away as we don't want any more accidents, please!'

All eyes fell on Sharon as she walked swiftly towards the Hotel and then headed at a fast pace into the Hotel lobby where we were all waiting.

She looked around the lobby and soon found Carlos, who had wrenched himself away from the earlier troubles with noodle soup.

After a few minutes Sharon announced to all that we could now get onto the coach outside and leave our bags with the driver.

Dad, also hearing Sharon and seeing the coach had arrived, announced with some urgency in his voice that the hotel was on fire.

'It's the coach!' he roared, 'Let's get the cases outside!'

Dad moved surprisingly quickly towards the Hotel door as if this place had all been too much.

With cases in hand and followed close behind by Mum, we headed forward and down the steps to the coach.

We were quickly followed by Dennis and Florrie, with Dennis grappling with the excess luggage that Florrie deemed essential for her short stay.

Jim and Doris, whose needs seemed simpler, just strolled down like they held just a few days of shopping from The Co-Op.

Dad, who seemed to be leading the escape, went straight up to the driver who obligingly took his cases and swung them rather gracefully into the hold of the coach. This was quickly repeated for the rest of us, and as we stood well back to allow others to relieve themselves of cases. Dad suddenly burst out laughing.

'What a holiday!' he said loudly while trying to compose himself, 'We owe it all to the Prudential!'

This started us all laughing but our merriment was soon interrupted by the rush of the descending crowd in the lobby who, like us, had started to move out to the coach. All the departing guests had seemingly, one common intent, to get out of the Flemington Hotel as quickly as possible.

I looked at Judy and said with a large smiling grin,

'Well, Judy, we're off home and back to a cold winter reality.'

'Thank God,' she replied, 'It may be cold, but I can't wait to get some good old English food in me!'

Feeling an awakening taste of fish and chips or a good roast dinner falling suddenly upon me, I continued.

'I'll buy you our favourite fish and chips from the shop up the road as soon as we get home and promise a large gin and tonic on the plane; how about that!'

Judy looked, almost gratefully, at me, then took hold of Karen's hand and said in a rather determined way.

'Well, come on, let's go, England awaits!'

Likewise I took Graeme's hand and followed close behind.

We ascended the steps of the coach and as we reached the top step, I turned my head for one last look at the Hotel.

I could see that guests were still pouring out of the Hotel entrance and milling around the coach, all seemingly trying to get their bags loaded onto the coach at once.

The poor driver was trying to deal with this, but I guessed he was well used to the weekly rush of people trying to leave the Flemington and seemed to be taking it in his stride.

A rather large woman, who had come up the stairs behind me,

interrupted my momentary pause.

'Get a move on!' she said in a rather rude and disgruntled voice. I recognised her as one of the Old Time Dancing Brigade.

'Miserable old bag!' I thought to myself, 'Fancy having to go home with any of that lot? Just our luck; perhaps they will do a dance up the aisle of the coach as we go along to keep us all entertained!'

I quickly moved on behind Judy and followed her down the coach till we reached Mum and Dad and the others who were seated about halfway down. Judy quickly put Karen and Graeme in seats next to Mum and Dad.

I sat down in the next row at the window and waited for Judy to compose herself and sit down. I looked out of the window and onto the people, still jostling to get onto the coach.

I thought over the events of the last ten days. Poor old Dad and all his expectations of Christmas turkey and a beautiful hotel.

Still, I pondered, in spite of the hotel and its crappy food, we all had a good laugh.

I realized I would look back on this holiday in some future years, probably still in disbelief of what had really happened. Although we had been unfortunate to stay in the dreadful hotel. Still, at least the weather had been beautiful, and everyone was sporting a bit of a tan.

Within a few minutes, the coach was full, Sharon, list in hand, started calling out names, which reminded me a bit of the old-school register.

After an eternity of checks, Sharon established to her satisfaction that all were present, then gave instruction to the coach driver to move on.

In an instant we moved down the narrow streets, but rather faster than seemed comfortable, I felt my teeth were slightly gritted.

Thankfully the coach journey was over very quickly, as we passed back over the route we had travelled in only just a few days ago.

As we approached the airport signs, we passed along rows of beautiful palm trees at the roadside, standing proudly in the sun.

I thought of the cold winter waiting for us back in England. Would it be snowing?

'Oh dear!' I sighed, 'The grim reality of it all!'

Still, we would all have some stories to tell, not to mention Dad's Trott's, which no doubt would be all around Sabey's as soon as Dennis and Jim returned to work.

I started chuckling to myself when I felt the customary nudge from Judy.

'What are you laughing at?' She enquired, smiling at me as if she already knew the answer to her question.

'Oh, just the events of our holiday,' I replied, smiling a little,

'What are we going to tell everyone when we get home? Nobody will believe us!'

Soon, we were in sight of the airport and, within minutes, were driving in and quickly parked, ready to get our cases again and lug them into the airport check-in.

I was quite excited at the prospect of going home, but my thoughts quickly went on going back to work and the cold grey winter skies of England. Somehow, the Hotel and all our problems seemed much smaller now and the thoughts of leaving the nice sunshine for the cold and dampness of England was getting less like a good plan by the minute.

I was shaken back into life by a nudge on the arm from Judy.

'We're at the Airport!' she announced rather firmly as though surprised we had got this far.

'Yes!' I replied, 'I wish we could stay in Spain for another few weeks; it's all gone so quickly!'

Everybody started to get up and move to the coach door, which had just opened. Quickly we were filing down the narrow corridor and down the steps to collect our cases.

`Goodbye Benidorm` - It was fun in the sun with memories, both the good and bad, engraved in our minds forever!

Chapter 19 – Return To Reality

We were at the terminal quickly, and to my surprise, there was only a small queue for the check-in.

'Quick!' I said to Dad, 'Let's get checked in now and into the bar.'

Check-in was completed in record time, and soon, our little gang was assembled around a small table in the bar to await the call for our flight. We had arrived quite early at the airport, and we had about two hours to wait for our call to board our flight home.

The time passed quickly, but after the welcome consumption of a beer or two, we heard the address system burst into life to announce, in surprisingly clear English, that flight 613 was ready for boarding.

After our earlier flight to Spain, the return journey was quite uneventful. No sooner had we been seated, settled and downed a few drinks the descent was in progress, and we touched down gently and back firmly and safely on UK soil.

The aircraft taxied gently to the terminal building, and the engines were shut down.

'Were here!' I said, quoting the obvious at Judy.

'Thank God!' she replied and gave me a big grin while squeezing my arm.

As we disembarked from the aircraft the shock of the cold was like a knife going through the body! I heard Dennis remark, with some fervour,

'It's bloody cold, I'm going to get the flipping heating on as soon as we get home!'

'Oh my Lord, what have we come back to? It's bloody freezing!' Jim followed on.

Sure enough, it was cold and as I looked around the tarmac where the aircraft had parked and could see a thin film of frost over everything and could feel the wind on my face like cuts from a knife.

As I breathed, I could see the condensed vapour coming from my mouth like steam from the kettle. Yes, we were home!

We walked across the tarmac towards the Terminal building and were more than pleased to get inside and onto the final phase to collect our luggage.

We passed through passport control quickly, and I started to feel like I was home at last, only the bags to collect and Customs then off in a taxi back to Mum's house and my little car. I wondered about its condition and if it would start after being left so long?

We walked the few steps onward to the baggage collection area and then assembled in our little group to await our belongings.

'Hope they're not too long!' said Dad a bit impatiently.

'Don't worry,' said Mum in her usual cheery voice, 'They will be getting everything out of the plane now, I expect, and it will soon be going round the moving belt thing.'

Mum's grasp of technical matters like 'Belt Things' always made me laugh. Thirty years as a Drawing Office Tracer had not added much to her understanding of mechanics.

Some further minutes passed on, and then suddenly the 'Belt Thing' burst into motion, and after a few seconds, a case appeared out of the hole in the wall, quickly followed by another and then another.

'Here we are,' said Dennis, who, since the flight, had remained uncharacteristically quiet. He continued excitedly.

'Not long now; we will soon be out of here and off home.'

Shortly, cases galore were pouring out of the hole in the wall. Suddenly, Florie announced excitedly,

'There's our case, Jim!' pointing frantically with a full thrusting finger in the case's direction.

'I can see our black one!' piped up Doris, soon to be followed by Dad, who had seen one of Mum's cases gliding along quickly.

'Can't see our ones!' Judy said, with an air of urgency in her voice. All could see her face clearly looking rather taught, with headlines becoming visibly strained.

In life with Judy, I had repeatedly learned she was a great worrier about all these kinds of events, and one in particular was going on holidays.

I looked on, almost straining my neck, but could not see any of our cases. We, of course, were not the only people anxious about our cases; the other passengers likewise wanted their cases quickly, too.

This became more apparent as many people were quickly jostling for position all around the conveyer belt.

The phenomenon was new to me as my air travel experience, apart from our outward journey, was previously confined to a trip to Jersey. This holiday was on holiday with Mum and Dad on an old Dakota DC3 at the tender age of 10 years.

Modern air travel with rushes to get your bags, the pushing and shoving, the rush for a trolley and so on was beyond my experience or understanding.

Around the quickly moving belt it was becoming very difficult to see round all the people crowded along the conveyer.

'Don't worry,' I said with an air of confidence, looking over to Judy and Dad, 'We will be able to get to the cases soon.'

Almost as I stopped speaking, our red case appeared like magic right in front of us, with Dad's just behind. I moved forward instinctively to get ready to collect Dad's and our one from the belt.

Other people were also trying to get their cases off the damn thing and, in the process, were knocking into one another. All together, it was a rather chaotic experience and

I decided to step back a bit and wait for the people in front to get their bags and move away.

After about ten minutes, in which my impatience felt like an hour, the space in front of me became clear. A rather large man in front of me had made a grab for his equally large case and, with some effort, had swung it around, almost mowing down a rather thin lady standing next to him and in the path of the thing.

I moved forward to assist the man and helped him manoeuvre the overlarge case behind him and onto the trolley he had parked close behind him.

It is said there's many a slip between cup and lip, and this example will serve as a reminder of this.

The man's case sat almost onto the trolley, but not quite. He had failed to notice that the strap going around the circumference of the case was damaged, and with the sudden movement, the strain had been just too much. The case toppled off the trolley and fell onto the floor with a thud. It rolled over and into a rather portly man standing alongside and opened, spilling some of the contents over the floor all around people's feet.

People started to move back, trying to get out of the way of the hapless owner's clothes and other things spilt out of his case. This seemed to start a whole train of further problems as people moving out of the way blocked in people trying to move their trolleys away from the conveyer belt.

Everything in the small area came to a halt in the ensuing chaos. The poor man with the broken case was soon bending down, busily trying to retrieve his things from around and under people's feet and put them back in the case.

Florrie, who was nearest to most of the stuff, moved forward to help him, quickly followed by Mum and another lady nearby.

Soon, the man's things were neatly packed back in his case, and Dennis, in the meantime, had done his best to repair the strap holding the case together. I looked to see; it was at best a real bodge up, but as Dennis explained to the man, in a famous last words fashion,

'It should hold together till you get home.'

The poor man was very grateful for the help and, after thanking everyone for their assistance, moved his trolley onwards and off to the exit.

With all our thoughts diverted to the man's case, we had all completely forgotten about ours. I looked at the conveyer belt, which still had a few cases going around. To think, just a few minutes ago, it was crowded around with people's cases and now left bearing our things.

I looked around to see nearly all the people had gone all fast heading towards the Customs area.

'Let's get our cases quickly!' I said to Dad, 'I think we have had enough of this for one day, don't you?'

Dad and I went over to the conveyer and waited for our cases, which were just on their way round to us. Dennis was first to retrieve his bags, then Jim reached out for there's which were quickly safe on a trolley.

'See you outside after Customs,' said Dennis and started off towards the exit, followed by Jim and Florrie.

Mum and Dad were next, and I helped Dad lift there's off and onto their trolley. Quickly ours were off the belt and likewise onto our trolley and having weathered the journey seemingly ok.

Judy, being true to form, always had this worry about losing things, and no sooner had our cases been put onto the trolley than she was examining them.

'This one's not ours,' she cried out in alarm, 'It's the same to look at, but it has someone else's name on the label, not ours!'

The feeling of shock and then panic set quickly in.

'It's the case with all Karen and Graeme's presents in it,' Judy went on. 'It's got my dresses and shoes inside as well!' She exclaimed.

Karen quickly heard this piped up.

'Are all our presents gone, Mummy?'

This was followed instantly by Graeme, whose face suddenly filled with the full anguish of a child.

He cried out, 'I've lost my Christmas presents!' and with that, burst into tears.

'Oh God!' I cried out, 'Let's go quickly to Customs and report this.'

We gathered ourselves together, and I moved off as quickly as possible towards the Customs entrance, pushing our trolley frantically, followed close behind by Judy and the kids, now both crying.

We arrived at the now-empty Customs, where a solitary man was standing behind a large table.

I pushed my trolley up to the table and turned to face him. He did not look a happy sort, stern-faced and official type stamped all over him.

'Someone's got our case by mistake,' I explained in a worried voice, 'This one's not ours, but it looks the same, I guess the person has taken our one by mistake!'

The Customs man walked round from behind his desk and looked at the label on the case.

'Mr. Duncan from Leighton Buzzard,' he informed us, 'Wait here please while I check this out.'

He then walked off and through a small door behind his desk. Within a few minutes, another Customs man appeared, equally as miserable-looking as the last one. He stood behind the desk and enquired in a rather vexed tone,

'Lost your case, have you?' Then remarked further in a droned voice, 'Why are the children crying?'

'All their Christmas presents are in the lost case,' Judy explained, close to tears herself.

'Well, don't worry too much about that!' the Customs man replied with a sigh, 'It happens here all the time, people picking up the wrong cases, and don't know why they don't check the labels?'

He continued, 'It's an offence you know, picking up the wrong baggage,' He then went on to a brief description of the offence and the seriousness of it all, followed by possible fines and the possibility of Prison terms.

I thought to myself and whispered quietly to Judy,

'Well, here's a good welcome home to England, I wonder if he had a Happy Christmas?'

The Tannoy system suddenly burst into life, and a man's voice crackled out.

'Will Mr. Duncan from Leighton Buzzard please come to the information desk immediately,' the message was then repeated.

Dad and I stood still, waiting in anticipation of the case's return. Judy was now crying with the children. Mum was trying to comfort them with her very best efforts. She spoke in reassuring terms, saying,

'I'm sure they will find the case soon, and I'm sure the man will soon know he has the wrong case.'

The Customs man just stood in silence, staring at all this with no sign of any emotion at the scene before him.

To my surprise, the door quickly opened, and the first Customs man appeared, case in hand, and put it onto the desk.

'Is this your case, sir?' He enquired in his official-sounding voice.

I reached forward to inspect the label, and to my eternal relief, there was our name on it.

'Yes, this is ours,' I replied anxiously.

Then he questioned in a stark tone.

'Well, have you anything to declare?'

'No, nothing,' I replied.

'What about those presents you talked about?' He continued.

'We bought most of those in England before we went on holiday,' Judy said, through tear-filled eyes, 'We only bought a few cheap things in Spain.'

'Well, open up and let's have a look,' He said, gesturing at the case.

I groped for the case keys in my pocket and quickly opened the case for the man to see.

Instantly, the Customs man's hands were rummaging inside and examining the contents. With a sigh of relief, I heard him say,

'Nothing to worry about here! You can go off home now.'

I gave thanks and quickly closed the case, put it onto the trolley with the other one beside it.

'Come on!' I said to Judy, Mum and Dad, let's go.

As I turned in the direction of the exit, I saw a man coming in accompanied by another Customs man. I guessed it was our Mr. Duncan to collect his case.

I thought I would not like to be in his shoes with all the trouble he had caused with the Customs men.

We made it hastily to the exit and breathed a big sigh of relief as we emerged into the terminal arrival area and into the sight of Dennis and the others.

'What happened to you?' Dennis cried out as we got close.

'Someone picked up our case by mistake,' I said with a sigh,

'What a drama! You can't believe what we have been through!'

Dad went on to graphically explain the events at the Customs to the open mouths of our friends.

'One thing after another on this holiday,' said Florrie, 'Let's all get home!'

Florrie quickly added with a note of sarcasm

'I'm surprised you men noticed the holiday at all with all that booze you put down!'

'Yes said Doris,' smiling as she spoke, 'Vincent Bar will notice their profits drop smartly this week!

With little to add, we went into the hand-shaking and parting kiss mode, and with goodbyes completed, we continued outside to a waiting taxi.

With luggage-loaded kids installed, followed quickly by ourselves, we sped off towards Mum and Dad's in Preston Road.

We were all strangely silent on the journey; I guessed everyone was just about played out after our travel and the mad experiences at the Airport. Graeme went quietly off to sleep and Karen just rested beside him.

In no time, we were turning the corner of Mum and Dad's road and Dad indicated to the driver in his inimitable way, and with finger strongly pointed to our house.

'It's over here,' said Dad to the driver, and in an instant, we had pulled up to see the house still standing, just as we had left it. My car was happily outside on the driveway.

Dad paid the taxi and we unloaded our bags quickly, I guess all were anxious to get inside and away from the cold. I helped Dad with their bags into the house, and as soon as the bags touched the floor, Dad shot off into the kitchen to switch on the heating.

Mum was quick to put the kettle on, and while everyone was sorting things out, I went back outside to put our bags into the Singer Chamois.

I talked nicely to the car in the hope it would start after being left outside for these long days in the freezing cold.

I sat down in the driver's seat, put the key into the lock, choked on it, and, with breath held, turned the key to start. To my surprise, in two turns, the engine burst into life.

'Thank you, God!' I said in earnest, so thankful that our car had not let us down. I left the car to warm up a little then switched off the key and returned back inside the house.

Mum had made the tea by then, and I joined Judy and them at the table and sat down. I paused and then looked at Mum and Dad, who both appeared a bit weary.

I thought, 'What a smashing Mum and Dad, taking us on this holiday?'

'Thanks, Mum, thanks, Dad,' I said with a slight quiver in my voice, feeling a bit overwhelmed by our return and thoughts of the long day.

'Judy, me and the kids have had a smashing time really,'

I grinned, 'Honest if you forget about the hotel, the Christmas dinner, dead OAPs all over the place, Jim and the Germans, and the children's show with Giorgio's flies undone, it wasn't bad at all! Also, to include the cases episode!'

Mum and Dad looked at each other and just laughed out loud, quickly joined by Judy.

'I think it's a relief it's all over, don't you?' I said.

'No, it wasn't so bad,' Dad replied with a grin, 'Was it Tiggy?'

'No, dear,' she confirmed, 'I think we all had a wonderful time, but it will be nice to get settled again now we are at home.

The time was quickly moving on, and I realised it was time to move and off to Dunstable, which was probably under snow.

'We must get off home now,' I said to Mum and Dad,

'The kids are tired, and so are we after the journey.'

We quickly got up and headed to the front door; I kissed Mum goodbye and thanked them once again for the holiday. Karen and Graeme were duly slobbered over, and with kisses from Nanny and Granddad, with parting completed, we got into the car for our journey to Dunstable and home.

We all waved to Mum and Dad as I drove off and turned into the main road, being careful to avoid the ice, which I could see was on the road surface.

I made a mental note to be very careful as I drove home; with the past events still fresh in my mind I was well aware not to tempt providence.

Judy and I were quiet during the start of our journey; the car was nice and warm, and Karen and Graeme had gone to sleep.

As I started to relax a little, I realised it was Saturday, and I had Sunday to get myself together and ready for my start back to work.

I thought there would be a few jobs to do in the house as usual and I could escape down the Highwayman for a few jars with my mates at lunchtime and relate all the tails of our holiday.

It seemed like no time at all, and we were in Dunstable, or Little Siberia as it was known locally. As we progressed further to our home, the darkness started to set in. The roads had got frostier and I could see that snow had settled on the

Downs, which surrounded our small town. I turned steadily off the main road, and soon, we were rounding the corner into Patterdale Close and our little home.

I turned my head briefly to Judy and said, with a smile on my face,

'Well, we're home at last, safe and sound!'

'Thank God for that!' Judy replied with a sigh,

'Let's get the kids unloaded and into the house, I bet it's freezing inside!'

Judy was not wrong on that point, and as we entered the house the coldness hit us. I made directly for the central heating switch while Judy went back outside to organise the kids out of the car and upstairs to get ready for bed.

After about an hour, the house started to warm up, Judy had made us a cup of tea and we were both feeling better after our long journey.

'I think an early night will do us good,' Judy suggested.

'Let's take our tea upstairs. The kids are sound asleep, and we can get a good night's rest!'

I needed no further persuading. I was very tired, and the thought of a good kip in my own bed sounded like heaven.

We were quickly in bed and I picked up my cup of tea from the bedside cabinet and drank it down. It sure tasted good, and I felt very happy to be home and safe with Judy and the kids. Although England was cold, it was still home and our little place in the world, Spain could keep its Hotel food, and my thoughts went to roast beef and Yorkshire pudding. And realising it was Sunday tomorrow, I looked over at Judy, who was lying still and quietly snuggled in the bed.

'Judy, 'I said, with some expectation in my voice,

'What's for dinner tomorrow?'

'I think we have some beef in the freezer,' she replied and gave me a nudge, 'I'll do a Sunday roast if you like.'

'Heaven, I said out loud!' almost tasting the lovely meat and gravy in my anticipation.

'That will put the Flemington food far behind us!' I replied.

Then continued, 'I better go downstairs and get the beef out of the freezer; it's so bloody cold. Still, I will be quick!'

With the job done I bolted up the stairs and back into bed.

We were soon both well tucked up snug in the bed and I leaned over to put out the light and settled myself down again.

As I lay still on my back, my thoughts quickly returned to Benidorm, and the many things that had happened to us raced around in my head; I felt a faint smile come onto my face.

'Judy,' I said quietly, 'That was a holiday to remember for sure!'

'Yes,' She replied, 'but poor old Mum and Dad, lots of their savings from the Prudential spent!'

I replied, trying to offer some consolation.

'Still we have lots of holidays in front of us, I wonder what the next one will be like?'

'Never mind the next one,' Judy quickly replied, 'I'm not over this one yet, and I think it will take me weeks of therapy to recover!'

I pondered for a few seconds and then turned over to look at Judy, and I said with a bit of a sigh.

'They'll never believe all that's happened to us,'

'All the crazy things on this holiday, it was like a nightmare, something from Alice in Wonderland.'

'I think it was Alice in Wonderland,' Judy replied, laughing as she said it, 'Certainly Dennis was the Joker!'

I rolled over onto my side to prepare for sleep again and further pondered over our days in Sunny Benidorm. I cringed to myself as I thought about the antics of Dennis, the Penguins, the Germans, the deaths and endless other events over our past days.

My thoughts started to drift to the funny side of all this chaos, and I started to laugh quietly at first, then out louder until I felt the customary nudge from Judy.

'What's up?' She asked. 'You are shaking a bit.'

'I'm laughing about our holiday, good God, what a comedy!'

'Maybe, one day, I'll write a book about all this!'

In Conclusion – A Better Way

Time passed on so quickly from our holiday in Benidorm and was followed over the years by further long travels off to the Greek Islands, Tenerife, Bulgaria, Portugal, and returns to mainland Spain.

All these holidays were considerably better than our Benidorm experience but remained at the low-budget end, catering to cash-strapped clients like us. These adventures were a lot of fun but normally involved 4 beds in a room, cold water showers, no air-con or other creature comforts. I still remember the searing night heat in our bedroom in Lesvos (Greece) with just small and ineffective fans battling to cool us down; air conditioning, I thought, was only for the rich and certainly not for us.

However, as sometimes happens in life, a cool wind of change can come breezing through, bringing the opportunity for far better things to come.

This wind, by chance of fate, came one day into our little house in Dunstable.

================================== .

It was a Saturday and a cold winter morning.

I awoke to the bright sun shining through the curtains. I picked up my watch to see it was just 7.15.

Judy was still asleep, and I decided to get out of bed and peer through the curtains. To my surprise, it had snowed fairly heavily during the night and the whole scene was just beautiful.

I could see clearly across the school field opposite and onto the road and pavements below, which was clear of any marks.

I decided to go downstairs and make a cup of tea for us, and while boiling up, I started to open the post, which had arrived yesterday, and Judy had put to one side for my later attention.

It was pleasing that little had arrived, and to my relief, I could not see evidence of any bills, only a larger envelope, rather thick in appearance. I picked up this thick envelope and got stuck into its opening with some interest. My knife slit quickly across the top end of the package and tipped out the contents onto the kitchen worktop. My eyes fell onto a folded letter, a small brochure and some photos which had all spilled out.

My hands quickly picked up the pictures, and as I eagerly scanned through I could see views of some beautiful grounds with a large swimming pool and various rooms of an apartment.

On further inspection, I could see this apartment was just fantastic inside with bright white furnishings, coloured matching curtains and two gorgeous bedrooms with two bathrooms.

The letter inside told of a seafront Timeshare resort on offer in the Costa Del Sol called Club Playa Vista, just 1,250 Pounds for 2 weeks a year.

Wow! I thought and read further to quickly soak up the info.

The pictures and the offer had made a significant impression on me, which was not hard to do after our various bad holiday experiences, and I decided to talk to Judy about this later.

I thought perhaps we should consider this offer; then again, was it real or just an advertising scam.

My mind wandered back and forth with dreams of the Costa Del Sol apartment and the beautiful pictures sent.

Should we take the offer? What about the money to pay for it?

During the evening, I talked to Judy about the offer. To my surprise, she agreed we should go for it and added, with eyes glaring, that she would never go on holiday again to stay in another [four-beds - in a room - shit hole] – as we had suffered before.

With our decisions now firmly made I took a loan on my Credit Card and paid for our weeks in luxury.

I waited for around two weeks and then started to worry if the offer was real; however, my concerns were put to rest when a big envelope appeared in the post containing our apartment ownership certificate and lots of information about the resort and local area.

With anxiety now relieved new dreams appeared of a holiday in our new apartment. Judy told me to get a booking without delay.

In the following years, we enjoyed exchanges to the most wonderful Timeshare Holiday Resorts in Spain, Portugal, UK and America. We stayed in the most superb high-quality Resorts with beautiful accommodations and fine facilities and service.

Who could have known that later on in my life, I would realise a dream when I moved to Bali in Indonesia, married my beautiful wife Ketut, and built two beautiful seafront Resorts as Members Clubs on Paradise Island.

But that's another story

www.balipalmsresort.com